Other Titles by Desserae K Shepston:

The Undoing: Book 1 of The Undoing Trilogy

The Adventures of Gatsby the Travel Cat

Travel Cats: tips for beginning an rv journey with your feline family

THE BREAKING

BOOK 2 OF THE UNDOING TRILOGY

By Desserae K Shepston

THE BREAKING

Copyright © 2019 Desserae K Shepston

All rights reserved. No part of this publication may be reproduced in whole or in part, stored in a retrieval system, or transmitted, in any form or by any means, electronic, mechanical, photocopying, recording, or otherwise, without prior written permission from the author.

Printed in the USA.
First edition: 2019
ISBN: 978-1-7334079-1-5

*For my parents,
who have always believed in me.*

PROLOGUE

CA5349 stood 20 rows back, the 5th CA Individual from the right. The sun shone down from its low angle in the sky, providing a little warmth in the chill of an early winter morning. CA5349 did not notice. CA5349 stared ahead with unfeeling eyes. Vacant. Looking at, but not seeing, the back of the head of the CA Individual positioned directly in front. If CA5349 were to look to his left or his right, he would see the same look on the other CA Individuals in row 20. The same look could be seen on each of the CA Individuals in this formation of 300.

As one, the formation began moving forward, though there was no one present giving command.

CHAPTER 1

Rebecca stared out of the window of the moving vehicle at the night sky. The moon tonight, waning crescent, displayed as a mere sliver, but the clear sky revealed a million blinking stars. She could clearly see the milky way, though her eyes strained to see the details on the ground. The inky black sky was only distinguishable from the ground by the presence of the stars. Rebecca still found this darkness a little disturbing, though by now she had made this middle-of-the-night trip countless times. She didn't need to see where they were, she could tell just from the feel of how long they had been driving that they would soon be approaching their destination.

Her Colossus phone had signaled an alert from Remy just after she had fallen asleep. The tone from the phone caused her to bolt upright. Rebecca was no longer a deep sleeper. She had become so accustomed to messages arriving from Colossus in the middle of the night that she was always on alert, even when sleeping. Most of the time, these alerts were practice drills. Tonight's message was unusual. They were being called to an urgent meeting at headquarters.

Rebecca looked around at the other three occupants of the car. No one spoke, but the apprehension they all felt was palpable. She could not make out anyone's features because of the dark. Remy was the exception, with his profile dimly lit in the glow of the dash lights. They drove without headlights. It was too risky to have them on. She couldn't fathom how Remy could see where he was going well enough to avoid most of the largest potholes on this wreck of a road. The faint light of the moon did little to illuminate the desolate surroundings. Turning in her seat to look behind her, she could just make out the outline of the second vehicle, with Bryn at the wheel and the other three passengers that made up their team of 8.

Troy broke the silence, asking the question that was on everyone's mind: "Hey, Remy. Mind telling us what this is all about? Not a big fan of surprises."

Remy replied in a tone that barely concealed his irritation, "I would if I could, but you know as much as I do. We'll all just have to wait a few more minutes."

Rebecca couldn't tell if his irritation was directed at Troy or at not knowing why they were being called out. It could be either, really. Troy hadn't quite grown on Remy yet. His sarcastic nature and need to know more than everyone else in the room could be hard to take for anyone who didn't know him well enough to understand that he was also well-meaning and would do anything to help those he cared about, as was evidenced by the fact that he was sitting in this truck right now, rather than tucked safely away between his bed covers. Troy heaved a sigh and crossed his arms in front of him. Rebecca smiled to herself and turned back to the window, resting her forehead against the cold glass.

The darkness pulled her thoughts from the present, drifting away from the truck and into the past. Had it really been just a few short months since this all began? Was it really only months ago, and not years, since her own brother succumbed to what Council was still calling a virus? Rebecca amended her thoughts: *Well, guess it is a virus of sorts. Just not a naturally occurring one. A virus created by BRO at the direction of Manglebee to wage a silent attack on citizens.*

She still had a difficult time believing this was her life. It was such a long way from the days when Jonathan used to torture her every morning to get her to wake up on time for school.

From when she would ride carefree on the back of her horse, Cedar, across the open fields around Quadrant 1. From social gatherings just for fun with the four friends who now shared in this new life with her. From the crush from afar on Daniel, who currently sat in the backseat with Troy. From a life of order, where what she would be doing tomorrow, next summer, in five years, and, basically, for the rest of her life, was pretty safe from surprises and unexpected turns.

Her mind meandered back to the first trip she made down this road. It was in this very same truck, with Remy at the wheel. Then, Daniel had been in the front passenger seat, and she in the back, blindfolded. Rebecca recalled being terrified but unwilling to show it. She and her friends had just infiltrated the secret BRO facilities, finding scientists' notebooks with strange genetic diagrams, vials of what was presumably the active virus, and a hallway full of unconscious bodies hooked up to machines. The very next night, Remy and Daniel had kidnapped her, taking her in this repurposed truck down these decommissioned roads to an abandoned building in a bombed-out ghost town from the days of The Reckoning. Colossus Headquarters for the Region 3 pod.

The predictability of her life ended for good that night, when she, Selby, Cassidi, Bendi, and Troy, along with Daniel, joined Remy and Bryn in the resistance group Colossus. Now, she seemed to never know what, exactly, her days would bring. Not even the regular schedule of school put order to her day. Within a few short weeks of joining Colossus, they no longer had to worry about juggling school and training. The masses had continued to grow increasingly restless, impatient for answers Rebecca knew would not come. At least not from Council. As the tally of victims swelled, so did the chaos. Council did the only thing it knew how to do to control the population: restrict the rights and movement of its people even further.

Schools were closed and all non-essential workers were told to stay home. Some of the workforce were reallocated to community safety and patrol, while others were put in charge of food rationing, since keeping shops open was not considered essential. Citizens were not strictly prohibited from leaving their homes, but movements were limited by available options and the constant watchful eyes of the newly formed patrol, most of whom thought they were doing a good thing, keeping the citizens of Montrose safe in the rapidly unraveling city. SMALS was even more active, apparently having been reprogrammed to accommodate the new restrictions. It had all happened so fast. It really was rather impressive how quickly the new systems were put in place. Now, Rebecca understood a little of how it was that Manglebee accomplished the swift takeover of the United States, its destruction, and the reconstruction of Anecor in its place.

The truck slowed and made a right turn, bringing Rebecca back to the present. Just two more turns and they'd be at headquarters. The unknown nature of their meeting set up a knot of nerves in Rebecca's stomach. Their training and trials had become second nature. There no longer seemed to be any real danger involved. She trusted their systems. She also trusted that their activities wouldn't be discovered, although she knew that it was probably not smart to let her guard down. Ever.

Troy cleared his throat and Rebecca looked back in his direction, expecting him to say something. Instead, she caught the quick, restless movements of him fidgeting in his seat. He must be as nervous as she was. She looked at Daniel and smiled at him through the dark as the truck came to a stop under some low-hanging trees alongside the headquarters building. Bryn pulled her car in beside the truck. This is where they parked when the garage was occupied. It was doubtful Council or anyone else would have reason to discover their use of this building, but it was best to use precautions, nonetheless.

"On a scale of 1 to 10, how nervous are you?" She whispered to Daniel, as they made their way to a back entrance.

"Uh, I'd say about an 11. When even Remy doesn't know what's up…well…makes me nervous. Seems like something big is getting ready to go down, and I just hope we're ready for it."

"Yeah. Me too."

"Hey, what are you two lovebirds whispering about up there?" Rebecca turned and glared at Troy, though of course he couldn't see it. She knew he was trying to be funny, but it hit too close to home. For her. She had no idea how Daniel felt. And she could only imagine that some of this for Troy was jealousy.

"You're hilarious, Troy," Daniel responded.

"We were just talking about how nervous we are…you know…because of not knowing what we'll find out in there, especially since Remy doesn't seem to know either."

Troy let out a light whistle, "Boy don't I know it. Just a little too much adventure for my taste. Do you really think Remy doesn't know, or was he just saying that so he wouldn't have to tell us?"

"Don't know for sure, but I'm thinking he doesn't have a *clue*. He's even more uptight than usual. And, as you know, my brother can be wound pretty tight."

"Yeah. I know that, too."

"What's this all about? Bryn wouldn't tell us a thing. Claimed she was in the dark," Cassidi asked the group as the other car's occupants, minus Bryn who had stopped at the truck to talk to Remy, caught up to them. They were waiting just outside the door, unsure if they should go inside without Remy and Bryn.

"Guess we all are, then. Remy basically said the same thing to us," Rebecca responded.

"Man, what are we all standin' out here for? Let's *go*…sooner we get in, sooner we find out," Selby chimed in.

"Just waiting on those two," Troy said, just as Bryn and Remy's footsteps could be heard approaching.

"Alright. Let's head in," Bryn said with a deep breath as she and Remy reached the group. She'd hardly had the words out before Selby was pushing open the door.

Inside, the lights were burning. The power source, Rebecca had found out, was a piece of equipment called a generator, rigged to be fueled by algae, which was easily grown in one of the adjacent buildings. It was what they also fueled their vehicles with, since the electricity used to power authorized vehicles was strictly monitored. Petroleum and natural gas were even rarer commodities in Anecor. While Manglebee was busy taking over the country and killing large numbers of its citizens in the process, he lost control of Alaska, thereby losing access to the largest, though still nominal, remaining oil reserves.

****

Manglebee's efforts had been concentrated on the main continent—they'd had to be—and during that time, Russia and China (now a confederation of states controlled by a single oligarchy), quietly sent troops and military equipment in to occupy the land. This meant that Anecor no longer had access to the natural resources in what had been Alaska nor in the now always ice-free Arctic Ocean. Not that those resources weren't nearly depleted already. What was left was increasingly risky and costly to extract. Manglebee let it go. There was nothing else to be done about it, no way for him to reclaim the territory he lost, but his message to the country was that he had no need of the land to the north. All the resources Anecor needed were right on the main continent.

Privately, he seethed. While it was true that the natural resources in Alaska were not too much of a loss over the long term, as it cost more to extract those resources than what they were worth, the land itself was of high value to Manglebee. With its sparse population and high mountains, it would have provided the perfect environment for his current projects. There would have been almost no risk of discovery given how much the land was separated and isolated from the rest of the country. His operations could have all taken place on that vast 663,300 square mile wilderness. Transport might have been a kink to work out, as the tundra was now softer than ever, having thawed in the warmed climate. But no doubt he could have figured it out. And he'd still have need of facilities such as BRO, or he wouldn't be able to conduct the kind of valuable testing they were currently engaged in.

****

The generator inside the room also supplied power for the computers, whose screens currently displayed the schemata for the BRO facility. Troy headed straight for one of the computers to have a look at what was on the screen, proceeding to furrow his eyebrows in confusion and disappointment when it seemed to show nothing more than what they were all already quite familiar with. Shaking his head, he rejoined the others, who were making their way into the unusually full seating area.

Rebecca looked around the room and noticed a few faces she had never seen before. She nudged Cassidi. "Hey… wonder who these people are. I don't recognize some of them," she whispered.

Cassidi glanced around as well, looked back at Rebecca, and gave a shrug of her shoulders.

"Alright. It looks like we now have everyone here, so let's all quiet down now and turn your attention this way," Melody called over the general din of the gathering of people. "I am sure you are all quite curious as to the purpose of this meeting, so we'll get right to it."

CHAPTER 2

Juniper opened the door to her little sister's room as quietly as she could. It wasn't quiet enough. "Heeeey, Juni," Mari said sleepily, as she rubbed her eyes and rolled over to face the door. "What's going on?"

"Shhhh. It's okay. Everything's fine. I just have to leave for a while. Not sure when I'll be back. But I couldn't leave without saying goodbye, now, could I?"

"Can I come?"

"I'm afraid not, Sweetpea. Not this time."

"You're not gonna get in trouble again, are you?"

Juniper inwardly cringed, but replied, "I'll be fine, don't worry. You just take care of Mom and Dad, okay?" Mari nodded.

"Now go back to sleep. It's too early for you," Juniper said, leaning over to kiss her forehead and pulling the covers back up over her arms and shoulders.

"Okay. Bye, Juni."

"Bye, Sweetpea."

Juniper gave her sister a quick hug, and then left her room quickly before Mari could see the tears falling. She knew the chances of her returning to her home today were slim. She had no idea what happened to the Disappeared, but she accepted the fact that she would almost certainly find out. Still. If her actions helped the Cause, she would do whatever it took. If her actions meant that Mari would have the possibility of more freedom, more choices in her life, whatever happened to her would be worth it. Her number had been drawn, and she accepted the responsibility. She knew when she signed up for this gig that this day would come. She did not expect it so soon.

Juniper was, by her very nature, a risk taker. She always had been. She liked to push the boundaries of what she knew she could do. She was forever testing the limits of the rules set by Council. She had been called in on more than one occasion for going outside of the boundaries of her assigned quadrant or wandering off into restricted areas. She was a curious sort, that was one thing, but she also did not enjoy people telling her what she could or could not do. She had trouble with authority.

Along with pushing the boundaries of rules and authority, Juniper liked to push her physical limits as well. In some ways, it went hand-in-hand with pushing society's limits. If someone told her she couldn't do something because she was a girl, she felt the need to prove otherwise. And she generally did. Only a few broken bones and scars so far. At 18, she could already outrun, jump, throw, or aim better than every girl she knew, and a good number of the boys, too.

She knew she got away with more than most because Council was keeping an eye on her for their own purposes. She showed promise. Only she didn't want *their* promises. She wanted freedom. More than anything, she wanted freedom. She often dreamed of escaping into the Borderlands with Lucash, living off the land and answering to no one. The only thing that kept her in Westlow was her family. She wanted the freedom for herself, but she wanted it even more for Mari. She knew she would always find a way, left to her own devices, but Mari she worried about. Mari was kind and gentle. She had a quiet strength about her, but not one that would be put to use in defying societal norms. She wanted more for her sister, who was half her age, than a Tier 5 life.

It was Lucash who suggested to her that they join the Resistance. She hadn't actually realized there was anything *to* join. Of course, she saw the Council News reports of those who promoted resistance or engaged in acts of defiance being carted off by Council Guards. Everyone saw them. And she applauded those brave citizens every time, a fact that worried her parents. Turns out they were right to be worried. When Lucash discovered that these were more than just individual acts of defiance, he knew he and Juniper would have to join.

****

The Resistance was not formally organized. More of a loose association of people who wanted to do something about the current conditions in Anecor. These were individuals, couples, and sometimes even families or small groups who sought freedom from the current restrictions on their choices. Anecor citizens who felt stifled by Manglebee's Vision. There was no trail to link the actions of any person in the group to a single leader or group of leaders, nor really to one another. Most people thought as did Juniper, that this was not an organized group. A person had to discover it through word of mouth. This was how Lucash found out about it.

He had been at work, of all places. As a Tier 5, he was relegated to manual labor. Not the hazardous work of Tier 6, who were responsible for the more dangerous jobs like mining or hazardous materials waste and recycling. He was part of a crew that would make repairs to infrastructure. This particular day, they were repairing a bridge that led from the Limited

Residential District into the main part of town. The Limited Residential District was set up in each city unit for those who were in Tiers 2 or 3, citizens who were in government, medicine, technology design, and engineering. Tier 1 citizens could only be found in the Capital and a handful of Major Metropolitan Units, of which Westlow was not one. Tier 4 were those who worked in what would be considered in the days of old middle-class jobs. They were of the educators, skills trainers, and farmers and ranchers variety.

Lucash had been behind the work truck, and further hidden behind a compartment of tools. Mario and Dervin hadn't known he was there, apparently. The two were talking in low tones, but Lucash had been close enough to hear. One of the men said something about a number being drawn and wondering when it would be their turn. Both men spoke with a bit of envy for the individual who had been responsible for blowing up the bridge, even though that person was carted away and likely dead. They marveled at how good a job had been done on the bridge by 632. It really was quite a feat to be able to accomplish such a task as a solo operator.

Council News had not shown this incident because of the destruction it caused. They were more inclined to report on the showier and less damaging acts. It made the individuals involved look relatively harmless, but the consequences blatantly severe. The message was clear: don't mess around with Council and the societal order if you wanted to stay "free" or, even, alive. No one knew for certain if those who were carted off were put in one of the prison camps or executed. Either way, it was not a happy fate.

The work crews who were placed on repairing the type of damage done in this act of defiance were threatened into silence. They were not allowed to discuss anything they witnessed on the scene to anyone. The area surrounding the site had been cleared immediately and cordoned off to prevent gawkers and to draw the attention away from what happened as quickly as possible. The crews were not given any details about the incidents, but they could speculate. And they could talk. Those who were placed on these crews, however, tended to keep quiet, as there were bonus vouchers involved for doing the work. Good crews got repeat jobs. And it seemed there were more and more of them these days.

But, Mario and Dervin knew too much about what happened to be merely speculating. Lucash stepped out from behind the truck after he had heard enough to understand that they had some inside information. The two froze, looks of horror and fear crossing their faces.

"Yer alright…I'm not giving you away. Relax. I just want to know what you know. And how you know it."

"Know *what*, exactly?" Dervin said, trying to cover his fear with defiance.

Lucash raised his eyebrows at Dervin, "Seriously? I was standing right here the entire time. So, talk, or I do. Your choice."

"Okay. Okay. Just…okay. You gotta keep this to yourself. Got it? Us being on this crew can't be jeopardized." Mario stepped in close, not quite threatening, but making a point. Lucash simply nodded in response.

There was some shuffling around, some uncertainty about what to say and how much, before one of them finally spoke. "We are part of the Resistance. Both of us," Dervin said, wagging his pinky finger and thumb between him and Mario.

"What? That's a real thing? I thought that was just a name Council gave to the people who do stuff like this, but I didn't know it was real."

"Yeah, yeah. It's real. It's not like you think, though. No one started calling it the Resistance until Council did…then folks involved just sorta took it on. But, like I said, it's not like you think," said Mario.

"How do you mean?"

"It isn't an organization in the way that we have a leader or a group of leaders. No one leads," said Mario.

"Then how does anything get done?"

"Well, we have a hidden computer site. Beyond my skills to know how it works, but it works. Anyway, people find out about it by talking to someone else already in it," said Dervin.

"Like now," Lucash said with a mild attempt at a joke.

"Probably sometimes. But more like friends gettin' to talking and finding out they're on the same page, so to speak. So, the one involved invites the other. That's how it happened with us. You gotta be careful though. Make sure you know who you're letting in on it," said Mario.

"But you're telling me now."

"Yeah. Like we had a choice. We are definitely putting our necks on the line here, though, and if this goes wrong, it means a whole lotta trouble for all of us," said Mario. "Truth is, you already heard enough to get us in trouble. And the way I figure it, if you didn't really have some sort of interest in what we're doing already, you would've just said nothing to us, and went off and told someone."

"And we haven't told you how to join exactly, either, and we won't, til we know more about you than the little we can guess from workin' with you," Dervin added.

"Okay. So, I'm interested. What happens when you join? How do you join?"

"You have to have the recommendation of someone already in it. That gets put out onto the site and once enough people give the okay, then the person is given a login and assigned a number. That way, no one but the person who recommended you ever knows who you are," Mario said.

Dervin chimed in, "It's all random. Once the magic number of members giving the okay is met, the program generates a login and ID number, which is sent to the contact portal assigned for the new member. The person who gave the recommendation is told their recommendation is approved, and then they tell the new member how to get to their portal."

"That's clever."

"You're telling me. I've been impressed with this whole operation. We don't know who did this. You know, how it all got started. It's all very secretive. So, once the new person gets into their portal, they're given their login and ID. Only the numerical ID is used, so no one on the site knows who belongs to any of the numbers. Not even the person who recommended him does, unless he told them, which probably happens most of the time. Numbers assigned are random, too. And then the program picks a number a couple of times a week. When your number is selected, it's your turn to act," Dervin said.

Lucash whistled a long, drawn out sound of wonder and amazement, "Sign me up. I'm ready to join now."

The other two laughed, still a little nervously, but much more at ease than at the start of the conversation. "Not just yet, Lucash. We need to hear your ideas, first. We need to know if you're someone we can recommend. So, we'll chat some more. Away from here. And then me and Dervin will decide if we agree to recommend you, and then which one of us will be submittin' the recommendation."

The three men arranged three meeting times, and places, over the course of the following week. Lucash didn't wait to tell Juniper. He told her that night. He knew she'd want in on it as well, and of course she did. So, at his first meeting with Dervin and Mario, he said he wanted to include his girlfriend. After telling the two about her, they agreed to have her join the remaining meetings. It would either be they would both be recommended, or neither would, though at this point, it seemed to Lucash a bit of a formality. He knew too much now for them to risk not recommending him and Juniper both. But they went along with it because they understood Dervin and Mario's caution. Plus, they liked the meetings. They were very informative, and Lucash and Juniper felt the excitement of becoming part of something bigger than their own imaginations had so far allowed.

****

After Juniper closed the door to Mari's room, she picked up the bag of supplies she'd need for this mission, shouldered it, and headed for the front door. Lucash was already waiting for her, as were Dervin and Mario. This was her show, but Lucash would be directly involved, and Dervin and Mario were there to help set things up. After Juniper and Lucash were accepted, the four members became good friends, spending a lot of time discussing the topics they read about on the member boards, coming up with ideas for what they could do when their numbers were drawn, and debating the positives and negatives of acting separately or together. In the end, they opted to work as two teams, with one team supporting the other when someone's number was drawn.

When Juniper's number was drawn a mere two months after joining, Dervin and Mario tried to convince the other two to join forces instead of acting as two teams as they'd agreed. Neither of them could quite believe Juniper had been called up so soon after joining when they had been waiting for almost a full year for Mario and 9 months for Dervin. Juniper and Lucash understood the feeling, and they knew they'd likely feel the same way. But they had decided on two teams for good reason.

No one ever knew what happened to the Disappeared. And they all knew that when it came their time to act, they would become one of the Disappeared. It was a sacrifice they had all been willing to make when they signed up for the Resistance. But, in one of their many conversations about what they would do when one of their numbers was called, they decided it might be a good idea to try to find out what happened to the Disappeared. Thus, the decision to form two supporting teams instead of one.

They had a plan. The supporting team would help the acting team to set up, but then, they'd stick close, remaining hidden, for that inevitable moment when the acting team would be carried off by the Council Guard. At that point, the supporting team would attempt to follow the guard, for as long as they could keep the guard vehicle in their sights. If they could manage to follow the guard vehicle until the outer limits of town, then they might be able follow the vehicle tracks to where the guard took the captives.

They knew it would be a long shot, yet they had to try. Knowing what happened to the Disappeared would be a big boon to the Resistance. They were sure it had been attempted before, but also just as sure that no one had been successful, or surely there would have been information up on the boards on the Resistance site. They spent hours discussing the best way to improve their chances of success, and they determined that their acts of resistance would be in locations that would be easier to track the guard. They were all in agreement that finding out where the Council Guard took Resistance members was actually more important than any individual act of resistance they could do.

Wiping the remaining evidence of tears from her eyes, she descended the front porch steps and walked to the edge of the walkway, joining the three men waiting for her. "Ready for this?" asked Lucash, giving her a rare public kiss, then looking at her eyes for signs of fear, trepidation, or wavering. They weren't there.

"Ready. Let's do this thing."

CHAPTER 3

Head Councilor Manglebee stood in front of the large monitoring screen surrounded by his 12 advisors, all of whom were standing just a few steps back from parallel with Manglebee. The room was quiet, and all eyes were on the operations being shown on the large screen in front of them. A group of CA Individuals stood in formation. All were dressed in uniforms of dark green pants and a slightly lighter shade of green for the top. All had shaved heads and wore identical combat helmets. It made it virtually impossible to tell from a distance whether the individual was male or female. In truth, the squad was nearly evenly split between the two.

"How many are in this squad?" inquired Manglebee.

"300, Head Councilor, sir," replied Lux. "We've determined that squads of 300 work best for manageability. We can go up to 500, if needed, sir, but it begins to get more difficult to ensure quality control."

"Is the program not sufficient enough to handle 500 individuals?" Manglebee said, single eyebrow arched, and a tone of condescension in his voice.

"The program is robust, sir. I can assure you that," Lux replied, his voice sounding more certain and stronger than he felt.

"Then I am afraid I do not see the difficulty. Enlighten me."

"It has more to do with oversight and monitoring. If we were in a traditional battlefield, out in the open, or even in forest where we understood the terrain and the potential maneuvers of our opponents, this program could handle squads of 1,000 or more. Those maneuvers are easier to manage. Squads are divided up into positions and roles. Defined tactics. But what we are planning for is different. It is less defined. We are heading into battle in ways that look more like raids than the traditional battle scenario. There are more grey areas. And we lose the predictability of responses, not to mention a loss of visual oversight. We can see through the eyes of any single individual, but to be able to do that with each small group that splits apart from the whole, or each individual…well, I'm sure you can see the challenge in staying on top of what is happening."

Manglebee gave a slight nod of his head, signaling that, for the moment at least, he would accept Lux's explanation. "Show me," he said, eyes shifting back to the screen where the squad stood, still in formation, seemingly unchanged from the first moment the group saw them flash up on the screen, despite the fact that they had, indeed, moved. In the time that the group had been watching, and Manglebee questioning, the squad on the screen had moved in complete unison from a staging area—which consisted of 4 temporary buildings where practice squads could be kept, with each building holding one squad of 300 CA Individuals—to the outskirts of a former city. The squad currently stood motionless, as if waiting for orders.

Lux raised the device in his hand and quickly keyed in a directive. Then he lifted his eyes to the screen, and held his breath, hoping it worked. At once, the squad began to move again, at first, in unison, though this time at a trot, and then they began to separate into smaller and smaller groups as they moved through the abandoned city. As they separated, they entered empty buildings or turned down side streets towards another part of the town, where they would enter other buildings in small groups.

"What are they doing in the buildings?"

Lux again returned to his device and swiped to another screen, where he tapped a selection, and then selected four random numbers displayed. Each number corresponded to a CA

Individual. Once the numbers were selected, the screen in front separated into a grid with four different views.

The top left quadrant showed a street view, with the hint of movement of other CA Individuals to each side. The street in front was strewn with cracks and potholes, but empty of people and cars. The buildings were crumbling, with vines and trees growing on and through them. There was a crushed plastic bottle in the middle of the road, cracked and misshapen, but otherwise still whole. The wind must have been blowing it around this city and street for the past 40 years or more, as plastic bottles were a relic of the fossil fuel age and disappeared from stores a full 20 years before The Reckoning. That no one had found it and put it in a museum or kept it for themselves (they could be sold for a small fortune in the days before The Reckoning) was incredible. You could see several of the men in the room give a little start at seeing the bottle. But no one said anything.

The second and the fourth quadrants revealed another street view, minus the plastic bottle, and the approach to what appeared to have previously been home to a business establishment. The CA individual in the fourth quadrant turned right where the road ended at the building and continued down another similar street. The CA individual in the second quadrant, however, approached the building. From the front, the building looked relatively intact. When the individual in uniform reached the door, the attempt to open it was not successful. The individual tried pushing and pulling multiple times, to no avail. Taking a step back, the CA Individual paused, staring straight ahead at the uncooperative door momentarily. Then, in one swift movement, the CA Individual lunged towards the large window to the left of the door and struck it with a baton grasped in the right hand that came into view in front of the individual. The window shattered, but the individual did not react, waiting, instead, for the shattering to subside, and then walking through the opening into the building.

In the third quadrant, bottom left-hand corner of the screen, the view was barely discernable at first, until the CA Individual's eyes adjusted with the internally implanted nanochips that simulate the low-light sensitive rods in the eyes of mammals, like cats, that can see at night. In moments, the barest outlines of an interior room in a building grew a little clearer. The CA Individual's eyes swept the room methodically, head turning left, then right, in a smooth and evenly-paced motion. The room appeared to be a bedroom. Or what had once been a bedroom. The outlines of a closet could be seen, doors slid open, and clothing compartments visible. The majority of the compartments remained nestled in their closed positions; however, two were protruding outwards on their rails. It was unclear if any items of clothing remained from the perspective of the CA Individual, and the individual did not move any closer to inspect, obviously uninterested in what remained.

The individual moved further into the room, turned to the left, and repeated the sweep. This time, before swinging back to center, the motion stopped. The CA Individual began moving closer to the bed. The bed should have been empty. The city had been abandoned after The Reckoning, with any remaining, living, citizens rounded up and relocated to City Units to await appointment to permanent dwellings and job assignments. The bed was not empty.

A flicker of surprise crossed Manglebee's eyes, but none of the Councilors showed a similar reaction. The CA Individual reached the side of the bed and the form in the bed. The right hand could again be seen raised in front of the individual's body. In the hand was a small, cylindrical object that resembled a metallic syringe, but a little larger. It fit easily in the individual's palm, which was gripped around it, hovering over the neck of the form in the bed. With a sudden, swift motion, the device struck the form in bed. There was no movement or response or reaction from the form in the bed.

"What was injected?" asked Manglebee.

"In this case, a blank since we aren't working with a living target. We have been working on different compositions of injections that can do whatever we need in any given situation. The device can handle liquids or solids; therefore, we can insert a toxic serum that would incapacitate or kill the subject. Alternatively, we could inject the various compositions of the virus strain we've developed should we need to for any reason. This method is already being tested in the field during the roundups on dissidents. We could also implant a device, a microchip, programmed for whatever we needed, should we find that necessary or desirable," Cord stepped in, eager to share, as he was still not back in Manglebee's good graces. He was actually surprised he was still there, but grateful, as the alternative was not something he wanted to consider.

****

Cord had been in charge of Phase I, the Bio-Programmming sector, of the MBD, heading up the efforts to build their numbers of operational CA Individuals, but getting the programming to work as quickly as Manglebee wanted had proved an insurmountable task. Instead of getting rid of Cord, as Cord had feared, when he did not get the numbers up fast enough, he had been switched to CA programmer, working with Lux on leading the team assigned to "train" the army for the tasks assigned in Phase II, the Operations segment of the MBD. Trevor had been placed as the new head of Bio-Programming. If given the opportunity to be honest without fear of repercussions, he thought Trevor far more suited to the task than he and had questioned Manglebee's decision to appoint him to head up this most important sector in the first place. His tactical skills, along with the programming background he had, were much more aligned with his current assignment. Perhaps that is why he was still around. Perhaps Manglebee recognized his error and had sought a way to correct it without losing face.

Perhaps.

Trevor was not one of the 12 Councilors. He worked for the Security Division (SD) and was something of a genius in that department. He should have been brought on in the first place, despite Manglebee's reluctance to bring anyone new into his inner circle. If there were any chance to build up his numbers to the extent he desired, however, he had to bring in Trevor.

Trevor led the AI team in the SD in Montrose. He had a background in robotics, and, prior to The Reckoning, Trevor had developed a number of technologies for AI "thinking" that had proved elusive before his involvement in the field. He quickly rose to the top and had acquired a bit of fame among technology nerds for his achievements. He was clearly at the top of the robotics field and had always been the right choice for the task originally assigned to Cord. Even so, there was a risk to bringing him on board. Manglebee had hoped someone else could do the job, but his hope had been mistaken. Cord just was not up to the task, and he was the only one of the 12 Councilors who might have been.

****

"What is the reasoning behind testing virus strains beyond our current delivery method? The remote injections seem to be the most effective means of ensuring the desired results?" Manglebee asked, with more curiosity than derision.

"Yes, the current delivery method from BRO *is* more precise and the most reliable for targeted injections, but for large-scale injections, programming for individual DNA profiles is much more cumbersome. We are working on strains that would be fast acting and capable of incapacitating the individuals without being contagious. We will not be able to get the targets to the point of near death, as is our current goal with our targeted delivery system, but if we need large-scale injections, we can get large numbers of individuals very sick, while still maintaining control."

Manglebee nodded his head slowly, "Good. I can see where that might be useful if dissent escalates further."

"Yes," Cord allowed himself a brief, though restrained, smile. "Some of the City Units are showing signs of escalating activity. The Guard are having an increasingly difficult time keeping up. Westlow, as you know, is one example. Even with the increase in the number of guards on duty, incidents are going up."

With this last comment, and as he continued watching the actions on the screen, a realization hit Manglebee. "*Why* are they not using weapons?" he said, with an inflection at the end of his sentence indicating that his earlier curiosity had turned to disapproval.

"Well, sir, we could train—" Cord began, but in catching the hard look of Manglebee, he quickly retraced his words and took a slightly different tack, "we *will* train them in the use of weapons. I...we...started with what you see before you as a means to provide a more stealth approach. And to provide more options for how to handle our targets. We thought we would give you another approach to build up your army, sir."

Manglebee's steel blue eyes narrowed as Cord spoke, never wavering, seeming not to even blink. When Cord finished speaking, Manglebee let the silence become uncomfortable. Cord's face grew flush and he shifted ever so slightly, from foot to foot.

"You *will* train this army in the use of weapons. This training will begin immediately."

"Yes. Yes, of course, sir."

Cord opened and shut his mouth a couple of times, as if to speak, though no words came out. He bore a strong resemblance to a toadfish, gasping for breath after being tossed abruptly from the water to the slippery, hot deck of a fishing boat.

"Do you wish to add something, Cord?" Manglebee dared.

"Just...um...well, sir, not really. Just...just a question, sir. If I may?"

Manglebee's nod was nearly imperceptible, but Cord dared to ask the question anyway, "Should we discontinue with the current training regimen, sir?"

"Am I to assume from that question that you cannot do both?"

"No!" Cord blurted hastily, "We can certainly do both."

"Then do both. But I want this army proficient in the use of whatever weapons we have at our disposal. Are we clear on this?"

"Yes, sir. Perfectly."

"Alright, then." Manglebee looked at each of the 12 men in the room and noticed, for the first time, that Trevor was missing. "I asked for this meeting in order to receive a full report on our progress. Why is Trevor not here?"

Henderson stepped up to respond, in a self-assured manner, his voice with a hard edge that would have been intimidating to anyone else, "He is outside waiting. You did not specifically request that he be allowed in this meeting. Therefore, I thought it best he waited outside until and if his presence was needed."

"He is ready with a report, I hope?" Henderson raised his eyebrows in response, as if to say *are you kidding?* Without waiting for a further response, Manglebee continued curtly, "Bring him in now, then."

Henderson pressed a button on the console located to his right, "Trevor, you are wanted inside." He released the button without waiting for a response from Trevor. The screen in front still showed the movements of the four CA Individuals. Manglebee's eyes stayed on the screen as the door opened, admitting Trevor.

CHAPTER 4

Trevor still had no idea how he had ended up here. He had been happy with his assignment after The Reckoning. He had enjoyed the security and the little bit of prestige offered from working in the SD (Security Division) for Region 3. In many ways, it was better than his previous life, the one he led before The Reckoning had changed things for everyone. Yes, he had prestige then, and more money than he needed. But he could have done without the fame. Yes, it was mostly only among other AI nerdy types, but it drew more attention to him than he had cared for, all the same.

Working with computers and robots was easy, it was the regular people who were hard. If he could have, Trevor would have worked happily in complete anonymity, but that isn't how it worked when you started solving problems no one else had been able to find solutions for. When the world for the citizens of the United States turned on its head, and the United States became Anecor, Trevor got his wish. He was assigned to live in Montrose and to work on developing and programming SMALS. He got to do what he most enjoyed, and he got to do it in peace.

Much to his surprise, he met and married Mica, who also worked for the SD, within two years of beginning this new life. They were of like minds. Both of them enjoyed what they were doing, enjoyed putting in whatever hours were needed, and then enjoyed nothing more than to come back to the quiet of their home in the Limited Residential District of Quadrant 1. They'd agreed that one child was plenty, so that was all they had. They had few friends outside of work, but they didn't need to. Trevor and Mica agreed: they'd had all they needed with their little family and the few work contacts with whom they would occasionally agree to get together for social gatherings, just to be polite.

Social situations always made Trevor nervous. Mica was much better at them, though she still didn't really care for them. He relied on her to be able to handle most of the small talk that happened in those situations. Trevor was not one to enjoy meeting new people or speaking in front of people, whether it was a small gathering or large crowds. He had thought he'd escaped that when this new life began. Indeed, after 20 years, it seemed he had. Life was exactly as he wanted it to be.

Until…

Just a few months ago, Trevor was ordered to a meeting with Manglebee and his 12 advisors. He was further ordered that this meeting was to remain a secret. Trevor was to tell no one, not even Mica. This meeting changed his life yet again. Only this time, it was far worse than anything he could have imagined before. And it wasn't the kind of thing he could turn down or turn away from. He couldn't tell Manglebee he wasn't interested, to find someone else. You just don't say "no" to Manglebee.

So, here he was, working on the MBD, heading up its most important sector, while also continuing to fulfill his role at the SD. He still couldn't tell Mica about it, and it was beginning to affect their marriage. She knew something was going on; his unusual nervousness (she did not know him in his old life, when anxiety was a more normal emotion for him), his sometimes-angry responses, gave it away. They told Mica he was hiding something without him saying a word. It wasn't bad enough that he was hiding this from his wife, but the work he was being forced to do went against every fiber of his being. And he was trapped, with no conceivable escape. Now here he was, being summoned into a meeting with Manglebee and the 12 advisors to provide another update on the Bio-Programming work. He wished he wasn't so good at what he did.

Trevor tried to cover his nervousness as he walked into the meeting room. He couldn't seem to control the perspiration that beaded up on his forehead and formed under his glasses, forcing him to push them up on his nose twice before he reached the group of 13 men standing in front of a large screen displaying the end results of his efforts, as well as any success Cord had had prior to him taking over. The robots (for what else was he to call them?) moved with efficiency, devoid of any of the human emotion one might find in a normal army, physical movements human…but not quite.

"Trevor, please, come forward. Thank you for joining us," Manglebee's voice came out in a tight, forced, politeness, and Trevor fought an unreasonable urge to laugh, quite inappropriately, at the absurdity of the comment. "I assume you have made some progress?"

Trevor's urge passed quickly as he was now being required to speak, "Yes. I, and the team, have made significant progress, Head Councilor."

"That is excellent news." Manglebee almost looked like the corners of his mouth might have turned up in the hint of a smile. Almost. "Elaborate, please," and this time the courtesy seemed to Trevor to be a little more honest. Honest. This was not a word to use in connection with Manglebee. Less false. That was closer to reality.

"Yes, yes, of course," Trevor said, clearing his throat and then lifting the device in his hand and calling up his most recent notes on the MBD project. He concentrated on stilling the nervous tremors in his hands, afraid Manglebee and the others would notice.

"The work of the staff on the immune systems and DNA have been most helpful in our progress on Phase I-B."

Manglebee raised his eyes, questioning, towards Nic, who headed up Level 2 scientists at BRO.

Nic responded, "I believe he is referring to Remy Morgan and Bryn Magee. These are the two scientists who have been working on what they believe is the anti-virus. However, we, or I should say the Level 3 team, have been using their work to help determine the correlation between genetic makeup and proper compositions for our current purposes."

Manglebee turned back to Trevor, simply waiting for him to continue.

"Yes, that is correct. I'm sorry, I was unaware of their names."

"Continue."

"Uh...okay...these two scientists, Mr. Morgan and Ms. Magee, have provided a great deal of data to help us narrow down the correct compositions of the serum based on genetic makeup. They have come close, we think, to finding what would be an anti-viral for the serum."

"And, tell me, Trevor, how is this helpful to us, exactly?" Manglebee asked, voice at the edge of a sneer.

Trevor faltered a bit. Not because he didn't know the answer. He did. He had the full report from Witton, since, though he was in charge of the whole program, Phase I-A had more to do with immunology and microbiology than physiology and AI. But he still faltered…because he had a flashing image of what it might be like to be on the wrong side of Manglebee, and it made his blood run cold. Then he thought of what might happen to his wife and son if Manglebee decided he'd had enough of Trevor. And his blood turned to ice. He tried to erase the images from his mind and turn his attention back to Manglebee, who he found staring at him with hard, steely eyes.

He swallowed hard, pushed his glasses up on the bridge of his nose again, and dropped his eyes back down to his device. "Yes, well. In their research, they have discovered which chromosomes the serum interacts with and, essentially, they are learning how to manipulate the chromosomes in order to build a defense system against the serum. If we take that same concept, the idea of manipulating the same chromosomes, but we change up how much and when we activate those alterations, then we will have better control over target responses, recovery, and programming."

"Have you succeeded?"

"On, let's see, 347 cases so far. The first 203 have joined the original 97 and are already in Phase II training. The remaining 144 are in Phase I-C."

"How many losses?"

"We lost 153, sir. Most of those were at the beginning. In the last 100 and…let me see here…27…cases, we have had a 100% success rate. I think we are there, sir, with Phase I-B."

"And Phase I-A? I notice you skipped over that in your report." Manglebee was restrained, but the room could sense a growing impatience. It was difficult not to feel a *little* sorry for Trevor. He did not yet have the experience to know how Manglebee would spot weakness in a person and exploit that weakness to bend a man to his will. He knew Trevor had started with Phase I-B for a reason, and he knew Trevor did not want to talk about Phase I-A. Witton had not had as much success there, and there was another discovery that he knew Manglebee would not want to hear. He'd rather just move on to discussing Phase I-C, where they had also had a lot of success — if you could call it that. But no. He drew in a deep breath, while trying to make it as imperceptible as possible.

"I'm afraid, sir, that we are still running into trouble with the initial step of getting the dosage precise enough to have the target go through the stages of the illness and then lapsing into the state of near death we need for most of our targets. It is very individualized for each target and depends not only on their genetics, but also on their current physical condition. There is little room for error and miscalculations on the smallest scale lead to death. In most cases."

By this point, the vein at Manglebee's right temple was pulsating. His jaw was tight. Trevor glanced down at his hands, expecting to see them balled up into fists, barely restrained. They weren't. Manglebee wasn't the type to throw a punch. Or at least Trevor didn't think so. First, he was far too composed for that. Second, he didn't have to.

"In most cases?"

"Yes."

"I do hope you plan to explain further what you mean by that statement."

Here it goes. Trevor braced himself. "Yes, sir. I'm afraid we've had a…discovery…that could complicate matters in the long term." It took all of Trevor's willpower not to take a step backwards before he spoke the next words. He really wished he had at least been able to soften the news with the report on his AI program before having to inform Manglebee of their recent discovery. What he really wished, however, is that he had never been made a part of Manglebee's devious plans.

"A. *Discovery*."

"Yes, sir. It appears, sir, that there are some who are…um…immune…to the serum, no matter how we change the dosing or composition. It doesn't make sense to the team.

Currently, they are looking into potential interactions from other chromosomal traits that might be protecting the targets from the effects of the serum altogether. Sir."

CHAPTER 5

Melody waited for the room to grow quiet and for all eyes to turn in her direction. And then she waited some more. She looked over the tops of everyone's heads, staring into some distance, appearing to gather her thoughts for what to say. This was unusual. Melody was one of the leaders of the group because she had the necessary characteristics for a person in her position. Few in the group would dispute her role. Melody was a take charge sort of person, rarely flustered, disorganized, or at a loss. She might not be any of those things now, true, but she was taking her time to begin speaking to the group sitting in front of her. Long enough for folks to begin looking around the room questioningly at one another with lots of shrugs and raised eyebrows, looks of concern and some of worry.

Melody had been with Colossus from the beginning. She had been one of its founders. Prior to The Reckoning, she had had a normal life. She had been married to a man who worked too much. She had two children who kept her busy playing taxi, counselor, maid, and sometimes jailer when she'd had to ground one of them for disobeying the family rules. And in her spare time, she wrote current event pieces for a digital media outlet. From the beginning, she had been suspicious of the handsome man with the crystal blue eyes and the velvet voice who wound a spell over much of the rest of the country, but she kept her opinions to herself. She wrote what she was told to write and braced herself for what she somehow *knew* was to come. She could not, however, have ever been prepared for the full force of The Reckoning and what it meant for her normal life.

Of her family, she was the sole survivor. It had hardened her. Instead of breaking her, it had made her stronger. Determined. She was a patient woman, so she would do it the right way. No striking out like those fools in the Resistance. What good did that do? No. Methodical. Careful. Slowly constructing the net that would bring him down and make him pay. Oh yes, he would pay dearly for taking away everything she'd ever known and loved. Melody's anger and pain were a constant presence, boiling beneath the surface of calm she put on display. Now was a moment when her patience had paid off. One more knot in the net was slipping into place. She'd soon have the next piece of the puzzle. If they were careful. If they did this the right way. Oh, she knew they were still a long ways off from bringing down Manglebee and the Council, but this next step was important. It would be a major accomplishment, if they could pull it off.

She drew in a steadying breath and brought her eyes down to the group waiting to hear what she had to say. She imparted a brief, reassuring smile when she noticed the anxious faces. "I am sorry to bring you all in here under such mystery, but this cannot wait, and I could not convey the particulars in a message. First, let me reassure you, what I am about to tell you is good news," she said, bringing looks of relief all around that changed almost instantly to curiosity and anticipation. "We have information now that we have been hoping to discover for a few months. With this new intel, we need to plan our next steps. Hence, the call for the urgent meeting."

The bodies. That has to be it. Rebecca looked at her group, and they, in turn, at her and each other. The same though crossed every single one of their minds.

"Zeche, can you pull up the BRO schematics for us?" Melody directed her attention to a rather rough looking man, probably around the same age as her parents, thought Rebecca. He looked like someone you would be afraid to run into in a dark alley. He had a scar running across his right temple, very dark stubble, and hair that was longer than hers that was matted into long, bunched locks, making it appear that it had never seen a comb or a brush. Rebecca had never seen him before.

Zeche pulled up his Colossus phone and punched some buttons, and the same image that was on the computers now displayed on the wall behind Melody. The same image they'd seen so many times it was permanently imprinted on their brains. It showed the layout of BRO, including the labs and the hallway of doors with the bodies in it that Selby, Cassidi, and Rebecca had discovered several months ago. While Troy and Bendi waited outside, the other three had gone in, in the middle of the night, to see what they could find. This hallway had contained room after room of people, but none were conscious. They'd hidden in three of the rooms while two men rolled in another male and a female, placed them in rooms across the hall from one another, and connected them to a bunch of nodes attached to screens next to the beds. They could not determine what had happened to them nor what would happen next, though one of the men had said something about running tests on the bodies the following day.

It turned out that none in Colossus had known anything about this wing of BRO. They had no access to the area and no contacts with anyone who did. Selby had taken Bryn and Remy into the area using his key card, which seemed to access any door in the building. When they'd gone in, they were unable to discover anything new. The bodies were apparently just hooked up to life support systems. The people were alive, but not conscious. They were in a sort of coma. There was no information in the rooms to indicate why these individuals were brought in or what would be done with them next.

They didn't stay put, either. New individuals came in, and ones who had been there a while moved out. The problem was, they couldn't figure out where they were moved to in order to find out what happened to them next. Even if they had hidden again, hoping someone would come in and take one of the bodies away, they had no way of following. There was simply no cover in the hallways. They couldn't just pop out of hiding and stroll casually behind the rolling cart. So, they'd been at a standstill for weeks now.

But, the image up on the wall didn't reveal anything new. Rebecca, Cassidi, Bendi, Troy, and Selby now looked at each other with confusion. Perhaps they were wrong, and this was something else entirely. Troy looked disgusted. Selby annoyed. Cassidi impatient. Bendi curious. And Rebecca a bit anxious.

Finally, Melody continued, "I'm sure this is an image you all know well by now. Up until recently, this is all we knew of the underground layout of the BRO facilities on the Morgan ranch. We know that there are three divisions within BRO, but those of us working on the inside have had no access to the Level 3 wing or to their information. Until our newest members came along, that is."

"Oh yeeeahhh…that's us…" Selby beamed, bobbing his head up and down as he spoke.

A few twitters could be heard around the room. Selby just smiled even bigger.

"Yes, we have our youngest members to thank for our current knowledge. Particularly you, Selby, as your key card is what has gained us access to the restricted areas of BRO. You are all also already familiar with their other discovery, which was made before they joined Colossus. Their brave act, though also reckless, I might add," and at this she gave a stern look at the five friends, "revealed new activity, about which we had had no previous knowledge, but which we have been unable to find out any more about. Until now. Zeche, next image, please."

Zeche complied. The next image to display also showed the BRO facilities. But bigger. And the new section was not detailed, just an outlined drawing of a large area, with no apparent rooms.

"Whooooa," Troy exhaled the word.

"Well, wouldja look at *that*," said Selby.

Bendi chimed in, "It's almost twice as big as what we'd thought."

Other murmurs rolled around the room along with exclamations of surprise.

"Do we know what the rest is being used for?" asked a female voice from the back of the room.

"Not yet. That is our next step, and what we have to begin planning. We do know it has to do with the bodies our young friends here discovered."

"How do we know this?" asked Remy.

"We placed a tracking device on one of the people in the room and waited for that person to be moved. We discovered that he was taken to a location we didn't know existed. Once we found this out, we had a team go out and use ground sensors to get an idea of what we were looking at. As near as we can tell, this is the outline of the structure. We do not know how, or even if, it is filled in. We don't know how many rooms or what they are used for. And, most importantly, we still don't know what they are doing with these citizens once they are taken there."

"S*ooo*, what's the plan?" Selby, as always, was ready to take action yesterday.

"That is what we need to figure out," Melody replied, with a somewhat strained smile. "The way I see it, this will involve a majority of us in this room at some point. We will have to find out what lies within this unknown area of the BRO facility. Map it as best we can onto our master schematic. Find out what Level 3 is doing with these people, and, hopefully, find a way to break into their computer records for details."

"Sounds like showtime for Troy," Cassidi whispered to Rebecca. "Wonder what the rest of us'll get to do."

As if on cue, Melody directed her attention to Troy, "We'll need your help here." Troy looked like a deer caught in the headlights. Any bravery he had gathered over the past few months currently escaped him. "Sorry, but you're the best person for the job when it comes to computers. So, I hope you're up to the task. You'll have Destin's help. She's almost as good as you are, and she's had some experience already with BRO cyber security." She motioned to Destin, who gave a little wave of acknowledgement.

Troy looked over at Destin, sizing her up. He just couldn't help it. He might be terrified, but he wanted to know who this girl was who was supposedly almost as good as he was in technology. He found it hard to believe that anyone was as good as he was. It was a little bit arrogance and a little bit just his experience so far. He'd never, other than his dad, seen anyone who was as good as him. And by the time he reached his dad's age, he was sure to surpass even him. He gave Destin the briefest of nods but kept staring at her until it got a bit uncomfortable for everyone in the room. Except Destin. She returned his stare. The only difference was, Destin showed no fear. The same couldn't be said for poor Troy.

"Ladies and gentlemen, mark this one down…Troy, at a loss for words…" Cassidi's comment broke the tension, and everyone but Troy and Destin laughed.

At the sound of Melody's voice, Troy finally broke his gaze, "Troy, can we count on you?"

"Uh. Okay. Sure. I'll see what I can do."

"Great. You'll have some time. First, though, we need you to make a few more copies of the key card chip. We'll need those quickly."

"*How* quickly? And how many are we talking?" Troy was regaining his composure. The key cards were a good diversion. They were easy enough to make and held no risk for him.

"We need them as quickly as you can make them. Five should do it. In the next three or four days, if you can."

"It can be done. Won't get much sleep," he grumbled, "but it can be done."

"It's likely many of us won't be getting much sleep, so you'll be in good company."

"Melody?" Remy gestured with his hand that he had something to say. Melody nodded. "This seems rather risky. Do you think it's a good idea to get these guys involved? They're just kids."

"Heeeey, I bet I got *way* more skills than you do. Of course, we should be *involved*," said Selby.

"You did seem to come with an impressive set of skills, Selby, I won't deny that. But I question your eagerness and your ability to make decisions in situations that present real danger," responded Remy.

"He has a point, Melody. Remy and I have to speak up here, as we feel responsible for bringing these guys on board, and, because of that, for their safety, too," Bryn added her concerns to Remy's.

"What've we been doing all this training for if we can't use it?" said Cassidi, looking to Rebecca for support.

"Right. We *have* been training now for more than three months. We've been in simulations; we've been called out on drills in the middle of the night. A *lot*. And we were the ones to find the bodies in the first place," Rebecca added. Her four friends, including Bendi, were nodding in agreement, as was Daniel. Was she scared? Yes. She was sure they all were. But she was also still determined to complete the task her brother, Jonathan, had left to her. He had had no idea just what he was asking, no idea how big a tangle he'd gotten her into. It was no longer about simply undoing the damage caused by the virus and BRO. It was now, apparently, about breaking the entire system. Everything they'd ever known in their own young lives could come crashing down around them.

"The way I see it, you *need* us. And we're members of Colossus, just like you. Am I right, or what?" Selby was not about to let Remy and Bryn cut him and the others out of the action.

"While I appreciate the concern you both have about the safety of this group, Selby and the others are right. They signed up for this, and we do need them. They've trained for it, and they've done well in their trainings. I do realize that the trainings presented no real danger, but they're designed to prepare them for situations that do. Just as they've prepared the rest of us. And I think we can all agree that they are safer as a part of Colossus than they would be if they were to take matters into their own hands." And with this last of Melody's comments, the gang of friends knew that they had won. Remy and Bryn knew it, too, and argued no further.

CHAPTER 6

"Now that we've settled that, let's move on," Melody said. "As I was saying, Troy, you and Destin will be working together on accessing the files on the computers we hope to find once we get inside this new area. You have a bit of time, but I'd like you to begin thinking and talking about how you might do this. Destin, share what you know about the BRO cyber security system with Troy."

Cassidi was watching this with amusement. *Well, this should be fun,* she thought, as she witnessed yet again the two forced partners looking both affronted and disgusted that they would have to work with the other. She gave Rebecca a little jab with her elbow to see if she was catching it all. She was. And she wasn't looking nearly as amused as Cassidi.

"Before any of this can happen, we need to find out what we're dealing with in this new section of BRO."

"So, we don't know anything except that there's all this extra room, and that they're taking these people there? Where, there? Do we know that, at least? So, we have somewhere to maybe start?" asked the same woman from the back of the room.

Zeche spoke up, this time, "Yes, that's basically what we know. The tracker is still operating, but the male was moved just the one time, four days ago, and hasn't been moved since. His location is approximately…here," he said, using the device to place a marker in an area along the far wall, "and he was taken into the area through a doorway at the end of the long hallway of rooms…here." He placed a second marker showing where the door was located.

"The first thing we need to do is to go in and get a layout of the land. Before we do anything else. No matter how tempting it is to just get straight to investigating what they are doing to the people they bring in here. That will take more planning and care, and we will be able to do that better if we know what's over there." Melody had to admit, she was impatient to find out as well. This was big news. But she refused to jeopardize her team unnecessarily.

"Why?" asked Selby.

"First, as you yourself know, BRO can be active day or night. We need to make sure we know what goes on in those rooms so that we at least have an idea of when they might be active. We need to know our options for getting out should something unexpected occur while we are investigating. And we need to have an idea about how many people are being kept there and for how long. Zeche, how long will the tracker continue tracking the individual you placed it on?"

"The battery should last another 7-10 days."

"That's good. If he gets moved again in that time, we can see where they take him. We can also work on placing trackers on other individuals in this new area."

"Who's goin' in first? To do this mapping thing?" asked Selby.

"You may go, if you wish, but I will require that Remy and Zeche accompany you." Selby gave a triumphant pump of his fist, and Melody continued, "We will need a few teams to approach this first task so that we can complete it as quickly as possible. I want two to three people to a team and coordinated schedules so that you aren't all swarming in there at one time. Each team needs to have one person who is good with the mapping technology. Destin, you can't do it because I really want you and Troy focused on your task. Ambir, Evan, and…let's see…Perce. You three will manage the mapping technology. That will give us four teams. Do we have volunteers to accompany them? We will need at least three, but I'd feel more comfortable with six."

"I'll go," Rebecca was the first to volunteer. This would give her something to do right away, and since she'd already ventured into BRO under the cover of night, she felt confident she could handle it. Daniel raised his hand up next, followed quickly by Cassidi. A few others raised their hands up as well. Though necessary, the job at hand didn't seem all that exciting to the ones who had been around for a while. They'd rather be involved in the next stage, so there was a reluctance to jump into the game now and miss out on a better opportunity later.

"Okay, good. Rebecca and Daniel, I'll have you both with Perce. Vee and Davi, with Ambir. And Cassidi and Mel with Evan. Time is of the essence here, but I don't need to tell you, your safety and that of this organization is paramount," Melody pointedly looked at each volunteer as she spoke. "We will reconvene here in three nights, at 1 a.m., to hear from our teams what we are dealing with. From there, we'll determine what comes next. I'll let everyone go now, so that our teams can meet to coordinate, and we can all get home before daylight."

With that, everyone started getting up from chairs or floor — or standing up from a position propped against a wall — and moving about the room. The 12 members who'd been chosen for this first task gathered up at the front of the room, where

Melody joined in their discussion. Bendi, Troy, and Bryn gathered together to wait for the others.

"So, what do you guys think? About the meeting? I *knew* she was going to say something about the bodies as soon as she said they'd gotten information they'd been waiting on for a while. I just *knew* it!" Troy spoke with excitement upon approaching the other two.

"Yes, I thought the same thing. I wish they had found out more, though. It was a little bit of a letdown to find out that the only thing they discovered is that BRO is almost twice as big as we thought," Bendi responded.

"It's the way of this work, as you'll find out soon enough. Even this is an important discovery, and we have all of you to thank for it," Bryn said.

"I see you stayed quiet, Bendi…lucky you, you don't have to do anything. Wanna trade?" Troy said, only half joking.

"I'm afraid I wouldn't be able to fill your shoes, Troy. Besides, I only stayed quiet because I thought I might be more useful on the next tasks."

"So true…*nobody* can fill these big shoes," and this time he was not even half joking. "But what do you mean you'll be more useful for the next task?"

"I don't know exactly how useful I will be, but more than now. If the next step involves figuring out what they are doing with those people, I might be able to help. You know, just because of my background. We also have the information from the scientists' notebook in the lab. The one that shows the work on DNA. I just thought I might be more helpful there than mapping out the layout of the building."

"Whoa, Bendi, look at *you*. You're braver than I thought!"

"Are you sure you want to do that?" Bryn asked. She had backed down during the meeting, but she was still worried about this gang. She'd grown quite fond of the little group and didn't want anything to happen to any of them. She also didn't want to be the one to have to tell any of their parents if something did.

"I want to help," was all Bendi said in response.

"I know if I'd been given the choice, I would've kept my trap shut, but not so that I could help later. This is getting too real now."

"So, you wouldn't want to help?" asked Bendi, in a tone that was as accusing as you could expect from someone who thought the best of everyone.

Troy at least looked embarrassed. "Well, uh, yeah, I'd want to help. Sure. But it's getting dangerous. I mean, I've sorta been drug along this whole time. None of it was my idea of…" his voice trailed off, as he began to feel more and more foolish. Here was quiet, unassuming Bendi ready to jump into the most dangerous situation so far, and he was talking about how he'd rather just sit back and not do anything. But the truth of it was, that wasn't entirely true. Not anymore. When they'd tackled the mountain that last time, and he and Bendi had stood guard outside, he'd felt a sense of purpose. He felt that what they were doing was more important than his fear. And he liked that feeling. The truth was, he spoke more from the habit of a lifetime of nothing more adventurous than the next programming challenge.

Before he could say anything further, Destin approached, looking surly.

"Hi Destin," Bryn opened the conversation, hoping her introductions might make it easier for Troy and Destin, who seemed to take an immediate dislike for one another for some unknown reason. Perhaps because they both had huge egos where technology was concerned, so they immediately saw the other as competition instead of partners.

"Bryn. Good to see you again," Destin managed the nicety, even though she was not in the mood for such pleasantries.

"I'd like you to meet Bendi Patel and Troy Sullivan. We were just discussing the meeting. You and Troy have an important role to fill here. We're lucky to have the both of you. But please do be careful," Bryn added.

"Haven't been caught yet. Don't intend to, either." Destin said this last as if she thought Troy might have other plans.

"Yes. Well. Good. I'm sure you'll do fine, but I suppose we ought to let the two of you have some time to talk about when you'll want to begin," Bryn said. "Troy, we'll wait for you and the others by the side door." And with that, she led Bendi away, glancing twice over her shoulder to make sure Troy was alright. Destin could eat him alive. And she just might.

Troy looked after them, feeling abandoned. He did not like Destin. He knew that immediately. But he was also immediately afraid of her. She made him very nervous. He swallowed hard, pushed his glasses up on his nose, and cleared his throat. He then wiped his hand on his pants leg and thrust it out to shake hers, not quite knowing what else to do. Destin simply stared at it. He let it fall back to his side.

"Uh. Okay. Well. How…um…how should we do this?"

CHAPTER 7

Troy sat glumly in the back of the truck, feeling sorry for himself and wondering what he ever did to deserve this. He was beginning to now wish he'd never gotten involved, forgetting everything he had been thinking just a half hour earlier about how good it felt to be doing something useful. All he'd done is try to help, and the thanks he got was to get stuck with that awful, mean, know-it-all Destin. Who cared if she was 4 years older? It absolutely did *not* mean she was smarter than him. So, what if she knew more about cyber security? It was *only* because he had never had a reason to know.

All of this had been for Rebecca, and there she sat, in the front seat, googly-eyed over *Daniel.* He knew he wasn't always very observant when it came to people, and it took him a while to figure it out, but he got there. An offhand comment from Cassidi helped. Or hurt. Troy thought, in this case, ignorance had been bliss. Not that he ever thought he had a chance with Rebecca. Nothing had ever changed in how she acted towards him from that embarrassing day at their 6th grade dance. But, at least, if she didn't seem to like someone else, he could pretend he had a chance with her.

"Troy? Hey, Troy...Earth to Troy, are you listening?" Rebecca's voice eventually broke through to him.

Troy jumped a little at hearing her say his name, obviously trying to get his attention, "Huh?...Uh, no. Not listening."

"You okay?"

"What? Oh. No. I'm not *okay*. Did you not *see* that monster I have to work with? These next few weeks are going to be a total nightmare."

"Oh, come on, she didn't seem *that* bad," said Daniel, with a bit of a smirk. He was enjoying Troy's discomfort a little. Troy could use being taken down a notch or two.

"Destin takes some getting used to. Her life hasn't been easy. She's a Tier 6. She's had to fight for her knowledge because her family doesn't naturally get the opportunity. They're out cleaning up the toxic waste leftover from the nuclear dump sites, while the rest of us enjoy a safer environment and a good education. Her mother died from exposure just last year, which is why she joined us, really. It's been hard on her," Remy explained. "Being with Colossus has provided her with a sense of purpose, yes, but also an opportunity to use skills that she never would have had otherwise. She is protective of that."

"Yeah. Well. Still, I didn't do anything to her."

"Yes, you did. At least in her eyes. It isn't your fault. But, imagine you're her, and a 15-year-old Tier 3 kid comes in, with more tech smarts than you, and that kid is given an important role, while you're assigned as his support crew, instead of lead, which you're used to. How would you feel?" Remy said this with far more patience than he usually demonstrated with Troy.

Troy sighed, but his face softened a little, "Okay, you're right, I wouldn't like it."

"And I saw you, Troy, you and she had the same looks on your faces. You're not so different from her in that you're used to being the one who has all the tech smarts in the room. Just try to understand her position. She's the same as you, but she didn't start from the same place as you. She's smart. Acknowledge that when you can, and it'll go a long way towards smoothing the road for you."

Troy groaned.

"Just…try. Okay?" Remy's patience was fading. "When do the two of you meet next?"

"Tonight. I *somehow* have to fit it in around making copies of the key card chips, but we're supposed to meet tonight."

"Okay. I'll see if I can't talk to her before then. As long as you agree to try cutting her some slack. And maybe ask her to help you make the key card copies. She probably won't do it but ask anyway."

"Fine."

"Hey, Troy…sorry this didn't go so well for you tonight, but I'm glad you're here. Thanks. Little bit scared for you, though, and *not* because of Destin. It's good for you to have some competition," Rebecca said with a smile, trying, as she often did, to smooth things over for Troy. She often felt more like his big sister than his friend.

"Scared? You're going in first. You should be more scared for yourself. At least when I go in, you guys'll already have cleared the way. I'm just breaking into a computer system. You don't even know what you're breaking into. What's your plan anyways?"

"Selby is actually the first one going in, because of Zeche. And Remy," she said as she glanced quickly to Remy, hoping she didn't offend him. He didn't seem to notice. "While you were sitting back there feeling sorry for yourself, we were all discussing plans. So, you wanna hear them now, 'eh?"

"I *wasn't* feeling sorry for myself. Just wishing I wasn't stuck with that evil…I mean, Destin. Wishing I wasn't stuck with Destin. But, *yes*, I do want to hear your plans."

"Okay," Rebecca smiled. Her efforts to drag Troy out of his funk and to distract him were working. "So, like I said. Selby gets to go in first, with Remy. I guess Melody wants Zeche to kinda direct this all because he was the one who started all this—"

"Actually, *you* guys can be blamed for starting all this, since it's you who stumbled upon the bodies in the first place," Remy said with a little laugh.

"Right. I guess. But, Zeche is the one who put the tracker on the body and has started the mapping of the extra BRO area."

"Are you always so serious, Rebecca?" Remy asked, feeling pretty good about tonight's meeting because this was *finally* some real progress, after months of standing still.

"Ha! You're one to talk!" Daniel burst out.

"Wait, what? I'm not *that* serious," Remy sounded a little hurt.

"Have you seen yourself for the past, oh, I don't know, two years?"

"Okay, enough of the brotherly love, let Becs finish," Troy interjected, annoyed.

"Sorry," said Daniel, "go ahead, Rebecca."

"It's okay. Not a big deal. So, me, Daniel, and Perce are next up, then Cass and the two she's with, and the other team of three will finish up. We split up what we're doing, taking different sections. Selby's team is checking out the first area, so when we go in, we're going to be in the part where the body with the tracker is," Rebecca said.

"Lucky you…are you okay with that?" asked Troy.

"Yeah. I don't think it's going be any different from the others. I mean, I doubt that that's the only body in there, and at least we know where he is. But I bet there's lots more in there."

"And who knows what else we're going find. I'm not worried about the bodies. From what you guys said, they aren't even awake. Not conscious. So, what can they do to us except creep us out?" added Daniel.

"Yeah, they're definitely creepy. But I feel sorry for them, too. Wonder what they did to get in there? I know we've talked about this before, but I'm still kinda wondering if these aren't the Disappeared," Rebecca said.

"I think you're right, Rebecca," Remy agreed. "It's the only thing that makes sense to all of us. If we're right, that's one mystery solved."

"But what are they *doing* with all of them?" Troy added.

"Exactly," said Remy, "One mystery solved, and a bigger one created. This web just keeps getting bigger. Glad we are getting somewhere. It's taken a long time to make as much progress as was made with this discovery, but at least it's forward movement.

I know Melody is really smart for doing things the way she does. She's careful, and we've hardly lost anyone because of it—"

"Except all those people dying from the virus," Rebecca said.

"Yes, of course, there's that. And that's one of the reasons she's so careful, why we're all so careful. It's one of the reasons we're doing all this. Colossus has grown in number, but if we weren't so careful, we would be wiped out by Council easily. Who knows how many would die if that happened? But I get frustrated, too. It's hard to move so slowly. And watch so many of the people in this city die from something we know is not from natural causes. Starting tonight, we'll get more answers. I hope."

"Not many, since all we're doing is mapping," Daniel sounded disappointed. He was not as eager as Selby and Cassidi when it came to their jobs with Colossus, but he was glad to be involved and wanted to be a part of the more important activities. *At least we're doing more than just training*, he thought. Like the others, he thought the training was becoming a bit boring and felt like it all was more of a game than the monumental task of bringing down a government and saving lives.

"We might be just mapping, but we're also going to be the first ones to see what's over there. There's a lot of danger involved, so don't take what we're doing lightly," Remy admonished. "We have no idea what we will find. Not only with the people they're taking over there, which we'll be the first to *see*, but also with **BRO** staff. We might know the basic patterns of activity for the areas we've been in, but what if it's completely different in this new section? What if there's a whole crew of staff over there round the clock? We have to be prepared for anything when we go in there."

"Huh. Didn't think of it that way, but I guess you're right," Daniel brightened a little.

"And that's precisely why you newbies have to have others along who've been at this a while longer," Remy grinned.

"Haha," Daniel deadpanned.

The truck grew quiet at that. It wouldn't be long before the sun came up. A bare hint of the brightening of the sky shown over the tops of the peaks to the east. Remy dropped Troy off first, as he was the furthest away.

Troy yawned as the truck slowed and then stopped in front of his house. No lights were on inside. Good thing. It was still too early for his parents to wake up. "Okaaay, time for sleep. Good luck you guys. Becs, I'll message you later, before you go in."

"Sure. Thanks, Troy. Get some sleep."

"Not a problem there," Troy said through another yawn.

Rebecca laughed, "See ya."

"Yep. See ya."

Remy made sure Troy was inside before he drove slowly away, out of the neighborhood and towards Rebecca's house. By the time they got there, everyone was dragging. The adrenalin from the night's events drained away and sheer exhaustion was taking over.

"Tonight will be a long night, Rebecca, so rest up today," Remy said as Rebecca started climbing out of the truck.

"I'll try."

"We'll be in touch, as planned, before we head in. If you need anything before then, message me, alright?"

"Yeah. Alright. Night guys. Or morning…but you know what I mean."

"Good night," Remy said, along with Daniel's, "Night, Becs."

Rebecca smiled at that. It was the first time Daniel had called her by the name her friends all called her. She liked it. She was still smiling as she made her way up to her front door, and turned to wave, before heading inside and straight for bed.

CHAPTER 8

Bryn again drove behind Remy's truck with Cassidi, Selby, and Bendi occupying her car. She had mixed feelings about tonight's events. On the one hand, she was relieved and excited to have some forward movement after the weeks-long standstill. Maybe excitement wasn't exactly the word. Bryn was a little too measured about what they were doing, and all too well aware of what they were up against, to allow excitement to overtake her. But there was a sense of anticipation. At the same time, however, she had an increasing concern for including kids in their mix. For, they were still kids in Bryn's mind. Very intelligent kids, but still kids, nonetheless. Too young to have the life experiences needed to make decisions in the circumstances they'd likely find themselves by being involved with Colossus.

"Can't believe you were all so nervous about tonight's meetin'! Good stuff, tonight," Selby said from the back seat. "Can't *wait* to get in there to see what they got for us."

"You aren't a little worried about what you'll find?" asked Bendi.

"Nope. Not really. All this training we've been doing is gettin' bo-o-oring. Now we get to put it to some use. Aaaaat *last*!"

"Those words make me exceedingly happy Melody is sending Zeche and Remy in with you. And I *hope* you *don't* have to put your training to use because that will mean that you've run into trouble," Bryn admonished. Of course, that didn't faze Selby. His enthusiasm remained intact.

"I second that," Bendi agreed. "I'm happy for you because I know you're excited about this, but I don't want anything to happen to you. Just be careful, okay?"

"Careful is my middle name. I was raised to be careful. Why do you think I wouldn't let you guys handle the big boy tasers? I just feel prepared, that's all. Geez, cut me some slack, would ya?"

"Sorry, Selby. I know you know what you're doing. But I still can't help worrying. This is new for all of us," Bendi responded.

"Thanks. I *will* be careful. That's a promise. To you. I was careful with Becs and Cass inside BRO, wasn't I? I'll be just as careful this time, too."

"I'm glad to hear you say that, Selby," Bryn chimed in, turning briefly to smile at him in the back seat. "It makes me feel a whole lot better."

"Yes, me too. Thanks, Selby."

"Cass...you okay over there? You been awfully quiet. That's not like you at *all*."

"Hmmm? Oh, I'm fine. Just listening to you guys ramble on...and on...aaaand *on*." Truth was, she hadn't really heard a word of what they'd said until Selby spoke her name. She'd been deep in thought. Wondering what Jonathan would think of all this. She was missing him terribly at that moment, as she was thinking about tonight's meeting and all that had happened since last summer to bring them to this point, to this world that was no longer recognizable to her. She regretted not ever being bold enough to tell Jonathan how she felt. But even now, the possibility of his rejection was too much, and she felt her cheeks flush in embarrassment. *You'll wander into a facility full of unconscious people and who knows what else and hardly feel a butterfly flutter, but just imagining a dead guy turning you down makes you nauseous. Way to go, Cass.*

Bendi spoke, interrupting her thoughts again, "How do you feel about going in again, Cass?"

Cassidi gave a little laugh, "Oh, I'm good with it. Figure that's what we're here for, right? And our hero, Selby, here, will clear the way for the rest of us, so what've I got to be worried about? We've done it once already, anyways. Twice for me, actually."

"That's right, you know I'll make sure it's safe for the rest of ya," Selby laughed. "Hey. Wait just a minute…Bendi?"

"Yes?"

"When are you goin' in? I don't seem to recall your name being called…" Selby didn't sound accusing. More just shocked that one of the gang wasn't going to be included in these new events.

"My name wasn't called because I'm not going in. I didn't volunteer."

"Wait, you're not? Why not?" Cassidi looked up in surprise at this as well. Apparently, she hadn't noticed that Bendi's name hadn't been called either.

Bendi proceeded to tell them the same thing she'd told Troy and Bryn. She finished up just as Bryn was turning the car onto her street.

"Good plan, my friend, good plan," Selby said proudly.

"Thanks."

"Yeah, you'll be good at that," agreed Cassidi.

"Thanks for the vote of confidence guys," Bendi said as she opened the car door. "Well, good luck. Both of you. In case I don't see you before you go in. I'm sure I won't see you, Selby, so be careful. Let us know how it went, please."

"Oh, you know it, you'll be hearin' from me as soon as I get out!"

"Good. Night everyone. Be safe." And with that, she closed the door gently and walked up the path in the dark to her house.

****

Bendi entered her house and made it up to her room without making a sound. Her parents, sisters, and brother were all certainly still sound asleep. Theirs was a quiet house in the early morning hours, but during the day, there tended to be a lot of activity. They were a close family, but all of them were also fiercely independent. They generally left one another to make their own decisions, unless advice was asked. Because of this, no one had thought twice about Bendi's comings and goings over the last several months. She knew, however, that they would probably have concerns about her involvement with Colossus, and certainly about her sneaking in the house at sunrise, so she was careful.

Once inside her room, Bendi found she wasn't tired yet. She was still too wound up from the night, it seemed. So, she pulled up the images of the scientists' diagrams from the BRO lab and looked up some resources on genetics and viruses. She might as well do something productive…see if she couldn't get a jump start on gathering more information that she might use during the next stage of their plan.

****

Selby continued to chatter away in a near monologue until they'd reached Cassidi's house. Cassidi continued to be rather quiet. It wasn't just because Selby was talking so much. That was just a good excuse for her to continue on in her own thoughts. He didn't require a lot of participation when he was on a roll like he was this morning. Bryn contributed a bit more than Cassidi, but she was content to let Selby talk. She was too tired to speak much, and she still had a while before she'd be home herself. Once Cassidi was out the door, she was relieved for just the one more stop before her own house and her own bed, with no one there but her cat, Gremlin, who would curl up at her feet as soon as she crawled under the covers.

****

Cassidi entered her house quietly but was surprised to see a light on in the kitchen. She paused, waiting to see if whoever was up had heard her come in. Apparently not. Or, if they did, they were choosing to ignore her, which was better than the alternative in her house. At least that had been her experience for most of her life. Her parents were inclined not to care what she did, as long as it didn't interfere in their own lives. But if she crossed some arbitrary line, they made her life miserable, so she did her best to tiptoe around them and steer clear when possible. It seemed to suit them all just fine. She went down the hall to her room and entered without turning on the light. She also didn't bother to change, falling into bed with her clothes on, and kicking her shoes off just before tucking her feet under the covers.

****

Selby finally ran out of steam once Cassidi exited the car. He stifled a yawn, and glancing up to see if Bryn had noticed, but her eyes were glued to the road in the early morning light. The sun would be above the mountains before too long. The light was now just enough to see by. Selby was looking forward to his bed and a few solid sleep hours before he'd have to make his presence known with his parents. He couldn't sleep too long, or they'd grow suspicious. He and his parents were early risers and they would notice if he stayed in bed too long. Likely, it wouldn't matter, he was sure to be too excited about tonight to sleep much anyway.

He opened the door, without giving it much thought, and discovered his parents, sitting on the couch, looking composed. But worried.

"Son." His father's voice came, low and strong. It was a statement that implied a question. *Where have you been and what are you doing creeping into the house at this time of the morning?*

His mom stood up quickly and came over to hug him, apparently relieved at the sight of him, "Oh, thank god, you're safe," but then she pulled herself back, looked at him more closely, and then gestured to the chair, "I think you'd better sit down, Selby. Something tells me you've got a lot of explaining to do."

Selby's father did not stand up. He also did not say anything else. His eyes simply followed Selby to the chair. Selby sat down, avoiding eye contact with his dad. His dad's face looked menacing in the dull glow of the single light turned onto its lowest level. He didn't think of his dad as a menacing man, but his look just then made Selby shiver slightly.

He didn't speak right away, and his parents let the silence stretch out between them. They were patient. They would wait until he was ready to talk. He stared at his hands gripping his own legs, gathering his thoughts and considering his options.

He was in a quandary. His parents were survivalists. They had been among a group of individuals who had seen something of The Reckoning coming, long before it finally did. They saw it in the violence erupting across the nation. In the wide divisions between political parties. In the fear tactics used by the politicians and the media. And in the ever-widening disparities between social classes. The Meyers and the others in their group were determined to survive whatever happened. For years prior to The Reckoning, they worked to develop and hone their survival skills, operating in secret. When The Reckoning erupted, they all went underground, lying low until it was over.

They were fully prepared to defend themselves, if needed, and, as it happened, it had been needed more than once. But they'd survived. All of them. And when it was over, they came out of hiding and blended back into society, adapting to the structure Manglebee set, and accepting their assignments without a fight. But they knew that this new nation was not any better than the old. Probably worse. So, the survivalists kept up their training, and the Meyers included their son in that training as soon as he was old enough to understand and participate.

Selby's skills and the tools and weapons at his disposal were what not only allowed the five friends to get inside BRO, but also provided Colossus with technology they did not previously have. The problem was, he'd kept it all from his parents. He'd done so for Rebecca. He was sure he could have asked for their help, and they likely would have given it. Or at least he thought so. But Rebecca hadn't wanted to involve them. So, he didn't. And now he was faced with either continuing to try to hide their involvement with Colossus or filling them in on what they were all doing.

It wasn't an easy choice. If he'd told them up front, they would have been understanding. Even if they hadn't agreed with it, they would have had a rational, honest, conversation about it, weighing the pros and cons between them. But he didn't tell them up front, so he knew if he told them now, he'd have to face their disappointment, and hope, in the end, he could get them to understand. And then, he'd have to face Rebecca's disappointment, not to mention the others in Colossus, when they discovered he'd told them.

If, on the other hand, he made something up, continued to deceive them about his involvement in Colossus, he risked them finding out anyway. His parents were *very* perceptive. They knew how to read people and situations. They would not have survived The Reckoning in the way they did otherwise. Either they'd figure out now he was being dishonest — which was highly likely, given that he was their son and they knew him well — or they would be keeping a closer eye on him and potentially find out later. Especially if something went wrong.

Making a decision, he raised his head and, for the first time since coming in the house, looked his parents in the eye.

CHAPTER 9

Juniper, Lucash, Mario, and Dervin made their way in the quiet of the morning hours to the nearest transit stop. At this time of day, it was primarily the Tier 5 and 6 workers beginning to make their way to their workstations or worksites out and about. It would be another couple of hours before the rest of the city began making their way to work or to school. Then the streets would be quiet again. The group figured that their best chance to follow the Council Guards was to make sure that the streets were as busy as possible, forcing the truck to move at a slower pace. It would also allow Dervin and Mario to blend into the crowd more as they attempted to follow the guard vehicle.

They fit right in with the other riders on the transit carriage, so no one looked twice at them, which made what they were doing easier. They'd be uninhibited in getting to their destination because no one would think them suspicious. They hoped that they could set up with relative ease as well. Their activity involved only a few supplies, which was why they were able to wait as late as they did to start. Their destination was the end of this transit line, which stopped at the delivery site for the ranching and agricultural goods that were brought in from the outer regions of the city twice per week. Today was the day for dairy products, among other things.

It was the dairy canisters that were central to their plan, as they intended to place red dye in one of the large vats, and then open that vat so that the dye spilled out onto the thoroughfare at a time when there would be crowds making their way to their work assignments. Real milk was only available to the upper echelons. Like meat, it was symbolic of the inequality of society in Anecor. It was evidence of one of the lies Manglebee told everyone on his campaign trail about getting rid of the ever-widening gap between the haves and the have nots. The red dye was symbolic of the blood that had been shed during the Reckoning, and since, in Manglebee's pursuit of power.

Juniper's bag carried the packets of red dye obtained on the black market, a laser cutter, two bricks, and a sign, painted on an old sheet, that read:

"WAS *THIS* WORTH THE DEATH OF SO MANY? ARE YOU FREE?"

The group of four would look like workers doing their job, along with the other workers milling around the dairy platform, up until it came time to hang the sign and cut a hole in the vat to spill the red milk. Dervin and Mario would help up until that point. The four of them would open the top of the vat, put the dye in, close it up, and move it to the edge of the platform, in the process mixing the dye into the milk. It would look like they were preparing the product for delivery to its destination within the city. After that, Dervin and Mario would retreat to a nearby location to watch the rest. That was the plan. Simple.

The transit carriage came to a stop against the bumpers at the end of the line. The doors slid open and the group of four filed out with everyone else, leaving an empty carriage behind. No one was waiting to get on at this platform, so it would begin making its way back to the beginning of the line to pick up another round of citizens. Other workers were offloading from carriages that came from other directions. The walkways and thoroughfares were getting busier by this time. In another half hour, they'd be filled.

"Stick close," Lucash instructed. It was the first words anyone had spoken since they had arrived at the transit platform at the beginning of their journey. They could not risk any discussion of their plan, and no one was in the mood to try small talk. Best just to stay quiet until they were off of transit.

"You sure you're good with this, Juniper? Lucash? Cuz me and Mario sure don't mind tradin' places with you guys," came Dervin's last ditch effort.

"Or maybe you need help? With the sign and all? We could do that," Mario added. "I'm also good with the laser."

"Not a chance," replied Juniper. "We need the two of you to get us out of this once we're taken away. If you do, or at least if you find out where they take us, you'll be heroes, you know."

"Let's get moving. I feel like we're starting to get some stares standing huddled together like this," Lucash said, nervously looking around as people glanced in their direction while walking by them.

Juniper nodded and then turned to lead them in the direction of the platform, with the other three following closely. They moved quickly through the crowd, but no faster than many of the others in a hurry to reach their worksites on time. When they got to the platform, they moved around to the back, where the regular workers would enter, and walked out with a number of others. There was row upon row of metal canisters. They would have been dropped off earlier that morning, and all of them would be gone by midday. They made their way to the front, but all taking slightly varied routes through the rows.

When they got to the front, Juniper made her way along the front row until she got to a vat that was not too far from the outside edge to allow for some cover while they worked. While they hoped to blend in, it still just felt safer to have a bit of protection around them, especially as they opened the lid and dumped the dye inside. That part was the riskiest part of the operation up to the point where Mario and Dervin would leave.

They all took their practiced positions, doing their best to look like they knew what they were doing. In spite of the now-present fear that gripped each of them. This was it. This was real, and at the end of it, only two of them would be going home. Juniper kept reminding herself that this was for the Cause and for Mari. She tried to remember any time in her life when she'd felt like this. She couldn't remember one. She still had no doubts about what she was doing. It felt right and important. But at the same time, she was now afraid of what would happen to her.

This feeling hadn't risen to her consciousness until they walked onto the platform. Prior to that, she'd been quite calm. No fear at all; just an acceptance of the outcome. But once she stepped out onto the platform, amid all the metal vats, the world grew surreal. The morning sun shone extra bright. The growing street noise pushed to the back of her awareness, but everything nearby was louder. She could hear her heartbeat in her ears and the sound of her breath on its way in and out. She could hear Lucash's boots strike the concrete, and when the metal from the strap of her bag hit the metal of one of the vats she was passing, she nearly jumped out of her skin at the loudness of it. Every worker she passed by was looking at her with suspicion. She was certain someone had already figured out they didn't belong there. Maybe they'd even already turned them in to the supervisor or, worse yet, perhaps the guard.

Juniper looked at Lucash and could see he felt the same way. That gave her some strength. At least she wasn't the only one. She couldn't tell how the other two were feeling. They seemed as they always were, and she didn't know them well enough to read the subtleties of facial expression and body language the way she could Lucash.

They were all standing around the selected vat, with Mario attempting to pry the lid off of it, and the other three with packets of dye in their hands, ready to pour as soon as the lid was released. They would have to work quickly and get the lid back down and locked in place so that it didn't spill before they got it mixed up and to the edge. That would be too soon and not nearly as effective. The drama of a stream of the substance spilling onto the street was what they were aiming for.

It was taking Mario longer than they'd hoped to release the lid. The other three were getting antsy and beginning to worry, especially with the level of noise his efforts were creating. Just as it was getting almost too intense, they heard a metallic pop, followed by a hiss of air.

"HEY! You over there, *what* do you think you're *doing*?" came a shout from the edge of the platform. They all froze. Mario with the lid finally pried open, but still in his hands, and the other three with their open packets of dye ready to tip into the vat.

"HEY, I asked you a question! Answer me! ANSWER me!"

All four looked around carefully for where the voice came from, unsure who it was directed at, until they saw a big burly man yelling at a young boy who had wandered onto the platform and was looking around at the workers and vats of milk, seemingly in his own little world. They all heaved sigh of relief. Juniper, Lucash, and Dervin quickly dumped the contents of their packets into the vat while the man was distracted. Mario closed the lid and pulled down the lever to reseal it. He had to put all his weight into it to get it to pull down and seal the lid, but he got it.

The four of them then took ahold of the vat on different sides and started walking it to the edge of the platform, with more motion than necessary in order to shake up the contents inside. The vat was heavier than expected, and Juniper was glad there were four of them. Other workers were beginning to move other vats out for transport as well. There were transport vehicles waiting at the edge of the platform. They weren't heading there. They were heading to an empty section where the contents could spill out onto the ground and the sign could be read by the passing crowd.

Now they were out in front for everyone to see. Including the Council Guard patrols. As soon as they got the vat to the edge, Mario and Dervin whispered, "Good luck."

"We'll do what we can to get you out fast. Just don't die beforehand," Dervin added, and the two men were off, slipping quickly and quietly into the rows of vats, to retrace their steps to the back of the platform, and then to the overhang of a building nearby, where they could watch and wait.

Juniper and Lucash pretended to be occupied while they waited for the other two to disappear into the vats. They checked their devices and looked at the lineup of waiting transport vehicles, keeping an eye out for the passing guard as well. So far, no one seemed to take note of their unusual position on the platform. Juniper took out the laser when the coast was clear. Lucash had the sign ready, in his hand, but still crumpled up into a large ball that he was having a hard time hiding from view.

Juniper activated the small laser cutter. She had to crouch down low in order to cut at the lowest possible point, so that all the contents would spill out. She really hoped they put enough dye into the milk and mixed it up well enough. Pink milk would not be good. They *had* put in a LOT of dye. It was supposed to be fast-dissolving and easy to mix. They'd find out soon enough. She started cutting. It wasn't as easy as she'd hoped. At first, all she saw was a glow, and then a darkening circle. What was happening? This was supposed to be fast!

"Hurry, Juni, I see the guards approaching, coming back on their pass this way."

"I'm *trying*, but this thing is slow! This metal must be thicker than what we practiced on!"

Her palms were starting to sweat. The laser cutter kept slipping in her hand, so she switched hands and wiped her palm on her pants. When that hand became sweaty, she repeated the action.

"*Juniper*, I hope you can go faster. That big guy from earlier just spotted us."

"I can't make this go any faster than it is," she grumbled. Just then, the laser broke through and an opening appeared, but not large enough. She had to keep going a little bit longer.

"He's heading this way, and he doesn't look happy. We have to go!"

"Almost there. Be ready with the sign."

"HEY! You two! What? What in god's name is going on?" Now there was no doubt who he was talking to. He picked up his pace and started trotting over, his size obviously inhibiting him from a full-on run. It might buy Juniper another moment or two.

"STOP! This instant! GUARDS!"

"*Now*, Lucash!" Juniper exclaimed as, at last, the hole opened up enough to allow a fast, steady flow of *red* milk. Juniper couldn't help the smile that formed on her lips. Lucash shook out the sign and draped it off the edge of the platform, placing a brick in each of the two corners as he did so. Then he winked at her, as they jumped off the platform, ready to run. Their goal was to make it as close to where Mario and Dervin waited as possible, giving the guys the best chance of following the guard vehicle that would surely intercept their escape.

They made it further than they thought, and almost believed they might get away. Juniper was actually beginning to laugh from the feeling of victory when a hand clamped around her arm in a vice grip that was so hard it stopped her forward momentum instantly and caused her feet to fly out from under her. She felt a pull in her shoulder. A muscle stretching. Or ripping. The laugh turned into a yelp and a grimace. She was yanked up on her feet roughly.

Juniper struggled, trying to twist out of the guard's grasp, to no avail. She tried using her heel to kick back into his kneecap, but he easily evaded her movements. Her reward for that was a twisting of her arm at the already injured shoulder. The pain buckled her own knees under her, and she felt like she might faint. She briefly thought that might be a welcome relief. No such luck. She was on her feet again, with a club of some sort jabbing her ribs, hard.

She looked for Lucash, a faint glimmer of hope that maybe he'd gotten away. He had been in front of her. But then she saw him, just ahead. He'd been tased. Apparently more than once, as he was convulsing on the ground from the electrical currents moving through his body. A guard was standing over him, waiting to yank him into the nearby truck when the convulsions stopped.

Juniper became aware of the crowd of onlookers. She had enough of her wits about her still to see if they were also gathered by her display. They were. *Good*, she thought, *at least we got the job done*. She also noticed Dervin and Mario in the shadows of the building the truck was pulled in front of. They looked like the rest of the onlookers, except maybe more afraid than curious. Still, Dervin tried to give her a nod of encouragement as they loaded her into the truck.

CHAPTER 10

The rear doors to the truck remained open. Juniper was restrained against the cold metal interior. Her shoulder throbbed. Each time she tried to move, searing pain shot through her body. Looking out the doors, she could see that Lucash had stilled, but they were not picking him up yet. She could see no reason for it, other than perhaps to let the citizens milling about to witness for a little longer what happens to those who rebel. The throngs of people now filling the street all looked the same. Harried and hurried. But Juniper could see the glances shifting sideways as they walked by. Looking without wanting it to be known that they were looking. Curious, but unwilling to show it openly.

Juniper's own gaze returned to Lucash, still unmoving on the ground at the feet of the guard. She was growing more worried. She didn't think the taser would kill him, but he was lying so still. Was she wrong about that? She narrowed her eyes to better focus and looked at his chest to see if she could see him breathing, but she couldn't tell.

What she did see now, however, was the Council drone that moved in close to capture the incident on camera. That is when the Council Guard dragged Lucash to his feet, and not at all gently. He could not support his own weight yet, so the two guard members held him by his elbows and moved him along, his feet splayed out behind making no attempt to keep up. His head was bent forward and lolling from side to side with the movements of the guard. She couldn't see his face and couldn't tell if he was really conscious or not. And then they tossed him…literally tossed him…into the back, hopped up inside, and attached him to the wall on the bench next to her. *At least I can touch him*, she thought, *let him know I'm here too*. She did just that and felt an almost imperceptible nudge back in response. She exhaled, not realizing until that moment that she had been holding her breath.

The drone sat just outside the doors, still recording. *I guess this means Mom, Dad, and Mari will all know what happened to me.* She had hoped that wouldn't be the case, that her stunt was a little too much of a jab at Manglebee to get recorded, but it seemed that that wasn't to be. *It can't be helped now.* She could only hope that they understood a little of why she had to do this, though she doubted it. She also doubted they would be all that surprised.

The drone pulled back, and she saw the recording light go out before it took off out of sight. The two guards checked their restraints a final time, jumped from the back, slammed the doors, and, apparently, moved to the front of the truck because they jerked forward and began moving down the road. There were no windows in the back, just metal benches with restraints attached to metal walls, so there was no way to know how long Dervin and Mario were able to follow, or if they were at all. Within a few short moments, she felt the wheels glide from the smooth surface of the maintained roads in the city to the rough terrain of cracked and sometimes broken concrete that began just outside the city limits on this side of the city. And then there was no more pavement, just dirt tracks. No one was allowed out this far. No one except for the Council Guard.

"Lucash?" Juniper whispered as loudly as she dared, unsure of what the men up front could hear. "Lucash? You okay?"

He apparently heard her because he mumbled an unintelligible response. He also managed to lift his head part way before it fell forward again, but Juniper thought that was a good sign. He was starting to regain muscle control. "They filmed us. Council News did. Don't know if they got the whole thing, but they got us being put in here. We did it, though, Lucash! It worked just like we'd planned." She'd wanted to tell him that she saw Dervin and Mario, but without knowing if they could be heard, she didn't dare. Lucash gave a grunt that Juniper could only assume was indication of his abounding joy at their success. Or something like that.

Juniper let her head fall back against the side of the truck and winced in pain as she did so. Upon hearing her, Lucash tried to lift his head again to check on her and made it a bit further this time. Enough for his eyes to meet her sideways glance. They held the gaze for a moment, taking reassurance there, and then Lucash's head fell forward again. Juniper closed her eyes. There was nothing else to do. She tried not to think of the pain ripping through her shoulder and the rest of her body at every bump. Instead, she replayed her last words with Mari or imagined Dervin and Mario following the truck's tracks. They'd not made any turns yet, so up to this point, it shouldn't be hard for the guys to follow, so long as they didn't get caught.

Juniper thought about the trackers, wondering, not for the first time, how Dervin and Mario would avoid SMALS? They'd talked about it, of course, and the plan had been to follow as far as they dared, to see if they could tell where they were being taken. The hope had been that it wouldn't be far, and they could defy SMALS for a time, returning to present themselves to Westlow's DAD at the appointed time and making up plausible story for why they were following the Council Guard truck out of town. They all agreed the best bet was to tell them a vague version of the truth: the guys thought they knew one of us, and curiosity got the best of them because they'd never imagined that someone they knew could be a *rebel*. Perhaps offer up some seemingly important tidbits about Lucash acting suspicious at work or something to throw DAD off their connection and make it less likely there would be any serious repercussions.

They'd been on the road for too long. The truck wasn't going terribly fast, but Juniper thought they had been driving for well over an hour. There was no way Dervin and Mario would still be following. Now a cold fear started creeping into her belly. Perhaps it had been stupid for her to think that the guys might actually be able to follow them to the end. For the first time in her life, Juniper felt a complete loss of control. At this point, there was nothing else she could do. No other action to take. No escape. No defense. Just sit and wait to see what happened. That was not at all her style.

"Was it worth it, Lucash? Do you think?"

She was surprised when he actually lifted his head again, and then he answered. "Yes. We can't doubt ourselves now. We did what we had to do. And, besides, we aren't dead yet. That means there's still a chance." His words came out slow and thick, but they were coherent. They were Lucash. She nudged herself just a bit closer to him, as that was all she could do. It hurt, but she felt better. His look said he did as well.

So far, the guards hadn't stopped the vehicle or given any other indication that they were listening to the conversation in the back. Perhaps there was no need to. With the rebels in custody and restrained inside a metal container on the back of a truck, what could their words matter now? And they certainly weren't going anywhere. They hadn't even bothered to lock the back of the truck.

"I don't think the guys could possibly be following us still. We've been going for a long time now," Juniper gave voice to her fear.

"No, probably not. But who knows? Those two were itching to be involved. Mario would try, unless Dervin was able to keep him in check."

"I'm not sure who I want to win that battle."

Lucash gave a little laugh, "Me neither. But it won't do us any good at all if they're captured too."

"Good point."

"They'll figure something out. Too stubborn and bullheaded to let this go just because we drove outta sight."

"Right again," she paused and looked at him. "I'm glad you're here."

"Me too."

"So, let's assume Dervin and Mario aren't coming to our rescue…what are *we* going to do? We can't just sit here and let them do whatever it is they're planning to do us. Like you said. We aren't dead yet. So, what's our plan?"

"I don't know, but it seems we got time to—"

Lucash stopped mid-sentence, his words interrupted by the slowing of the truck. The same thoughts crossed both of their minds: had they arrived at their destination? Or was it possible that they were overheard, and now the guards were coming back to silence them? The truck came to a complete stop. Lucash looked at Juniper and pursed his lips in a silent *shhhhhh*, and then he dropped his head forward, pretending he was still incapacitated. Juniper understood immediately.

The doors opened again, but Juniper could not see anything but dirt tracks behind them, with clouds of dust still filling the air from the spin of the wheels, and a few scrubby trees, stunted and brown from the ongoing drought. The scene disappeared quickly when the two guards filled the entryway as they jumped back into the back of the truck. Without a word, one guard approached her, and the other guard, Lucash. He remained still and unmoving. Juniper did as well, until she saw the injection device coming towards her neck. She struggled against the restraints, to no avail. Lucash somehow managed to stay perfectly still, even as the guard jabbed his neck.

CHAPTER 11

Trevor sat at the kitchen table with Mica. It was just the two of them this morning. This seemed to happen with regularity these days, as their son was often out with his friends, taking advantage of school not being in session to spend long periods of time at one friend's house or another's. He couldn't blame him. He'd have done the same. But now he wished for the presence of another person to break the uncomfortable silence in the room. He and Mica weren't arguing. They hadn't had another fight. They just weren't talking. The sound of utensils clinking against plates was the loudest sound in the room. Trevor cut his meat into small pieces, but then just pushed them around on his plate.

He had no appetite after the morning meeting. He kept replaying the reaction from Manglebee when he'd heard that there were some who seemed to be immune to the virus. The number of individuals wasn't high. So far, they'd only discovered fewer than 50. Given how many had been injected, it was a low percentage of the total number of cases, and thus the ratio in the population was likely equally as low. But Manglebee was still positively furious, acting like it was Trevor's fault that this had happened. True, he should have had the list of names from Witton, but it hadn't occurred to him to get it. He assumed the numbers were all that was important. Well, that and the information that Witton and his team were investigating the reasons these individuals might be immune based on their genetic structure. It wasn't an easy task since they didn't have the people to actually test, but they were working with the information they had from the extensive medical records kept on file.

Manglebee had accused Trevor of being incompetent, at which point he had had just the briefest glimmer of hope that maybe Manglebee would release him from his duties. It was very brief. His hopes were dashed almost immediately when, rather than sending him on his way, Manglebee instructed him to contact Witton then and there to have him send over the list. It seemed he wasn't going to be returning to his normal life any time soon.

Witton hadn't responded right away. When he did respond, his message to Trevor had stated that he wasn't at BRO, so he didn't have immediate access to the list, but he would head there now. *Let Head Councilor know I'll get is as quickly as possible, but it could take me a couple of hours to get there. I'll send it over when I do.* Trevor reluctantly relayed the message to Manglebee, and then braced himself for the reaction. It came. And Trevor was relieved when Manglebee then dismissed them all, rather than have them all wait the two hours for Witton to send over the list.

Trevor was sent back to Montrose and arrived home in time to sit down for a late lunch. He was certain the list would be getting to Manglebee any time now, but he did not know what to expect after that. Manglebee hadn't said. As if on cue, his phone buzzed. He looked up at Mica, expecting a look of exasperation from her, but instead, he saw that her attention was entirely on her plate as she slowly ate bites of her food. He directed his attention to the message on his phone. It was from Henderson. Manglebee was demanding another meeting. Now.

CHAPTER 12

Rebecca awoke to the sounds of her parents downstairs in the kitchen. There was laughter. That had been a foreign sound in their household since Jonathan's illness and death. More than just an absence of laughter, there was a serious lack of conversation in general, with her parents keeping to themselves much of the time. Every once in a while, they'd disappear for a day, leaving Rebecca to fend for herself. Where they went was a mystery. They would check on her wellbeing frequently, always asking her how she was doing and telling her that she could talk to them if she wanted, but it was almost perfunctory. She knew they loved her, that they did truly care about how she was doing, but she didn't think they really had it in them to take care of her right now. They could barely take care of themselves.

But now, they were apparently in the kitchen. Together. And there was laughter.

She crept down the stairs quietly, not wanting them to hear her, fearing she'd break whatever spell was cast upon them. She sat against the wall, knees tucked up, just beside the entry to the kitchen, where she'd be out of site. She could smell the aroma of spices. And pasta, a family favorite. They were actually making pasta, for lunch, it seemed, as it was just now half past 12. It was late enough in the day that Rebecca's stomach growled at the smell of the cooking food, and she wrapped her arms around her stomach in an effort to quiet it.

"…remember that time we'd come home to find Jonathan, oh, I think he was maybe 5 or so, sitting on the floor with dry noodles and the marinara sauce, trying to make himself some dinner?" Her mom was laughing as she said this.

"Ooooh, yes. And what a mess that was to clean up. Poor Vicky, she felt so bad. She thought he was in his room. She was sure she would be reprimanded for that. But…hehe…no harm done. Just a little mess. And Jonathan finding out uncooked noodles don't taste so good!" her dad reminisced as he stirred the sauce.

"Oh, that boy, he always had a mind of his own. He sure thought he could do anything, didn't he?" Her mom asked, voice warm with the memories.

"And he could. It sure seemed like he could. But he was also a good kid. He was a good son, and a great big brother to Rebecca, though I'm sure she wouldn't always agree!"

"No, especially not right after he woke her up for school. She never liked mornings, but he made sure she was always up to catch the transit on time for school. Poor girl," They both chuckled over that.

He was the best brother, Rebecca thought, with a smile, *even when he was waking me up from a dead sleep…*

Rebecca sat listening to them for a few minutes more. They continued with their walk down memory lane. It made her so happy to hear that they'd gotten here, to this place where they seemed like themselves again, and where they could talk about and remember Jonathan without all the tears.

"Should we wake Rebecca now, so she can have some of this while it's hot?" her mom asked.

"No, not just yet. Let her get a few more minutes of sleep. We'll still wake her when it's ready, so we can all sit down to eat together.

With that, Rebecca went back up to her room to await their knock on her door. Their family only occasionally used the communication pads, especially with her being the sound sleeper she was. Or had been. She longed for the days of a solid, hard sleep, but those days were gone. Rebecca tiptoed up to her room, looking forward for the first time in months to the meal she would shortly be sharing with her parents, as a family. She knew that today Jonathan would be at the table with them, not as a sad memory this time, but, rather, as a happy presence filling the room just as it did when he was alive.

****

Lunch had been exactly as she'd hoped. Her parents' good mood lasted, and they all had stuffed themselves until they could barely lift themselves from the table. Rebecca had no idea what brought all this on, but she was glad for whatever it was, and hoped that it lasted. After dinner, her parents each had to go their own ways. Her dad had some work to do. With the new restrictions in place, her dad's work with the Citizen's Advisory Division was even busier than usual. Her mom was going to catch up on some work as well. Boring stuff, she'd said, but stuff she'd put off for far too long.

Rebecca decided to pay a visit to Cedar. She had hours to kill before it was her turn to go inside the BRO facility with Daniel and Perce. She couldn't spend them just sitting around waiting. She needed to get out for a bit, get some fresh air and feel the cold air on her face and the warmth of Cedar as she ran across the fields. Before she could get Cedar out of the barn, her Colossus phone buzzed. Her heart skipped a few beats. Her first thought was that something had gone wrong, but no one had gone into BRO yet. Selby, Remy, and Zeche still had almost four hours.

She pulled out her phone and looked at the message. Daniel. Now her heart skipped a beat for another reason.

What are you doing? Can you meet? To go over tonight's plans again. The wait is killing me. Maybe the time will go faster if we waited together.

Rebecca tried not to get too excited at the thought. He was just bored and anxious, after all. It made sense to get together to go over plans. This was their first real assignment with Colossus. Waiting out some of the time in the company of a friend might help pass the hours. That was all it was, surely.

I can meet. I was just taking Cedar out for a ride. Meet me at the river where the road goes up to your place? That way I can still exercise her. And we'll be hidden.

She waited for his reply, leading Cedar out of the barn as she did.

Sure thing. See you there soon. Leaving now.

She sent him a quick response: *Me too. See you there.*

Rebecca was glad Selby had disarmed their trackers all those weeks ago. So far, what he'd done worked. They'd all just left them disarmed anymore because of their involvement with Colossus. His method was better than what Colossus had been using, so the device and the technique were replicated within the rest of the organization. *They really are lucky to have Selby*, she thought, *we all are*. With that thought, she hopped on Cedar's back, taking ahold of her mane, and giving her a nudge of encouragement to get her moving. It didn't take much, and soon she had her worked up to a gallop, as they made their way across the fields towards Daniel.

While Daniel was closer to their meeting place, she had ridden Cedar fast enough that she still was the first to arrive. She had slowed Cedar to a walk for the last few minutes so that she would not be overheated when they stopped, and now Rebecca led her to the river so that Cedar could drink her fill before grazing on the nearby grass. The afternoon sun warmed the chill of the late winter air.

No longer did they get the mountain winters of decades past. Rebecca had heard about those: snow for months, sometimes several feet falling in the mountains during a single storm, and temperatures below freezing even during the daytime. This weather still occurred in some places on the planet, high up in the mountains of the most northern and southern latitudes. But here, in Montrose, while they still got snow in the mountains, it was measured in inches rather than feet. And it often melted off in the afternoons as the temperatures rose above freezing. Occasionally, they'd get a freak snowstorm followed by colder than normal temperatures. This was a cause for excitement and celebration when it occurred. Even the adults in Montrose could be seen packing up an arsenal of snowballs and joining in a good-natured snowball fight.

Today, though, was a typical Montrose winter. It was cold enough to see her breath, and she'd had to wear a winter jacket and hat to ride Cedar. But now, as she sat by the water, out of the shade of the trees and in the sun, she unfastened her jacket and removed her hat, letting the heat of the sun seep into her skin and warm her from the outside in. She closed her eyes and tipped her head back, enjoying the quiet of the afternoon for the moments she waited for Daniel, hearing nothing but the wind rustling the leaves in the trees and the water flowing rapidly over the rocks strewn across the river in front of her.

For the moment, Rebecca was able to forget everything but the sun and the wind and the water. Her mind was just…empty. She felt Daniel approach but remained as she was. He sat down beside her without a word, recognizing her calm demeanor for the peacefulness it signified, then laid all the way back in the grass, arms crossed under his head. The silence between them was comfortable, and neither was in a hurry to break it.

When at last one of them spoke, it was Daniel, still lying on his back with his eyes closed, "This sure beats waiting around the house watching Remy pace like he's in a cage. Even Dad noticed."

"*Way* better than waiting at home. What did he say? Your dad, when he saw Remy."

"Asked him why he was pacing like an animal in a cage. Remy just said he had a lot on his mind with work. Which is basically true. Dad's used to him saying stuff like that, so he just went back to what he was doing."

"Are you afraid of your mom and dad finding out about all this? It almost seems impossible that they haven't yet."

"Oh yeah. I'm afraid of that, like, all the time. I think it would kill them to know that the ranch is being used like this."

"Not to mention *both* their sons working with Colossus."

"Heh, yeah, can't really even think about that part. Knowing what Council is doing with the ranch would kill them but knowing what we're doing with Colossus…well…pretty sure they'd kill *us*. How 'bout your parents? What do you think they'd do if they found out?"

"I think they'd be terrified. They just lost Jonathan. Me doing anything that might make them lose me, too, would be too much. I used to not worry that much, though, because they've been so in their own little worlds after Jonathan died that they barely noticed me. Or each other, even. They barely even noticed when I turned 15 last month, which was fine. I almost forgot, too…would have, probably, if Cassidi hadn't remembered. But now, it might be time to worry about my parents."

"Because of what we're doing tonight?"

"Yes, that. But also because of today. Today they were basically *normal*. When I woke up this morning, or lunch time actually, I could hear them *laughing* in the kitchen. They were cooking together, and they were actually talking. Remembering things about Jonathan. My mom didn't cry even one single tear."

Rebecca couldn't believe she was saying all this to Daniel. She hadn't even been sure she was going to tell Cassidi because it all felt so fragile. She was afraid that if she talked about it, it would make it all disappear, like it never happened. She wanted to hold on to that feeling of the three of them making up a normal family. Even though they had talked about Jonathan, it didn't feel like his ghost was haunting them. It just felt like memories. Or more than that, but it wasn't sad. She wasn't sad, and her parents didn't seem to be either.

Yet, telling Daniel felt easy. Maybe because it wasn't something she had thought about. She never would have even considered the idea of telling him anything so personal. She would have thought it would make her feel too vulnerable. Instead, it had been easy. It had seemed like the most natural thing in the world to do, and rather than feeling vulnerable, she felt relief. Relief that speaking it made the afternoon feel more real, not less. Relief that she felt nothing from Daniel but kindness and understanding.

As if to emphasize this last, Daniel rolled over onto his side, leaning on his arm and propping his head in his hand, looking at her now, instead of the sky. "It must be crazy hard for you. Losing your brother and then feeling like your parents weren't really there anymore either."

She glanced down at him and, seeing the kindness in his eyes, turned away again in case she started to cry. "It is. But only sometimes. It's been months, and we have all this insane stuff happening now. Life doesn't feel real anymore. And sometimes, I forget why I'm doing this. That I'm doing it for Jonathan. I feel bad for forgetting. But with all the training and planning and just being a part of Colossus, it's like sometimes there isn't room in my brain to think about Jonathan, or to miss him. Is that bad?"

"No. No, of course not." With this, Daniel laid a comforting hand on her arm, "It's just how you deal. You're still doing this for Jonathan, but you can't think about that all the time. I didn't know him, of course, but he was in some of my classes, and I saw how he was with you. I bet he wouldn't want you to think about him all the time."

Rebecca smiled, "You're totally right. He wouldn't."

Daniel removed his hand from her arm and rolled back over onto his back. Rebecca felt the absence where his hand had been, pressing warmth through her jacket and shirt and onto her skin. It made her shiver a little with the now heightened perception of cold where warmth had been. She hoped he hadn't noticed.

"I wonder what Jonathan would have thought about all this," Daniel mused.

"I know. I wonder that, too. I think if he could see me, he'd be happy to know I listened to him, for once. And proud of me for doing stuff that scares me."

"Like what?"

"Well, first thing would have been climbing up that mountain. He was a rock climber, but I'm terrified of heights. And you almost made me fall over the edge that first time you found me up there," she teased.

Daniel laughed, "I remember that. I had no idea you were scared of heights, but I remember I had to catch you because you jumped completely out of your skin when I said hi."

"Do you blame me? I didn't hear your footsteps. Didn't even know you were there until you said something to me as I was *spying* on your ranch! It's like you did it on purpose. Like you wanted to scare me."

"Honestly? Not really. I *did* sneak up on you on purpose. I wanted to watch you without you knowing I was there right away. I was curious about why you were there. And about you. Didn't exactly think about it when I did say something. Just thought I needed to let you know I was there. I'm glad you didn't fall over the edge, though," he turned his head in her direction and grinned at her. "But I'm sorry for scaring you. How long have you been afraid of heights?"

"For as long as I can remember."

"It's really cool that you were able to climb up that mountain."

"Thanks. I was terrified. It was just as bad trying to look over the side. Thought I'd lose my breakfast. Except I didn't eat that morning because I was *so* nervous. But I did find out that the binoculars helped me. I could look through them without being super dizzy. I'm really glad we use roads and trails now, that's for sure."

"Me too. I don't want to have to see you pass out or lose your lunch." Now he was teasing her, and she laughed right along with him.

"What do you think we'll find tonight?" asked Rebecca, her thoughts shifting to their plans for the night.

"Bodies," Daniel smiled.

"Haha."

"Seriously, though, I wish I knew what else besides that. I keep thinking about what I hope we *don't* find. But I hope we find something. Something that gives us a clue about what's behind all this."

"Yeah, me too. I know I don't want to run into any BRO people. I've seen some of them. Once was enough for me. I called one Zeus because he reminded me of a Greek god because, I mean, he was just HUGE. That's someone I hope I never see again."

"Let's hope not."

Rebecca looked at her watch. It was only an hour before Selby would be heading in with Remy and Zeche. How had so much time passed just sitting here talking to Daniel?

Daniel saw her glance at her watch. "Do you have to go?"

"No. Not yet. But probably soon, in case my mom and dad come home and wonder where I'm at. Probably should eat, too, I guess," Rebecca said, but added, quickly, "But I've got a little while longer," in case he thought she still really wanted to go.

"Good."

"Do you need to see Remy before he goes?"

"I will. Let's go over the plans for tonight. It'll be good just to review them. Then we can go. I'll still have time to see Remy and you can get some dinner. Can't have your stomach making noises while we're in there tonight. Might give us away…" he winked at her and she grinned in return. And with that, they got down to their presumed reason for meeting in the first place.

CHAPTER 13

"You guys aren't gonna like what I have to tell you…" Selby said to his parents.

"Somehow, I didn't think we were, Son," his mom replied, "but you best go ahead and tell us anyways."

Knowing there was nothing else he could really do, Selby told them the truth. All of it. From beginning to end, including Jonathan's plea to Rebecca. To their credit, they listened without interruption. Their faces passive, he couldn't tell what they were thinking. But he kept going until the story was told up to the current chapter, finishing with informing them of the plans for tonight.

"So, that's…that's it. I wanted to tell you; I really did. But Becs…"

"You still should have told us. It was wrong of you to promise Rebecca that you would keep this secret from us, your parents. Even more so because you went behind our backs to use our equipment. You know how valuable it is, and how difficult it would be to replace it if anything were to get lost or damaged," his father spoke for the first time, quietly. He sounded more disappointed than angry. *That*, thought Selby, *is worse*.

"Yeah…I mean, yes…," his parents hated the word 'yeah', "I know. I just didn't really know what to *do*. Becs just lost Jonathan, and she needed my help. I knew that. And I didn't want her to get hurt. Or anyone else."

"What about this group you're involved with now? Do they not have any concern about the danger they are putting you children into? And what do they think about you not telling us?" his mom asked.

Selby wanted to point out that they weren't exactly children, that all of them were 15 now, except for Troy, who would catch up to the rest of the gang later that month. But he thought better of it, saying instead, "Oh, they worry alright. At least Bryn and Remy do. Maybe not so much Melody. She's too worried about takin' down Manglebee. But she's also seen us train. We're good. All of us, and she thinks we're ready for this. You've trained me pretty much my whole *life*, and I knew a lot going in, but the others, well, they're fast learners. They're good, too," Selby said, hoping to reassure his parents. "And," he added, "they don't know who I get the equipment from. I wouldn't tell 'em. Told 'em I wouldn't betray my source. They know nothin' about the group or about your background or survivin' The Reckoning."

His parents both sat quietly, absorbing the information Selby provided. Selby sat waiting. He knew better than to interrupt their thoughts or overstate his case. At last, his father leaned forward, resting his elbows on his knees and loosely clasping his fingers together, steepling his pointer fingers and tapping them together lightly.

"When we trained you, it was with the idea that, at some point in time, it might be necessary to use the skills we've taught you to survive the collapse of this country, just as we had to during The Reckoning. The skills are for survival, not for initiating conflict. Your mom and I, and the rest of us, did what we did to survive. We blended in, hid, fought when we had to, and then when it was safe, we came back out again," he spoke the words in a low and measured tone, so that Selby was not quite sure where he was going with this lecture.

"What you're doing now seems unnecessarily dangerous. You are purposefully placing yourself in a situation that is life-threatening. To you and to your friends," his mom added. "While it is commendable that you wanted to help Rebecca, it seems like you and your friends have allowed yourselves to get carried away and involved in an operation that is above your heads and beyond what your experiences have left you capable of dealing with."

"What guarantees have the leaders of this group…Colossus, you called it?" Selby nodded and his father continued, "What guarantees have they given for your safety? What measures have been put in place to ensure you children are as safe as they can make you?"

"Well, they're sendin' us in with experienced people. Like, I'm going in with Zeche and Remy. They wouldn't let me do anything stupid. Not that I would. But that's why Melody is makin' us go in with at least one person who's done this sort of work for a while."

"I guess that demonstrates that they aren't entirely inconsiderate of your safety and inexperience," his mom said, "but, I'm still not sure I can support your participation in this group. This goes against the principles of survival we've worked so hard to instill in you." She looked to Selby's dad, who indicated his agreement with a nod of his head.

"But this is *different* from what happened to you back then. It's different than The Reckoning!" Selby exclaimed, fearing he'd have to defy his parents in the end because there was no way he wasn't going tonight, or that he'd walk away from Colossus now. No *way*.

"Do you think that we didn't face imminent danger, Son? That people we knew and loved weren't being threatened or killed? Every day, we faced the reality that our *government* was now waging war against its *own* people. The people they were supposed to protect and serve. It was a violent time, and we knew our best chances were to lay low, wait it out, and defend ourselves when we needed to," his father's voice rose, just a little, but enough that Selby knew he was getting upset and impatient.

"Okay, maybe it's kinda the same, but not exactly. You guys at least *knew* you were at war, you knew that Manglebee was sending his army out to either make people do things his way or kill them if they didn't. If Becs hadn't gone to check this stuff out after Jonathan told her what was up before he died, none of us would know we were at war with Manglebee again. We'd just be watchin' everyone around us die, waiting for our turn. We wouldn't even *know* to go into hiding because we wouldn't know it was our own government killing us with this virus-y thing! And if Colossus hadn't found us, we wouldn't've had the training and we wouldn't know everything we know now about exactly what BRO is doing for Manglebee! Don't you see, this *is* about survival now?" The words flowed out in a torrent. Selby didn't even pause for a breath in his rush to be heard, afraid his parents would cut him off.

His dad sat back against the back of the couch again and let out an audible breath. His mom's eyebrows raised in surprise, and then knitted together in thought. Another silence, but in this one, Selby felt he'd gotten somewhere. He held his breath as he watched their faces, afraid to move a muscle, feeling their decision was teetering on a brink and the slightest nudge from him could send them down the wrong side again.

"Well," the word came out clipped, followed by a deep sigh and a shake of the head, "you have made an excellent point. I will concede that this does seem to be different in nature from the last time. Can you give your mom and me some privacy for a few minutes?" said his dad in a question that really wasn't a question. "We will call you down when we're ready for you."

Selby made sure to keep himself calm and composed, face in neutral, as he rose from the chair and walked upstairs to his room. Once in his room, with the door closed behind him, he gave out an almost silent whoop of celebration. While he didn't know what exactly his parents were discussing right now, he was certain they saw his point, and he was almost as certain, because of that, they wouldn't forbid him to participate.

Selby paced his room. It was fully light outside, and he knew he should be on the verge of collapse, but he wasn't. The adrenaline was still coursing through his veins from both the night's events and the meeting with his parents. He hoped that their conversation had a good end and that he'd be able to sleep afterwards so that he'd be on his game that night. It was a big night for them. The answers they all sought would not come from tonight's expedition, but they'd be one step closer to getting them.

Becs...oh, no, he thought, stopping dead in his tracks, and then falling onto his bed...*what do I tell her now? Oooohhh, she's so gonna kill me...I promised...*he let out a groan. Surely, she'd understand. There was nothing else he could have done. She'd see that. Right? He looked at his watch. She was probably still sleeping now. Maybe it would be best not to let her know before tonight anyway. Because he'd be going tonight, even if it meant his parents kicked him out of the house. He allowed himself a small smile, thinking that was now not likely to be the case. He'd wait to tell Rebecca until he could talk to her in person, and after they had both completed their tasks tonight, since she was going in right after him.

Now that that was decided, he allowed his mind to drift back to his parents' conversation downstairs. This sure was taking them longer than he'd like. What could they have to discuss for so long? It seemed to him their discussion should be pretty straightforward. He was right. They were wrong. He should be allowed to continue as planned. End of story. He got up from his bed and started pacing again. He was like a leopard in pen. His long, lanky limbs seemed to fill the room, and within a matter of a few strides, he was across the length of the bare, concrete floor, where he flipped directions with a little less finesse than his limbs normally would exhibit for lack of adequate space to freely move in.

At last, his mom's voice came through on the communication pad on his wall. "You can come on down now, Selby, we're ready for you." His mom sounded even more formal than usual, which made him anxious about what they'd say when he got downstairs. Suddenly, his certainty in their response evaporated into thin air. He set his jaw, as he set his mind, determined that they would not sway him from his course. When he felt ready, he made his way downstairs.

Selby's parents still sat in their same places on the couch, same expressions on their faces, so that it seemed time had stood still when he went upstairs. He took his seat again across from them, but sat rigidly, barely able to contain the nervous energy in his body.

"We have discussed your situation and your deception, and we have come to some decisions. First, while we commend your loyalty and desire to help your friend, we cannot condone your deception, no matter how noble your intentions. We are sympathetic to your reasons, but this cannot happen again. Under no circumstances. Ever. No matter how good your reason, you are not to use our equipment without our knowledge and consent."

Wait, his dad's words made it sound like he would be able to still use the equipment, that they just had to know about it and give the okay. So, did that mean? For the second time this morning, he found himself holding his breath, waiting for what was to come next. Daring to hope…

"Second, if what you've told us about Manglebee is true, then we will also allow that you are right that this probably is different than The Reckoning and calls for different tactics. What you, your friends, and Colossus are doing could be important. It seems that our survival is at stake, but the war is being fought on secretive turf. If so, we have to fight back." His mom's voice sounded urgent.

Hold up, Selby thought, *did she just say "we?"*

"Yes. You heard me right. In order for you to be able to continue your involvement with Colossus, your dad and I must be included as well. I'm sure your group could use our skills. And we will at least have a little comfort in knowing we can provide some protection to you and your friends."

"But it isn't up to me! I can't just say yo…include my mom and dad because they won't let me stay in unless you do. Colossus doesn't work that way."

"We understand how these things work," his dad chided. "We expect that you will set up a meeting with the head of Colossus, however it is that that happens. You can tell them we have skills that they will find useful."

"I doubt I can convince Melody to meet with anyone, but Bryn and Remy maybe could, and I know I can get them to meet with you. Probably."

"Alright, then, do that. We realize you have big plans for tonight, and you said this Remy you were just talking about is going along with you. He seems a responsible sort from what you've said. We will allow you to proceed with your plans tonight, but you will have to talk to him immediately afterwards."

"Okay…okay…I can do that," Selby had no idea what Remy would say, but at least he could confront that situation after they finished with their task tonight. "Uh. So. It might help if I told Remy more about you, about your background and stuff. Especially if I told them that it's you guys who trained me and have the goods they've been using since I came on board."

"As I am sure you can imagine, we are more than a little leery of disclosing too much about ourselves to outsiders, but we recognize that in this situation it is likely to be the only way forward. We will have to trust your judgement about the character of the people in this group. It's a risk we realize we must take if we expect to be included in this fight," his father said, his apprehension clear in the tone of his voice. Just then, Selby realized his parents were scared. Not just for him, but for themselves, too. It shined a different light on them, made them seem more vulnerable than he ever thought they could be. That fact made him feel almost protective of them. He now knew what it must be like to be in their shoes, as parents to a child they trained to think for himself and defend himself and who they now had to, on some level, trust to do just that.

"I promise, you can trust these guys. I'll talk to Remy tonight, after we finish up at BRO. Bryn isn't going in, but I'm sure she'll be waitin' to hear how things went down, so I can probably talk to them both."

"Okay. We trust you. Now, I think you need to get some sleep. It sounds like you had an eventful night, and you need to be fully rested for tonight. So, eat something, then get upstairs to bed," his mom said, as she stood to head into the kitchen, presumably to find some food for him.

"Yep, I think I can do that. Thanks, Mom. Dad." Just then, a thought occurred to Selby. "You guys…uh…you guys won't tell anyone else, will you? In your group? Or any of the other parents?"

"No. For now, we will keep it to ourselves. We can see how letting others know would complicate things, and we understand the need for Colossus to be secretive. So, no, we won't tell anyone else," his dad said, "for now." Then he, too, rose from the couch and headed towards the kitchen.

So. That's that, I guess, Selby thought, shaking his head, *life sure is strange.* And he moseyed in after them, feeling at once the weight of the night and these most recent events dragging his eyelids down and making his legs feel like lead. He hoped he made it through lunch without crashing right there at the table.

CHAPTER 14

The Council Guards had resumed driving the truck immediately after injecting Juniper and Lucash. The two were stunned when they were still alive and conscious after the injection. It also left them confused. The truck rolled on, jostling over bumps and potholes in the road.

"What do you think *that* was about?" Juniper asked once the guards had resumed driving.

"No idea. But I'm sure we'll find out soon enough. Just glad it didn't kill us, whatever it is," Lucash responded.

"Yet."

"Right. Yet. Which means we still have time. Maybe it's another kind of tracking device or something."

"Yeah," Juniper said, without much conviction. Somehow, she could not help but feel that Council would be up to something far more sinister than just another tracking device. They wouldn't get off that easy. No way.

"Yeah. I'm sure you're right," Lucash responded, reading her thoughts. "So, what do we do now? Just wait?"

"No. We plan, just like we were starting to do before they so rudely interrupted us. We don't know what it is yet, so we might as well continue on with sorting out our next moves. Except it might be more urgent now, since we don't know what this'll do to us."

"So. You think there's any way out of this?" Lucash asked.

"Well, they aren't locking the back doors, so if we can get out of these bindings, we can just jump out. Make our way back, or hideout in the Borderlands."

"But, the trackers…" Lucash began.

"I've been wondering…would they work out here? In the Borderlands? I mean, I wonder if there's a signal out here at all."

"No way of knowin', 'cept to try it, right? Maybe they don't have a signal out here, since, who in their right minds would ever come out this way? Most people wouldn't know how to survive out here."

"Exactly my thinking…I've thought a lot about you and me escaping out here and living off the land, before we joined the Resistance. We could do it. I'm sure we could. One of the things

I always wondered about is if the trackers work out here in the middle of nowhere…"

"Council counts on keeping us afraid of them to keep us in line, but how much of what they say is real?"

"Well, we know the trackers are real…"

"Uh, yeah…how many times have you been called in front of DAD now?"

"Too many to count…" Juniper gave up trying to keep track of how many times she had received a message from SMALS about her wanderings, and then, subsequently, the command to appear in front of DAD.

"Willing to risk it? Getting caught out here, if we can get out of the truck?" Lucash asked.

"I'm game if you are. But how do we get out? How do we release these bindings? And *why* is it so hot in here?" Juniper's face was flushed, and beads of sweat were starting to appear on her forehead.

"Wow, Juniper, you're really sweating, and it isn't even warm in here. No heat at all. You feelin' okay?"

"Feelin' really hot. Must be nerves and all the excitement."

"Since when have you ever reacted this way to a little excitement? Anything else wrong?"

"Got a little headache, and my whole body hurts. But that's been the thing since the guard ripped up my shoulder and yanked me around. Nothin' I haven't been through before, though.

Headache is probably from that, too. And getting tossed all over the place in this truck," Juniper said as the truck clunked over a particularly large pothole, causing them both to bounce around on their seats, straining against the straps holding their hands and feet in place. "So, how are we getting outta here? Any ideas?"

"You sure you're okay? You really don't look so good."

"Well, thanks. Neither do you," Juniper responded with as much sarcasm as she could muster.

"Okay, I get it. We'll move on. It's just that it's makin' me nervous that those injections might actually *do* something to us."

"Me too. All the more reason to act quickly. If something does happen, I don't want to be in the hands of these brutes if we can help it at all. Rather take my chances sick and dying out on our own in the Borderlands. So…back to the same question…any ideas?"

"Just one. I'm not sure if I can cut these bindings loose with my knife, or if I can even reach it, but if I can, I say we jump and hope they don't notice."

"And hope the trackers don't work here."

"Right."

"Where's the knife. Didn't even know you brought one, by the way, but, good thinking."

"I almost didn't…didn't want it used against one of us, or have it discovered, since I'm not supposed to have it on me unless it's for work. That alone would be cause for the Council

Guard to kill us on the spot. Decided to risk it anyway. It's hooked to the inside of my pants at the waist, jabbing me good in the side right now."

Their bindings were tight enough to allow for little movement of hands or feet, with hands strapped to the bench and feet strapped to the base of the bench at the ankles. They both worked their hands to see how much movement they could gain in each direction. Not much. It quickly became evident that Lucash would never be able to reach up to his waist, no matter what he did. Juniper, however, had more wiggle room with her tiny wrists. She maneuvered her body as low as she could go, working against the pain that ripped through her shoulder and shot down her arm, across her back, and up through her neck. She ignored it all.

She also felt very light-headed, but she didn't dare say as much to Lucash. Sweat was now pouring out of every pore in her body. She finally was able to reach Lucash's pants, but not far enough up to get to the knife. She collapsed back against the back of the truck in exhaustion.

"You were almost there, Juniper. Let's try something else. Maybe the two of us, if we scoot our bodies closer together, we can work it out that way. If you can just get your hands to reach the bottom of the knife, that would help provide some leverage to push against."

"Okay. Just a sec. Let me catch my breath." Juniper spoke with her eyes closed. "How are you doing?" She asked.

"Me? Oh, I'm fine. Feel mostly normal now after that taser shock. A little banged up. But other than that, I feel normal. Maybe what you're feeling has nothin' to do with the injection they just gave us. Maybe it's just you're getting sick cuz of all this excitement." Lucash had never known Juniper to be sick, and she was not one to be affected by stress, but what else could it be? Sweating in the chill of the truck, flushed skin, headache: they all were symptoms of the kinds of illness people often got these days.

The warming of the planet meant that more people got sick, but there were always anti-virals to help in the recovery. If it was a virus. If it was a bacterial infection, not much could be done. At one time, there had been antibiotics to help, but with the overuse of these medications in the past, they had lost their effectiveness. Many scientists warned that the same could happen with anti-viral medications, but no one listened. Research on nutrition and genetics was making progress, and the hope was that some day it would be possible to engineer food and people in a way that would eradicate illness and disease from the planet. Thus far, research progress had not kept pace with the evolution of viruses, bacteria, or food shortages caused by the changing climate.

"That's actually heartening. I can handle sick. If you're feelin' fine, then I bet the injection was something else." She opened her eyes, turned to look at Lucash, and said, "Okay, let's give your idea a go."

With that, the two shifted in their seats so that they were touching at the hips. Juniper could feel the knife. Now, if only she could wriggle her fingers up high enough to reach the bottom…She strained against the binding, tears of pain springing to the rims of her eyes. A little further…

Just a little more…

The truck hit yet another bump in the road, throwing the pair off balance. Juniper cursed, and Lucash let out a groan of frustration.

"Let's try again, before we get thrown around again," Juniper said.

"Do you need a break?"

"No! No. Let's do this fast. We don't know how much time we have, and I *really* want to get out of here. Ready?" Lucash nodded his head once in response. They both readjusted their bodies again, attempting to move back into the previous position. Once there, Juniper made a final thrust of her hand to shift it so that her fingers just met with the base of the knife.

"Got it!" She exclaimed in a tight voice, the effort to keep her hand in place a struggle. "Okay, see if you can move down against my fingers. Hurry. Not sure how long I can hold this."

Lucash was already in motion as Juniper gave the instructions, and the knife slid out from his waistband and into the space where their legs met. The knife dropped to the bench as they slowly moved apart, and Juniper snatched it up before it fell to the floor with the next jostle of the truck.

"Got it!" Juniper said again. Sweat was running rivers down her forehead and her hair was damp from the effort.

"Can you manage the cutting? Or should I try?"

"Don't know if you can reach. Let me just try to get your one hand free, then you do the rest."

Juniper opened the knife and slid it between Lucash's wrist and the binding. It was a tight fit and didn't leave much room for maneuvering. She hoped she wouldn't slice his hand but couldn't be too worried about that. They just had to get out. The truck slowed again. Lucash and Juniper froze, holding their breath until they realized they were just turning a corner. The first one since leaving town. Juniper worked faster, using the last of her strength to get through the binding. Once she at last accomplished the task, Lucash took the knife from her and made quick work of his other three bindings and then her four. Triumphant, they gave each other a quick hug, Juniper falling into Lucash.

"Let's get you out of here and into a place with cover. I hope there's trees out there. You really don't look good at all. Here's the plan. I'm going to crack open the one door and see what we're dealing with. Then you're gonna have to jump while I hold the door…so it doesn't go slamming open in the wind. Then, I'll slip out, holding on to the door handle. Close the door, then jump. K?"

"Sure. Glad you're able to think straight right now. Let's do it," said Juniper.

Lucash looked her over and silently willed her the strength to make the jump without breaking anything. He held onto the side of the truck to stay upright over the roads, thankful that the rough ride meant slower speeds. Grabbing the handle, Lucash gave it a quick pull, holding tight while he eased the door open. The noise was not as loud as he feared. Looking out, he could see they were entering mountain country. Good. It would be easier to hide once they got off the truck.

"Okay, Juni…we're in as good a spot as we could hope for. You're gonna jump, then head off on the left for the trees there. Get off the road quick and stay low. I'll do the same and come back to you. Got it?"

Juniper was by then standing just behind him, gathering up her reserves to make the jump. "Got it." Lucash helped her maneuver in front of him as he kept a tight hold on the door. He opened it enough to allow her to ease through. Juniper squinted in the bright light of the afternoon sun as it headed down towards the horizon. It seemed so much brighter than normal. The cool air hitting her face felt wonderful, though. She had just enough time to take note of the wind, the sun, the dirt road stretching out behind them, and the trees that were her safety. And then she jumped.

CHAPTER 15

It was still daylight as Selby began to ready himself for the night's task. Glancing out the window, he could see that darkness would be falling quickly, as the sun was beginning to sink behind the mountains to the west. Antsy, he rummaged through his pack to ensure everything was in order. Twice. He fidgeted with his Colossus phone, waiting for the signal from Remy to head out to their meeting place.

Selby didn't want to go downstairs yet, where he knew his parents were waiting to see him out the door. They'd been full of advice and caution, filling his ears and overwhelming his brain with a litany of tactical maneuvers should he run into trouble, questioning the plans arranged for the night, and multiple reminders to speak to Remy after their mission and to hurry home when they were finished. His parents, normally of calm, cool, and collected demeanor, were now an uneasy combination of clucking hens and generals at war as the time for his departure grew nearer. They had made him more nervous than anything he had done with Rebecca or Colossus so far, and he wanted his last interactions before leaving for the night to be as brief as possible.

When his phone finally did signal the alert from Remy, Selby was out his bedroom door in a flash. But quiet. Hoping he could sneak out.

No such luck, of course.

They lay in wait, eyes on the stairs as he reached the top step.

"Is it time?" asked his mom, a worried note in her voice, but her face seeming almost impassive.

"Yep. Gotta run. They're expectin' me in ten minutes."

"You'll remember everything we told you, won't you?" his father was saying, as both his parents stood up to approach him, wanting, he was sure, to run through the list again.

"Yep," replied Selby and, tapping his head with two fingers, he added, "it's all right here. Won't forget a thing." He was out the door then, and almost had it closed before he swung it open again and ducked his head back inside, "and don't worry. I'll see ya soon."

The sun was beneath the ridges of the mountains and a brilliant sunset lit up the sky. Deep reds and oranges threw the mountains into an ink black silhouette, and as Selby jogged off in their direction, his shadow-shape joined theirs.

Selby could just make out Remy's truck as he rounded the corner towards their meeting place. Remy must have seen him as well because he heard the truck start up. When he approached, he could see that Zeche was already there as well, so he climbed in the back seat of the cab and added his pack to theirs on the opposite side of the bench.

By now, dark was settling in, though it was still early. Most people would be sitting down to eat their evening meals right now. They were counting on any weekend workers already making their way to their homes and families by the time they reached the BRO facilities. They were driving up to the ranch. They'd get as close to the facility as they dared, park the truck, and then hike in the rest of the way.

"Are you sure you're up for this, Selby?" asked Remy.

"What? You need to ask?" Selby replied indignantly.

"No. I suppose not."

"Just make sure you do as you're told, kid," Zeche said, "I'm the only one who can get this place mapped, so I can't be worried about what you're doing, too."

"I know, I know. Have a little confidence, man. I think you'll see I'm a pretty level-headed guy, even if I do like me some adventure, too. Just not a person who likes to sit around waitin' for stuff to get done when you could be doin' stuff instead, ya know?"

Zeche grunted a response that sounded like it could have been agreement.

Remy drove the truck past his house and down a track that faded away at the edge of the mountainside. Remy kept going.

"This used to be the road back to the valley, but we quit using it, so it's grown over. BRO workers go in another way, so they don't go past our house. Supposed to be for privacy for the family. But, of course, it's really to keep my parents from seeing too much," said Remy, as he flipped on the truck's lights for the first time.

"Yo, you sure it's okay to have the lights on?" Selby asked.

"We're safe. Too much tree cover for any of the drones to detect from above, and no one else would be using this road," Zeche replied.

The "road" was nothing more than flattened grass and weeds where Remy, and perhaps others in Colossus, had apparently driven on occasion. The road that had once been was no longer in evidence. As they drove, branches from the trees swiped the sides of the truck or struck the windshield and dragged across the roof. None of that slowed Remy. He seemed confident of what he was driving through and unfazed by the beating his truck was taking. And Zeche was equally as unaffected by the terrain. He pulled out his device and opened up the schema of the BRO facility, preparing the program for mapping the space they were headed into.

"So, how's that work?" asked Selby.

"It's pretty simple once you get used to it, really. The device does most of the work. See here, you aim it at what you're mapping, take the measurements, and enter in the codes for the object. Real easy for a building because there's usually not much to it but walls, doors, windows. But you can also add in other stuff if you want. More details. Won't do that tonight, though, we don't have time. I'll just enter in some notes if we find anything in there worth noting."

"Uh, yeah, like a lot of half-dead people?"

"Yeah, like that. I'll map the rooms first. Then we'll take stock of what's in them. If there's more than one room. I'll take notes, take some photos, and then we'll move on. Shouldn't take us long."

"Think I can learn how to use that program?"

"Sure, you could. Always good for more people to know it. Like I said, it isn't hard once you get the hang of it. Then it's just practice to get faster at it." Zeche seemed to relax with Selby as they talked. He demonstrated a couple of functions as they drove but didn't get far before Remy was pulling the truck off into a clearing. Zeche deleted what he'd just entered, but left the program open on the device, locked the screen, and then grabbed his pack and placed the device in it for the hike down to the entrance.

They all got out of the truck, shouldered their packs, and switched on headlamps.

"Stick close. We'll be in the trees the whole way down, and the trail is almost nonexistent, but the terrain isn't too bad," said Remy.

"How far we got before we're there?" asked Selby.

"Not far. Maybe twenty minutes. Try to stay quiet, in your walking and talking both. If someone happens to be outside, they might hear us. Sound travels in this valley, and it seems even louder at night."

Remy took off into the trees with the other two following close behind. It was true that everything seemed louder at night. The sharp crack of stick breaking under the weight of someone's shoe sounded like the electrical crack of lightening in a stormy sky directly overhead. A whispered voice could be heard from several feet away. Selby tried to walk lightly, but it seemed his every move caused a disturbance in the night. He kept waiting for Zeche, who was walking directly in front of him, to harass him about it, but Zeche just kept walking.

The forest seemed so much more alive at night than during the day. Insects zipped around, dancing in and out of the beam of his light. More than once, he caught the eerie light reflected from the eyes of small animals, or the multiple pricks of light cast from the spiders' eyes in the brush. Selby noticed more on this walk in than on the previous one, when he'd first made the trip inside BRO. The hike in now was much easier, but, for some reason, he was more nervous this time. Wearier of being discovered.

A movement off the trail to the right caused Selby to jump. He wasn't the only one. Even Zeche twitched at the sound. All three came to a halt. Listening. The sound came again. A slow movement. Branches snapping. Leaves crunching.

Headlamps off. Breath held.

The sound stopped. Almost as soon as they did. It wasn't too close, and it was impossible to tell what it was. It was too loud to be the scamper of the small animals found in the area, and the large animals had disappeared long ago. The three crouched low to the ground, not daring to speak for a few tense minutes. They waited, unmoving. It was all they could do until they were reasonably certain it was safe to move again.

"Can you either of you see anything?" asked Remy, voice just barely audible, as he peered into the darkness of trees and brush.

"Nothing," said Zeche.

Selby just shook his head.

They continued to crouch and squint into the darkness until Selby felt his legs going numb.

At last, Remy stood, "Stay here a minute. Listen for it again when I start moving." He walked away quietly and was quickly out of sight, footsteps fading into the dark after his shadow.

Zeche and Selby remained still, listening. The forest was quiet. Quieter, it seemed, than before they'd heard the noise. Selby imagined the forest creatures listening for the intruders along with them. He was sure that what they heard was real, but now there was nothing stirring in the night.

"We need to start moving. Time is getting short if we expect to get this done before the next group arrives," Zeche said, obviously a little annoyed at Remy's order to stay back. He'd taken no more than two steps in the direction Remy had gone when footsteps led Remy's form back into existence in front of them.

"Anything?" Remy whispered, noticing, but deciding to ignore, Zeche's look.

"Still nothing," Selby said.

"Let's move," Zeche added. "We are losing time with all this waiting and you wandering off."

"Yes. Let's move. I did not hear anything else or see anything in the direction we're going. Whatever it is, it's gone."

"Or whoever it is," Selby added.

"Or whoever," Remy agreed. "We're really close. We need to be even quieter now, if at all possible. Especially if someone might be following us."

"Eyes and ears open," said Zeche, prodding Remy forward with a gesture.

They switched their lights back on and took off with halting, ginger steps, still expecting something to come at them. Nothing did, and after a couple of minutes, they resumed their previous pace, though with even more caution.

Less than ten minutes later, they came to the bottom of the mountain and joined with the double track road Selby recognized from his first trip in. They'd not gone more than a few steps further, reaching the top of the rise where Troy had kept watch behind a tree on the previous adventure, when Remy came to an abrupt stop and pulled the other two back into the cover of forest.

The reason became quickly apparent. A truck was at the entrance and the doors were open to the back of the truck as well as to the entry to the BRO facility. Several people were milling about, looking the truck over, inspecting the inside, the undercarriage, and even climbing on the top.

"How could you *not* notice two people escaping?" came an angry voice from a figure who's back was to them.

"They were restrained. We injected them. There was no way for them to escape," was the reply. The voice was angry as well, but equally perplexed.

"Well they obviously did, now, didn't they? You had to have neglected a crucial precaution or they'd be right where they should be, and we wouldn't be having this conversation. What injection did you use and when?"

"The one we were given to use. Don't know what it was. Some white coat from here came up to us just as we were headed out for duty. Asked what district we were headed to. Told him we were being sent to beef up Westlow patrol cuz of all the trouble stirring in those parts lately. 'Good,' he says. Puts a syringe in my hand and says, 'then you'll be able to test this out for us today. Use it. Then take the prisoners to BRO instead of the prison facility.' We did as we were told. We injected them about an hour from here. Assumed it would incapacitate them, but they were still restrained. I don't understand how this happened."

"Then I suggest you start searching and hope that you find them before sunup. I can guarantee you won't want to be forced to explain this to Council."

"No, I assure you I don't. I've been down that road before. Do you know what the injection was supposed to do?" The guard spoke without the deference of someone who was at the mercy of a superior, though he spoke with a person who was obviously in the position to give orders.

"I assume it was the trial we are running on a synthetic virus. It should have, as you noted, incapacitated the prisoners quickly, making them too ill to travel. I don't imagine they could have gone far. I will send two men with you to assist you in the search." The man in charge waved over one of the men nearby still looking through the empty truck. "Listen, I need you to grab one of the others and go with these nimwits to search for the prisoners. They've been injected. If they can move at all at this point, it won't be fast."

"Got it," the man replied, shooting a disgusted look in the direction of the guard before turning back towards the truck to tap another man to join him.

The one in charge gave the order for everyone to clear off the truck while the two guards and two BRO workers conferred next to the still open rear truck doors. Once everyone was out of and off of the truck, one guard and one BRO worker climbed into the cab while the other two hauled themselves up in the back, shutting the doors behind them. The truck engine revved into life and the driver backed the truck up, turned around, and bounced down the dirt tracks past the three hiding in the trees. The remaining BRO workers disappeared inside the facility.

CHAPTER 16

The twelve advisors plus Trevor stared down the length of the table at Manglebee, waiting for him to break the deafening silence. He was, apparently, in no hurry. Manglebee sat with the list of names in front of him. The list of individuals who demonstrated no response to the viral injection when, by all accounts, they should have succumbed.

The vein at Manglebee's temple pulsated.

Without looking up, he finally spoke, "Are you certain that the individuals on this list are immune?"

"Well, uh, I think so." Trevor spoke with hesitation, uncertain if it was him who should be speaking up.

"You *think* so?"

"Yes. I mean, as far as I am aware, this is the conclusion the team arrived at. I am not sure what else it could be, sir."

"Did anyone even consider the possibility that the issue could lie within the delivery system?"

When no one answered, Manglebee looked up from the list and stared down the table.

"No? There are 6 men at this table working on this project and not a single one of you thought of this? Trevor? You're in charge of ensuring that this entire program operates according to plan. You are supposed to be the master of robotics. How. Is. It. That you did not have the program for the robotic injectors checked?" Manglebee's voice was low and even as his gaze rested on Trevor.

"S-s-sorry, sir." He did not mean to stammer. He hated the weakness Manglebee brought out in him. "I will set the technicians on it immediately, sir."

"Yes. You will. You are to head to BRO to oversee their work, and I expect that you will not leave until you are certain one way or the other about the results. Now. Get out of my sight."

Trevor scrambled to his feet with a loud scrape of his chair.

CHAPTER 17

Darkness had fallen not long after Juniper and Lucash jumped from the truck. They followed in the direction of the truck, hiding in the trees along the road. This seemed the best chance to discover where Council takes the Disappeared. Juniper was growing weaker by the minute. Her fever was intensifying and her headache growing to unbearable proportions. She valiantly continued her efforts, but by the time they reached the place where the dirt track split, she was unable to walk more than a few feet without stumbling.

As Juniper's knees buckled under her, Lucash caught her before she hit the ground.

"You can't keep going, Juniper. You're burnin' up and you can't walk ten steps without crashing to the ground."

"I'm—" Juniper trailed off, knowing it was useless to speak words that were clearly untrue.

Lucash led Juniper deeper into the trees, scoping out a spot to set her where she would be unlikely to be discovered. By now, they were certain their trackers were not functional here. It was a great piece of information. A weakness in the system that would be valuable to the Cause. They were unsure, at this time, whether their trackers were not functional just in the Borderlands or anywhere outside of their own City Unit. Either way, they knew the Resistance would be able to use that knowledge to their advantage.

Trouble was, their phones were not operational either. SMALS couldn't locate them with either their trackers or their phones. But they also could not message one another or anyone else. Not that that would matter anyway. Communications weren't private on Council phones, so that would never be a safe way to relay anything of importance unless it was coded, a skill neither Juniper nor Lucash had. It also meant there was no way to sign onto the encrypted Resistance site to seek help there. They were truly on their own out here in the Borderlands.

If only they could just get to where that truck went, they'd at least have the most vital piece of information they sought. They could figure out what to do next *after* finding out where they were to be taken.

"Wait here a sec." Lucash took off back to where the road forked. He stood just inside the trees, listening and looking for signs of people. He was met with darkness and only the sounds of nature at night. Lucash ventured to the split in the tracks and, in the dark, tried to ascertain which direction the truck went. His eyes had grown accustomed to the lack of light, and he was just able to make out what looked to be a continuous run of tire tread laying over the tops of other tracks that veered off to the right. He made his way quickly back to where he'd left Juniper.

"Okay. You'll be good and hidden here. Don't even think about trying to get up. You're really sick, and we can't risk you bein' found because you pass out along the way. Can you do that?"

"Yeah. Where are you going? Which road? Need…to…know. Just…in…case."

"It looks like the freshest tracks lead off to the right, so that's where I'm going. I'm hoping the destination isn't too far. Looks like we're gettin' close to another City Unit. There's a hint of lights in the distance. Looks like that's where the main track goes to. Another reason I'm takin' the track to the right…betting they'd not be takin' prisoners there."

Juniper gave a half-hearted chuckle through chattering teeth. "Betting you're right. Better get going. Don't want to wait here for you all night."

Lucash saw her chattering teeth. Taking off his own jacket, he covered her up with it, tucking it around her sides. He pushed up needles and leaves around her, hoping it would provide her some more insulation. He wished he knew what else he could do to keep her warm and ease her raging fever. He gently pushed her hair, damp with sweat, off her face, laying his hand across it to check once more on her temperature. He hadn't really needed to touch her to tell. The heat was radiating from her skin. He leaned over and kissed her forehead.

"I'll be back as soon as I can," Lucash whispered, his face still close to hers. "Try to sleep. Please." Juniper gave a little nod, already closing her eyes. Lucash took one final look before turning away and climbing out from the hiding spot. He arranged the opening to look undisturbed and shuffled the leaves and needles around to cover any trace of footsteps. Only when he was satisfied that Juniper's hiding place was as safe as he could make it did he turn around and make his way back out to the edge of the trees.

Without his jacket, the evening air drew a shiver up his spine. He'd move much quicker now, though he would still have to watch his step. Stepping just outside of the trees, he surveyed the landscape again. The lights in the distance still created a soft glow. It looked like the City Unit sat in a valley. It crossed his mind to take Juniper there if she didn't recover. He was sure it was a big risk, but maybe someone would help them without turning them over. Of course, there was the possibility that the trackers would pick up again once they got close enough to civilization.

He shook his head to clear his mind. He couldn't consider that yet. Maybe she'd feel better after a sleep. Right now, he was losing valuable time. The track he was following led into the mountains, where no lights shown. Lucash moved back to the edge of the trees. He thought he'd move faster if he stayed right at the edge. No dodging around trees in his path. He took off at a trot and found himself quickly warmed from the movement.

****

The terrain Lucash traveled over was rough going. Running turned out not to be as easy as he'd hoped. Between the rocks and roots and the thinner air, he was having to pause frequently to catch his breath. He knew he was being louder than he should as well, so he decided to slow down his pace. Slow, but steady would likely get him there nearly as fast as these rapid bursts followed by standing still.

So far, this road seemed to be it. He hadn't seen any other roads branching off of this one, which provided him some relief.

At some point, he would have to end up in the same place as the truck, wouldn't he? *But what if this road just keeps going?* he thought, and then pushed that thought away almost as swiftly as it had entered.

Now, Lucash was keeping a steady pace, only stopping occasionally to listen for any sounds that might indicate he was getting close. All was quiet, until he caught the sound of movement coming from above him to his left. He froze. Looking up through the trees, he caught the sight of lights before they were extinguished. They weren't lights from a vehicle. Those were people up there, and they did *not* want to be seen.

Lucash held perfectly still, waiting to see what they would do. There was no doubt they'd heard him. He did not want to draw any further attention or give any indication of his location. Though he really wanted to know why it was they were afraid of being seen, too. He did not take his eyes off the area where he had seen the lights. He could not see, but he could hear some movement and the murmur of voices speaking in hushed tones. It became silent again. The lights didn't come back on, but Lucash wondered if they'd moved on without their lights. As he sat debating whether he should start moving again, he heard the sound of voices again.

Moments later, the lights came back on. He could see now that there were three lights. Three people. He hadn't been sure before. When they started moving again, it was in the same general direction he was headed.

Why?

He was forced to wait a little longer to begin walking again. When he did start out, he slowed his pace even further, more mindful of the noise he was making and hoping the others were far enough ahead that they would not hear him again. He kept looking to see their lights again, but it wasn't those lights that he saw.

The sound of the engine came to his ears only a second before the trees in front of him lit up from the cast of the headlights. He flattened himself to the ground before he had time to think.

Lucash continued to lie there after the truck had flown past. It was the same truck he and Juniper had been in. He was sure of it. The fact that the truck was passing him going back the way he came from could mean only one thing. They'd discovered that he and Juniper had escaped.

Now, he was faced with a choice: continue in the direction the truck just came from and see if the destination comes up quickly or turn back and get to Juniper as quickly as he could.

The three lights moved above him again, going in the opposite direction.

Now there was no doubt. Whoever these three people were, they *had* been heading to the same place he was, and they were turned around by the passing of the truck. This, of course, only opened up a host of other questions. Questions he had no way of finding the answers to now. Or ever, most likely.

So, back to the task at hand.

If he saw the three individuals walking back so quickly after the truck had come by, he was hoping it meant that the destination was near. Juniper was hidden well. They'd come a good distance from where they jumped. It could take hours before they ever got close to the spot where Juniper was hidden.

I'll run ahead no more than five minutes, and then I'll turn back, no matter what. Lucash reasoned that those five minutes wouldn't change the risk to Juniper, but if he got to the destination, he would at least know *something*. He moved as fast as he dared, feeling he was safer now that the truck and the others on foot were headed the other direction.

His decision to keep going was quickly rewarded. Lucash rose to the crest of a hill and the garage doors came into view. *Yes! This has to be it! No place else to go...but what is it? And what could they possibly be doin' in there?* He looked around for another way in but did not wander far enough to see the other door. At least he had a location. He and Juniper could come back here when she was feeling better. See if they could find out more. Then they'd have to figure out how to get that information to The Resistance.

And now to keep from being re-captured.

CHAPTER 18

Rebecca had been preparing herself to meet up with Daniel and Perce for their turn at going into BRO when her Colossus phone signaled an urgent message. This time she realized her concern wasn't necessarily misplaced since Selby, Remy, and Zeche would be in the middle of their mission at that moment, hopefully preparing to move out so that they could meet Rebecca and the others to brief them on what they'd discovered ahead of their own trip in. Instead, when she uncovered her phone from under her bed covers, she found a message from Remy instructing her to drop whatever she was doing and get to the meeting place right away.

She'd done just that.

****

It had been a very long night. Again. And if they couldn't come to some sort of agreement soon, Rebecca felt she'd just have to curl up on one of the chairs and get some sleep right there at Headquarters. She probably wouldn't miss much. They'd been talking in circles for what felt like hours now.

She'd reached the meeting place before Perce, but Daniel was already there. She was relieved to see Selby and Zeche with Remy. No one was hurt, that was immediately apparent, but they were all three fidgeting and anxious. It was fully dark outside, yet they kept looking around them as if searching for something. She'd been instructed, in hushed tones, to turn her headlamp off and keep it off. And keep quiet. Had someone spotted them?

None of them would talk until all three of the second group were there, so they waited in silence for a long 20 minutes. At last, Perce arrived. Remy explained what they'd seen and said they were all to head over to Headquarters right away. Zeche had been in contact with Melody, who had instructed them to make their way as soon as they could. The other 6 members who were to make trips into BRO were meeting them there as well. Melody said they'd wait to let the other members of Colossus know until she'd decided what to do in light of this new information.

The tension in the room was high. Rebecca, Cassidi, and Daniel hadn't spoken much up to this point. As the newest members, they were unsure of how much they should say. Selby, of course, had no trouble voicing his opinion.

"Look, man, I *still* think we should find 'em before BRO does!"

"And do *what* with them, exactly?" Zeche said through clinched teeth.

The mission for the night had had to be called, for obvious reasons. Melody and Zeche wanted to try again the next night, and they did not want to try to locate the escapees. Melody, ever safe and deliberate in her actions, did not feel that action was in the best interests of Colossus and their mission. Zeche agreed.

"We will not spend our valuable efforts searching for Resistance members. As far as I'm concerned, the more of them off the streets, the better. They do *nothing* but stir up trouble. Imbeciles." Melody was never one to be generous towards the Resistance. Not even now, when she knew two people were being taken into the BRO facility, would she offer up any support.

"Are you sure they were from the Resistance?" asked Perce. He was undecided. Not quite convinced they should seek out the missing captives, though he saw some potential benefits to doing so.

"Almost positive," Remy responded. "The guard told Karl he was sent to Westlow because of *increased activity* there. I can only assume he means Resistance activity. What else could it be? They're the only ones that I know of doing anything that would anger Council enough to send the Guard out in force."

"Maybe. But not all of the Disappeared are from the Resistance. Some people just get taken off the street while walking along minding their own business," Vee chimed in.

"True. Though I'm bettin' they've done *something* to put themselves in Manglebee's bad graces. Wouldn't take much," said Ambir. Vee shrugged and then nodded her head in a brief acknowledgement of assent.

"Does it really matter if they're from the Resistance or not? I mean, come on! Now's our chance to get more information about who they're bringin' in. What else we gonna do today but sit around 'n wait to see *if* we get to go in tonight? Seems like a waste of time to me," said Selby. "Becs? Cassidi? You guys gonna back me up here, or what?"

Cassidi and Rebecca looked at each other, and then around the room. All eyes were pointed in their direction, and no one appeared as if they would prevent either of them from speaking up. Rebecca realized not a single person had shot down Selby when he spoke. They seemed to accept his right to voice his thoughts on the matter.

As if reading her mind, Selby added, "Both of you are part of Colossus, too. Right? So, you gotta *contribute*." Rebecca looked to Remy at this, and he nodded in her direction.

"Okay. Well, we don't know if the two people the guard were bringing to BRO were part of the Resistance, but I think it would be good for us to find out," she could see Melody's face harden further as another member sided against her. Rebecca looked away quickly before she lost the nerve to continue. She wasn't sure contradicting the leader was a good idea, but she went on anyway.

"If we find them, we get more information. What if they aren't part of the Resistance? Then maybe we get a clue about why people are Disappeared. Maybe something to tell us why they are bringing people to BRO. Also, they're from Westlow. Not Montrose. Maybe that's important, too."

"Why would that matter?" asked Vee

"Because they got injected with something. We don't know much about what's happening outside of Region 2 other than what we can find out from the other Colossus pods. Right? So, as far as we know, they've only used the virus on us. But what if they're using it someplace else now? And we don't know who these people are they're bringing into BRO, or why. I just think if we can get more information, we should get it," said Rebecca.

"She's got a point," said Vee. "Maybe this really is something we should do. Might help us more than we think right now."

"If it's the virus they got injected with, then they're probably already too sick to move. Might help us find them," Cassidi added. "If they're sick, Remy, could you and Bryn help them? Otherwise, what's the point? If they die, we don't learn anything. Not that you don't make a good point, Becs, like Vee said. I'm just sayin' if we can't help them, then what?"

"I think we might be able to help them. Hard to say. If they've been injected by the virus, maybe. If it's something else, probably not. We think we're close to an anti-viral for what they're given people here in Montrose, but we can't be completely sure. We don't get to test it on anyone. Just samples. We also don't know exactly how they're manipulating the virus based on individual health profiles, so even if we figure out the anti-viral based on the samples we're given, we don't know if it'll work on everyone."

"Seems to me this would be a perfect opportunity to test it out," Davi spoke up. "It's just one more reason we should be out there looking for these two. We're wasting time here arguing over it when we could be spending this time out there."

There were several shouts of agreement around the room. Selby's was the loudest.

"How would you propose we even begin to search for these two? We've talked on and on about why, but no one has said how. How do we begin to look for two sick individuals out in the Borderlands when all we know is that they came from

Westlow and they were injected, according to the guards, about an hour away from BRO? That doesn't narrow it down much for us," said Evan. He was also undecided, though now it sounded like he was leaning more towards the "no" group.

The room grew quiet, until Melody spoke up.

"Right. No one has even considered the how of this. You all seem to have forgotten who is in charge here. I've been listening to all of you go on for an hour now, and no one has convinced me to change my mind on this one. Evan, however, has made a keen observation that should convince all of you that attempting to look for these two is not an option."

"But, what if we—" Selby started.

Melody cut him off, "*Furthermore*, if we start looking for these two, then that means Council is also looking for us. We put ourselves out there directly in their search sites. If we somehow managed to get *unbelievably* lucky, and we find them, then we have another layer of concern. It is unlikely Council calls the guards off once Manglebee discovers there are two missing prisoners. Even if it is likely that they won't survive. He'll want confirmation."

She paced the front of the room a few times, staring up at the ceiling, hands clasped behind her back, as she did so. She had made up her mind about searching for the two escapees, and there would be no moving her at this point. But she still seemed to be considering *something*. When she stopped, she turned to see more scowls than not glaring back at her. She might be the leader, but few in this group did her bidding without question. She was glad they had the ability to think for themselves. It was often necessary. Sometimes, however, it made her job a lot harder.

"Now. What we *will* do next is to set up watch outside the garage doors to see if they bring the escapees back. Remy, are you supposed to report to work today?"

"Yes," he looked at his watch, "in about 5 hours."

"Sorry you won't get much sleep today. But you'll need to go in, of course. I want you to see if you can gather any useful information. If Karl is still hanging around, I want to know. I also want to know if you see anyone around today that isn't normally there. I have two possible leads I want you and Bryn to follow up on, if you get the chance. Two names with some possible information for us. They're skittish, from what I understand, so they won't talk if they don't feel totally safe in doing so. Don't scare them off."

"No. Of course not," Remy responded, not bothering to hide his irritation.

Rebecca raised her hand up indicating she wished to speak. "Yes, Rebecca?" said Melody.

"The rest of us, those who were supposed go in last night…do you want us to be the ones to watch the doors?"

"Not just yet. You will rotate through, two at a time, beginning with the groups who were supposed to go in tonight. The rest of you rest up. If the truck hasn't returned by tonight, the rest of you will rotate in and see if you can find an opening to head in and do the job."

"Melody," Zeche interjected, "we're gonna need to be careful here. Karl told the guard that if they didn't find the escapees by sunup, which is in just a few hours, then they'd have to tell Manglebee. I wouldn't be surprised if BRO got a personal visit from Manglebee or some of his minions today."

"Yes, of course. All the more reason we need to keep someone posted. I doubt Manglebee's visit, or any of the other Council members for that matter, will be made into a PR stunt for public viewing. He'll be brought in secretly. *If* he makes a personal appearance. That remains to be seen. He much prefers to intimidate people on his own turf. Now, since it will be light soon, I suggest you all get going. We need to have the first two people posted as soon as possible."

After a brief discussion, the rotation order was set, and Cassidi joined Rebecca, Selby, and Remy.

"I can't *believe* she doesn't want to look for those two. Don't get that at *all*," Selby was saying as Cassidi approached.

"I'm surprised too. I think it makes sense. I know she's careful, but I'm still kinda surprised," said Rebecca.

"She reminds me of my folks, man. Always so caref—" Selby cut himself off midsentence. His parents. He'd forgotten all about them and what he was supposed to be asking. He slapped his forehead, "Awwww noooo. Man. My folks. Ah man, totally forgot!"

"Forgot what?" Cassidi asked. Selby just looked from Rebecca to Remy with a stricken look on his face. "Come on…out with it! Forgot what?"

"Ah, Becs, I'm sorry. Sorry man, I didn't mean for it to happen."

"Sorry about what? Would you please just say it? You're kinda scaring me a little right now," said Rebecca.

"I'm supposed to ask Remy and Bryn something. But Bryn's not here, so I guess it'll have to be just Remy. And they're gonna kill me cuz it's so late now. And Becs'll probably kill me too. Or first."

"Selby!" Cassisi nearly shouted. "Get a grip and just get on with it."

"My folks know," Selby blurted out.

"*What?*" the other three responded simultaneously. Now Rebecca looked stricken, and Cassidi and Remy shocked.

"How? How do they know?" asked Rebecca

"Yeah, and how are you still *here*?" Cassidi added. "And by that, I mean how are you still *alive?*"

"Yes, I think you need to start explaining," Remy said.

"Yeah, well, I'm pretty surprised myself I'm still here, alive and all. They were waitin' for me when I walked in the door from our last meetin'. In the living room. I thought about makin' somethin' up about where I was, but you know my folks. That would *not* have worked. Doubt I coulda come up with a convincing enough story, so I went with the truth."

"You *told* them?" Cassidi nearly shouted at him.

Rebecca was speechless. Though her reddening cheeks gave indication of what she was feeling. It took a lot to upset Rebecca, but she had counted on her friends' secrecy. This felt like betrayal.

"I…I…I'm really sorry, Becs. Honestly, if I thought I could've told 'em somethin' they would have believed, I really would've. I'm *really* sorry, Becs."

"Okay," she said, in a voice that indicated that it really wasn't. She just didn't want to talk about it. Not now. Not here.

"I seriously can't believe you couldn't come up with *something*. Anything would have been better than putting all of us in danger, don'tcha think?" said Cassidi, not willing to let him off the hook and not caring that she talked about it in front of anyone there who might be listening.

"Cassidi. Keep. Your. Voice. *Down*." Remy, however, did care who heard. "Selby, you're obviously still here. How is that?"

"Well, that's the thing. I *am* still here. My folks weren't happy at all when I told 'em. I was thinkin' they'd try to make me stop. I wouldn't've though. I woulda come tonight no matter what."

"But they didn't try to stop you? Is that what you're saying?" asked Remy.

"Nope. Well…they did at first. Said that they thought we were in over our heads. And that they didn't teach me these skills I got so that I could do all *this*," he said with a sweep of his hands around the room, "They thought we were startin' things, that this wasn't about survival, like what they did. But I set 'em straight on that."

"Wait a minute," Remy said, "you mean to tell me your *parents* taught you these skills? And what do you mean, 'survival'?"

"Yeah, survival. Before The Reckoning, my parents started learnin' survival skills. They joined a group of people who called themselves 'survivalists.'" My folks, and these other people, well…they thought somethin' was gonna go down just from everything happenin' in the world back then. Before The Reckoning. So, they started messin' with technology to make the kinds of things I've been bringin' here…and learnin' how to defend themselves. They were prepared when The Reckoning started. But they didn't fight. Not unless it was to defend themselves. They hid out in secret places, and if they were threatened, they fought back. Almost all of 'em made it through

The Reckoning. So, they taught me all this stuff growin' up cuz they didn't trust Manglebee at all. They wanted me to be able to defend myself if the same sorta thing happened again."

Rebecca stood still; face gone passive, but a hard look in her eyes. She listened without saying a word. Selby's eyes kept darting to her face and turning away again almost immediately. He knew she was mad and didn't think his words were helping, like he hoped they would. He didn't know what else to do. Hopefully, she'd get over it. Cassidi was with Rebecca. That bothered him less. Cassidi's temper often flared out as fast as it started. She would get over it. Because he had seldom seen Rebecca angry, and because she was the one who felt responsible for all of them being here, Selby was less sure about her.

"And they were *fine* with you coming tonight?" asked Cassidi in a disbelieving voice. "Or did you do what you said you would and come anyways. Because if that's the case, we're all going to be in for it. Can't believe you could do that, and your parents wouldn't do anything about it."

"No, you're right, I probably couldn't've done that. Didn't have to. After I explained to them that what we're doin' *is* about survival because Manglebee is already wagin' a war against us, it's just that most people don't know it, they sent me off to my room so they could talk. Man, that was some hard waitin'. They made me wait forever. When they called me back down, they said they agreed with me that this is about survival and all. And then..." Selby's voice trailed off.

"And then *what?*" Cassidi and Remy both asked with impatience.

"Well...then they said I could stay with Colossus."

"We've gathered that already," said Remy.

"Yeah. They said I could stay with Colossus IF they could be part of it too."

Rebecca's head snapped up, a look of shock crossing her face. Then she looked to Remy to see what his reaction was. He looked just as shocked as she felt.

Selby continued, "they said I could come tonight if I promised to talk to Melody about them joinin', and they said I could say what I just told you about them bein' survivalists. I said I didn't know if I could convince Melody of anything, but that maybe you and Bryn could, so I'd talk to you. They agreed with that. Said I had to talk to you as soon as we were done with our mission tonight. Completely slipped my mind until just now. And I'm sure they're waitin' for me at home now to come back with an answer. This wasn't supposed to take all night."

"No, it wasn't. Will they be out looking for you or talking to any of our parents since you aren't back yet? That would *not* be good," Rebecca broke her silence.

"I don't think so. They said they saw why this needed to be kept a secret, so they wouldn't tell anyone else. At least not now."

"And what's that supposed to mean?" Cassidi asked.

"Well, I think they just want us all to be safe. I don't think they'd say anything unless they had to."

"I just hope you not showing up tonight doesn't make them change their minds," Rebecca said.

"Nah, not this fast. Remember, they've trained me. They might be worried, but they wouldn't do somethin' until they were sure there was trouble that couldn't be dealt with. So, Remy...what'cha think? Will you talk to Melody? Before she leaves?" Selby noticed Melody getting her coat and belongings together, looking like she would leave at any moment.

Remy ran his hands through his hair and blew air out through pursed lips. "That's a lot to ask. I'm not sure what she'd be too keen on the idea coming from me. Though there are advantages to it, if she could hear them. I just don't think tonight is the night to ask. Not with all this going on. And not when...not when I'm not sure..."

"Not sure about what?" asked Selby.

"Not sure about what to do right now," he then lowered his voice to just above a whisper, so that they all had to strain to hear. "I'm not sure I agree with Melody's decision tonight, and I'm not sure what I'm going to do about it."

CHAPTER 19

Trevor arrived at the BRO facility in the dark. He'd messaged Mica saying he was called into work and didn't know when he'd be home. She did not respond. No surprise there. He didn't blame her at all. And he didn't know how much longer he was willing to continue jeopardizing his marriage for Manglebee. This was making his life miserable, and for what? To stay alive doing Manglebee's dirty work? That was no kind of life.

Yet, here he was. Pulling the BRO vehicle into its slot in the parking area of the garage. He had messaged the technology team who ran the delivery system and ordered them in immediately. He turned off the vehicle and rested his head back against the headrest, closing his eyes to the all too familiar interior of BRO. He needed just a moment before going in to face the team. And it only lasted a moment before a tap on the glass started him upright. One of the team he'd called in had seen him pull up just as he was plugging in his own vehicle to the charging station. Trevor sighed, pushed the button to open the door, gathered his belongings and his strength, and climbed out of the vehicle.

The large garage area was quiet. A few of the BRO vehicles were out of their slips, but that wasn't unusual. BRO vehicles were shared among the scientists and other workers in the facility. They were not for personal use. They were stationed between the BRO facility and the transport stop where the BRO workers arrived from their homes. It was impossible to tell from the cars in the facility who was around. He plugged in the vehicle he was driving.

"Did you come on your own?" Trevor asked, though the answer was obvious. He was only trying to fill the air with sound and avoid talking just yet about why they were there.

"Yes. Just me. Not sure who else has made it here yet. What's this about, anyway?"

Trevor sighed. "Let's just wait until I have you all together."

"Oh. Okay. Sure."

They reached the entry to the facility and walked the rest of the way in silence, Trevor using his card to open up the doors to each section as they went. There were few people around this time of day, so most of the hallways were dark until they entered. They reached the programming room in the restricted access area and found the others there waiting.

"Well, good. You're all here," he said as he made his way in.

He moved to the main console so that he could address them all.

"Sorry to have brought you all in. Direct orders from Head Councilor Manglebee." That caused them all to sit up a little straighter. "Head Councilor is concerned that there might be a problem with our delivery system. As you all know, we have discovered that some of the individuals we are sending the virus to have shown immunity. Not many, but a few." God how he hated this work. He hated himself as he heard the words come out of his mouth. This was not him. He wondered how many of the people in front of him felt the same about the work they were doing here.

"What does that have to do with us?" asked a woman sitting just in front of him.

"Well, uh, I'm not sure that it does, but we have to check our system's programming just in case. Head Councilor is concerned that there might be an error in the programming, rather than individuals who are immune to a virus programmed to attack their particular health profile."

"There can't be an issue with the programming. That doesn't make sense. It's happening so few times it seems random," said the man who had walked in with him.

"It is improbable, but not impossible. Nonetheless, we are to check our programming out thoroughly. I have been instructed to stay here until we are absolutely certain of our results, either way." There were groans around the room and sounds of disgust. "I know. I'm not thrilled about it either, and I'll be here right along with you. I suggest we get moving. The sooner we start, the sooner we can all go home."

They all moved up to their workstations and switched them on. Trevor did the same. While he was waiting for the computer to power up, he checked his shirt pocket for his phone, only to find that he'd left it in the vehicle.

"Be right back. I have to run back out to the lot," he announced on his way out the door.

Retracing his route, Trevor's steps echoed off the walls of the empty halls. He hurried through the passageways and doors, wanting to get back and get this all over with. He was thinking again about how long he could keep this up, and whether he should defy Manglebee and just tell Mica everything, when he arrived in the middle of a chaotic scene in the garage. He ducked back inside the door, not wanting to intrude, and sensing that his presence would not be welcome. He did not leave, however. He kept the door cracked just enough to be able to see and hear what was happening.

Prisoners had escaped. *Good for them* was his first thought. *This might take some of the heat off me when Manglebee finds out* was his second. He felt some relief. Maybe two had gotten away. That would be two people he wouldn't be responsible for destroying. Two people who might have a chance. Yes, they'd likely never survive. He doubted the virus would kill them. The injection they'd been given was too generalized for that. But two young people on their own out in the Borderlands had little hope of surviving. There wasn't much left out there to survive on. But death would be preferable to what would happen to them if they had made it here. At least that was his opinion.

He felt ever so slightly better just knowing that two people had found the escape he longed for. Even at the likely cost of their lives. Trevor wondered if he could ever be as brave as that.

Trevor turned away from the door, deciding his phone could wait. He did not want to walk into the middle of the scene playing out before him. He only got a few steps away before changing his mind, returning to the door, and then entering the garage. He couldn't leave his phone in the vehicle. Not with Manglebee breathing down his neck right now. Trevor realized he also couldn't risk someone here driving off in the vehicle he had been using and taking his phone with them. So, he went after it. He needn't have been concerned. The group of people in the garage were far too preoccupied with their crisis to notice him.

Trevor quickly retrieved his phone and re-entered the building just as Karl was ordering the guard and a BRO employee to go in search of the missing prisoners. When Trevor reached to door to the programming room, he opened it to find chaos greeting him a second time. All four team members looked up as he entered.

"Uh, Trevor…you gotta see this. Not sure how this is happening, but—" said the same woman from earlier.

"What's happening?"

"Not sure, but it looks like someone is altering our programming as we speak. Someone is in the system."

"What? That can't be!"

"But it is. Come see for yourself."

Trevor walked over to the computer where all four of the programming team were gathered, leaning over the shoulder of the young man seated at the terminal. He stared at the screen, then squinted, leaned in closer, and stared harder, not believing what he was seeing.

"This can't be! Our security system—"

"Bypassed. Apparently."

"I thought our encryption was unbreakable."

"So, did we. It had been, up until now. I don't know how this person is doing it. They have to be insanely smart to crack it. None of us could do it."

"Nor could I," said Trevor, shaking his head in wonder and confusion—and, if he were honest, admiration.

"Could this be the issue? Could it be that this person has been infiltrating our system all along, and that's why some people have not responded to the virus?"

"I…I don't know. The changes they are making would certainly have an impact, but we'll have to check to see if they match up with what's happened in the past. Check the profiles of the individuals who have been found to be unresponsive, look at their dosages, and compare it to what's happening right now. One thing that doesn't make sense—" said Trevor.

"Is that the changes are being applied on a bigger scaler this time and not just the random few we've seen before."

"Yes. Exactly. Can you see where they're coming from? Where the changes are being made?"

"We haven't been able to yet. We're working on it. Someone sure knows what they're doing."

"Good. Keep trying. Also, let's get started right now in looking at those changes they're making and comparing it to the profiles of the people who didn't react to the virus," Trevor added, as he moved towards his own computer to help. "I'll start on that, if one of you wants to help, then the rest of you can be working on figuring out where these changes are coming from to see if we can find who is doing it."

"I'll help you," one of the men volunteered. The other three acknowledged this and each returned to their own terminals to begin to work on unraveling this mystery. No easy feat when they were up against someone obviously smarter than anyone else in the room.

CHAPTER 20

"What are you planning, Remy?" Daniel asked with some trepidation. He wasn't sure he wanted to hear the response. Rebecca moved closer to Daniel, without thinking, sensing his discomfort with the situation. She felt much closer to Daniel after their time by the river, but still not confident enough in what it all meant to consciously acknowledge this newly formed bond, not even to herself. Not even when Daniel shifted his own body towards her enough that their arms were now touching.

"Not sure." Remy glanced around the room. There was still grumbling, in pairs, or disgusted sideways glances in the direction of Melody and Zeche, mostly. But everyone appeared to be moving on, accepting Melody's decision even if they didn't agree with it. Remy wasn't entirely certain he could do the same. "Let's go. We shouldn't talk here, anyway."

When they reached the truck, they found Davi there waiting for them, leaning with his back against the passenger-side back door, arms folded, head tilted back, and eyes closed. His face was a grim mask, contradicting his casual stance. He heard their approach, opened one eye to check to see who all was there, then closed it again. "So, are we going to let them get away with this? Or are we going to take matters into our own hands?" he asked with a tone of nonchalance.

"No way, man," Selby offered immediately. The others shot him a warning look.

"What do you mean? Are *you* planning something?" Cassidi shot back, not willing to trust his motives as readily as Selby.

Davi opened his eyes and stood up, facing the group. "Thought you guys seemed to feel about this the same way as me. I'm not thinking Melody's word has to always be the final word. Was I wrong to think that?" he asked, eyes narrowing on each of them in turn.

Selby opened his mouth to speak, but Rebecca gripped his arm, hard, to stop him. He turned to look at her and she shook her head no. After his earlier revelation, he wasn't about to do anything to make Rebecca angrier at him than she already was.

With some effort, he closed his mouth and drifted to the back of the group to reduce his natural inclination to speak out.

"I wouldn't say you're wrong, at least not about us thinking like you about going to look for these two. But I'm not sure about the part about Melody. We're still pretty new at all this," said Rebecca.

Remy, who had been silent up to this point, stepped in, "You aren't wrong. At least not from my perspective." He turned to Rebecca, "You guys don't have to do this. Whatever this turns out to be. You *are* new, and it's certainly a risk."

"Colossus is important for what it does, but it's more important to me that we get somewhere. I owe it to Jonathan, and there's too much at stake to always be so cautious. So. What are we going to do?" Rebecca responded, knowing right then that she wanted to do this, regardless of the consequences with Colossus. Things had been moving too slow lately. Melody was too careful. Now, they had a chance to find out more, and maybe even to save two people. That sure sounded better than waiting around to see *if* they could go inside BRO and resume their previous mission.

"Davi, how did you get here?" Remy asked.

"Rode in with Mel. She's already on board."

Remy looked surprised at that. Mel hadn't voiced any opinions in the meeting, "Okaaaay," he said, slowly. "Let's head back to the ranch. We'll talk more there. Any of you want me to drop you off at home?" He directed the question to the others.

"If Rebecca is in, then I'm in, too," said Cassidi.

"Yep, me too," Selby added, with a look to Rebecca to check her reaction. There was none. This would take some work on his part to get her to trust him again.

"Count me in," Daniel replied.

"Right…let's head out then. Meet you there, Davi," said Remy, making his way around the truck toward the driver's seat.

****

They decided to break up into two groups, since there were so many of them and because Remy would have to make an appearance at BRO, especially if Karl was there. He'd expect to see Remy, and Melody would be looking for him to report to her. He also needed to talk to Bryn, both about Selby's parents and about what their plans were. Selby would also have to go home to talk to his parents and fill them in on the night's events. He could put it off no longer. Rebecca, Cassidi, Daniel, Davi, and Mel would start the search, and Remy and Selby would join in the efforts as soon as possible. After a nap in vehicles that brought them to the edge of daylight, they piled into Remy's truck and made their way around to the road leading into BRO.

There had been a lot of discussion about their approach to the search. Admittedly, this search was potentially futile. The pair could have gone anywhere. They reasoned, however, that with the terrain and the road, they would have been unlikely to have made it too far off the road. Especially if the virus is what they had been injected with. They'd never have the strength to climb, even if they had the skill. And the latter was doubtful considering the two were from Westlow. Prior to tonight's meeting, none had known where Westlow was located, but Zeche had pulled the City Unit up on his mapping portal for the group. Westlow was in the plains. Any outdoor recreation opportunities would not involve climbing mountains.

How far could the two escapees have gone once injected with the virus? The virus would probably be fast-acting—there would be little use for it otherwise—but not as strong. If they were experimenting with dosages, though, they would not yet have perfected the virus structure, so it was impossible to say how the injection would affect the pair. Remy wasn't privy to this side of BRO's operations, so any thoughts he had on it were only a little better than guesswork.

The group had come to the conclusion that it would be unlikely that the pair would have headed back the way they came. That would lead to a quick recapture. The trackers would be unavoidable to anyone without the technology Colossus was using, compliments of Selby. The group had also figured out that the escapees would likely have discovered by now that the trackers didn't work in the Borderlands. They'd probably want to stay in the Borderlands as long as they could.

With all of these factors, the group decided that their best bet was to backtrack down the road the Guard would have had to take between Westlow and BRO, but not all the way back to the place the one guard had said they'd stopped to give the injection. The main group would spread out from this point, with Mel and Davi going back towards Westlow and the other three moving out away from the road. Remy and Selby would meet the group at the drop-off point, and they'd all take it from there.

The sun would be creeping up over the tops of the mountains before long. Remy drove while the others kept a sharp eye out for signs of the Guard and the two BRO workers who joined them. There was no way of knowing the approach they would take to searching for the two prisoners, other than knowing they'd start from the location of the injection because that had been said during the confrontation with Karl. They hoped the Guard and BRO workers would assume the prisoners would head back towards Westlow.

Hopefully.

If not, they'd have a really hard time escaping being seen and an equally difficult time explaining how 7 people happened to be in a truck at daybreak wandering around on the dirt roads of the Borderlands.

Rebecca, Cassidi, and Daniel sat in the bed of the truck. Cassidi and Rebecca were propped on the edge by the cab, while Daniel squatted at the rear, keeping a watch on the road behind them. There was little discussion for fear of distraction from their duties as lookouts, but, occasionally, Rebecca could feel Cassidi's eyes on her, prying for information. Information about what, she didn't know for sure, but she would guess that Cassidi, ever perceptive when it came to Rebecca, had noticed something in her interactions with Daniel. Cassidi wouldn't be one to let that ride without saying anything. Rebecca was glad she was safe for now. There would be little opportunity for Cassidi's questions.

Rebecca kept her eyes diligently on the sides of the road, not acknowledging the lasers boring holes in the back of her head from the other side of the truck's bed. Right now, she had a job to do anyway. Her focus was where it needed to be, on the task at hand. Once she made the instantaneous decision after the meeting to go along with Remy in search of the missing pair, she did not look back. There was no doubt that this was the course she had to take. For Rebecca, her mission had grown beyond fulfilling her brother's promise. She realized this now.

When she had spoken to Daniel about the guilt she sometimes felt because she often forgot that she had been doing this all for Jonathan, she hadn't quite understood that she was now doing it for her own reasons as well. That understanding came with her decision to go along with Remy. She *did* owe it to Jonathan, yes, but not just because she promised him. She also owed it to everyone who continued to lose loved ones because the progress of Colossus was monumentally slow up to this point. And she owed it to those who continued to lose their own battles with the virus and with Council.

While she didn't necessarily agree with the tactics of the Resistance, Rebecca also felt that Melody's approach was far too careful. There was not a single person acting within Colossus who didn't understand that their own safety, their own lives, were on the line by participating in efforts to bring down Manglebee and Council. Melody went too far to ensure the safety of Colossus members, letting others take the fall instead.

The truck bounced and joggled over the road. The peaks behind them glowed with rising of the sun. The purple glow of BRO's virus delivery system had faded into black before they'd even set off from the ranch. Rebecca looked in that direction as if they were still visible, contemplating the damages the miniature robots would have inflicted while a small group from Colossus was arguing over whether they should try to save just two.

Just two. *Is it worth it?* she asked the still dark trees before her? *Yes*, came the reply. Even just two. Even without the potential for the information they might provide. *But what if…*the thought began forming in her head…*what if these two could also help Remy and Bryn by giving them a way to test the anti-viral they've been* *working on? Could they help more?* She knew Melody would never go along with any plan that involved large-scale action against Manglebee. Not yet. And maybe not ever. It seemed she was always waiting for Colossus to be big enough and strong enough to be certain of taking down Manglebee and Council. But would they ever be? Would Melody ever be satisfied enough with their progress, or would her caution always get in the way?

Rebecca knew she could ask that of herself as well. She thought of Selby. She was angry with him for telling his parents, but more than that, she was afraid. She was afraid that by telling his parents, he'd put two more people in jeopardy. She was afraid his parents might tell hers. This well of fear was the source of her anger. Not Selby. If she had been in his shoes, Rebecca was certain she would have done just as Selby did. No, it wasn't fair that she was mad at Selby. And, truthfully, his parents might be a huge help to them. They weren't like anyone Rebecca had ever met. Not even within Colossus. She only hoped that they, too, wouldn't be as cautious as Melody.

As the truck slowed, Rebecca was hoping that Selby's conversation with his parents was going well.

So far, so good. No signs of the Guard vehicle and no sign of the two guards or the two BRO workers. The three hopped out of the back quickly and gathered on the driver's side, near Remy's opened window. Mel and Davi joined them.

"All's clear so far. Make sure you all remain alert. You could have an unfortunate encounter at any time," Remy warned.

"Don't worry about us. Just go do what you have to do and get back here with Selby so you guys can help," Rebecca said and then, upon seeing the worry in Remy's eyes, added, "We'll be careful, and we'll be in touch if anything comes up."

"Good. I'll do the same. Let's hope we can get messages through if we need to. Otherwise, just plan on meeting back here in three hours. I'll stash the truck…" he looked around for a good place and spotted some fallen boulders a short distance away, "…over there, behind those rocks. We'll have to cover the tire tracks from the truck, but we should be well enough hidden there." They all followed the direction of his gaze to the where they'd meet and responded in the affirmative. "Okay, I'd best get going so that we can all get off this road. Keep me posted."

"Yep, will do, now get outta here, would ya? We got work to do," Cassidi said with the flash of a smile that Remy actually returned.

"Watch your step," Daniel called out as Remy turned the truck around, "especially when you come back out here." Remy gave a wave in reply, and then he was off. The group of five watched as the truck rolled much more quickly back the way they'd come, kicking up dust in its wake.

"Okay…what do you say we get this party started?" Davi said as he turned his attention towards the only place the pair could have taken cover: the trees and rocky terrain at the base of the mountain's incline. The opposite side of the road stretched into the valley bottom, with a river running through it, all the way to Montrose. No place for cover there. This might be easier than they'd feared.

All five of them crossed the short distance between the road and relative safety.

"Message us if you need us," said Mel, "and good luck."

"Same to you," Rebecca replied.

And with that, Davi and Mel peeled off to the right to follow the path of the road, while the other three moved deeper into the trees.

CHAPTER 21

Destin had picked up Troy at their predetermined meeting spot. When Troy left the house, only his mother was there. His dad was gone, as was often the case these days. With all of the extra measures in place because of Council's secretly orchestrated attack, Troy's dad's extra duties kept him at work for long hours. That seemed to be the case for several of his friends' parents as well. All of them were grateful for the freedom this provided as they became more heavily involved in Colossus. Troy's mom, while home more regularly, seemed often not in the mood to be bothered with Troy's actions. His parents, always close, were now obviously fractured, but Troy didn't have time to be worried about that.

Now, all he was concerned about was surviving his time with Destin. She had been waiting for him on the transit platform, still in her work uniform, looking as surly as ever. She and her dad were still required to work. Council did not want Tier 6 citizens with too much free time on their hands for fear of an organized retaliation. So, they worked, though on a reduced schedule. Today had been Destin's turn. Seeing Destin's dirty grey uniform and her wary stance brought home to Troy the differences between the two of them Remy had spoken about. But her glare in his direction ensured that his opinion of her did not soften enough for him to let his guard down.

They had ridden transit across the city to her living sector, a place Troy had never given much thought to because it was worlds apart from his own. It was also a place he was only now able to enter because of his disabled tracker. As they crossed from the commerce region into Quadrant 4, the difference between his world and Destin's became even more apparent. Ramshackle houses in various states of disrepair and care lined narrow streets crowded with bone-tired workers making their way to homes with barely enough food to compensate for their hard labor. He braved a look in Destin's direction, but she was staring out the window, a hardened look on her face. She would not look at him.

They were working at her place because she had a Colossus computer secreted away in a hiding place in her room, which also doubled as the living room. Her father now slept alone in the only bedroom of their small house. He'd offered Destin the room after her mother died, but she refused to take it. When Troy and Destin arrived at the house, Destin's dad was already at the nuclear waste plant for his shift. Their shifts often varied between daytime and overnight hours, with little predictability to their schedule. This, again, was by design. It kept the population off-balance and tired. And without a consistent group of coworkers, they were less likely to form into any sort of organized groups.

Tonight, he and Destin would be programming the key cards. Shockingly, and unfortunately, she'd agreed to work on that with him. If they got that done, they'd log onto the Colossus computer, and Destin would begin giving him lessons on breaching BRO security.

Despite her obvious resentment at having to work with Troy, Destin was attentive in learning how to program the key cards. She was a sponge. He had only had to show her what he did once, and the next one she'd done on her own flawlessly. He had never met anyone who absorbed information as rapidly as he did. It left him feeling both insecure at meeting his match and elated at the prospects of what they could accomplish if they combined forces. He also felt the beginning twinges of admiration at what she could do even in the circumstances she had to endure on a daily basis. He wondered if he would be as strong if he were in her position.

"Wow. You're good, Destin," Troy said as she completed her first key card.

"Of course, I am," she replied in a tone of disgust. But Troy thought he caught just the barest hint of a smile before it sank back down into the more familiar scowl.

That gave him the courage to say, "I've just never met anyone before now who is as good as me at this stuff." She didn't respond, but their interactions grew a little less tense after that. Troy had to acknowledge that maybe Remy was right about Destin.

****

With the two of them working, they did manage to get all of the key cards done in one sitting. They worked faster than either of them would have on their own, each instilling in the other a competitive reaction that wasn't altogether unfriendly.

"Well, um…thanks. That went fast," Troy said as they finished the last one. "Uh, do you want to hold on to these?" Troy added.

"No. You take 'em. This was supposed to be your thing, so you get to be responsible for making sure they get to Melody."

Destin's voice sounded almost accusing, but Troy had the feeling that she was making her own gesture of goodwill.

Troy collected them all and put them in the protective case he'd brought along just for this purpose. Destin walked over to the shelves that lined the wall on one side of the room. The shelves held an assortment of items, all neatly arranged, along with some containers. Troy realized that this shelving unit took the place of closet, as there was none in the room. These were Destin's personal items.

Feeling a little embarrassed, Troy shifted in his seat so that he was turned a little away from Destin, allowing her to discreetly remove the computer from whatever location she had it hidden. Troy did what he had felt uncomfortable doing before; he had a look around at the rest of what could be seen of the place Destin called home. It was small. It could use a number of repairs. But it was clean and organized. There was no clutter, in spite of the lack of space to store anything. It was then that Troy understood that there was likely little that the father and daughter had need of storing.

He felt the weight of Destin's life as she sat down next to him. Composing his features, he turned back towards her to give her his attention as she opened the computer and turned it on.

Destin logged in and checked to ensure all encryption and discovery protections were on and functioning before continuing. When that was complete, she turned her focus back to Troy. "Okay, I've been working on this for months now. It's taken a lot of work to crack their security systems while also remaining undetected. I need you to pay attention and do only as I say. Do not try any other stunts because you think you know better than me how to do this. Trust me. You don't. And I've likely already at least considered any method you could suggest. As long as I have your word on this, we can continue."

"Uh…um, yes. Of course," Troy responded, a little taken aback. "I trust your methods. After what I saw today with the key cards, I don't question your skills."

"I need your word."

"You've got it. I will only do as you say."

"Good. Let's get started then."

Troy was nervous about what they were about to do, afraid that somehow her methods would not work this time. It wasn't that he didn't really trust her skills even though he said he had. It was more the idea of the consequences if she was wrong. He'd have been equally as worried if they were using methods he'd discovered.

Once Destin began, Troy focused entirely on Destin's words and the screen, not wanting to miss anything.

This was also a little exciting, he realized. New turf. Something he had not done before. It was a new technology challenge. As he sat there, the nervous feeling drained away, to be replaced by an attentive calm. He was entering a new world, and the journey was a new adventure. A far more exciting one than climbing up the side of a mountain in brush so dense it had to be hacked through. This adventure was much more to his liking.

Destin surprised him by saying, "You're not so bad at this. Not quite as good as me, but not bad."

A compliment from Destin. He was sure those weren't easy to come by. He allowed himself a small feeling of victory.

They worked away for a few hours before Troy had sufficiently grasped the ins and outs of bypassing BRO's security system for the layers Destin had mastered. She had yet to breach security for Level 3's systems, which is what would be needed in order to access the data for the bodies. They didn't even know for sure where those systems were located within BRO's network. It was possible the systems were not connected to rest of the BRO operation. It was possible that the data was stored only locally, on the computers that had to exist somewhere in the Level 3 High Security area. But it seemed highly unlikely. They needed too much of the data the scientists in the first two levels were gathering. It had to be somewhere. And if it existed, and they found it, then perhaps they could breach it.

From right there in Destin's living room.

Destin told Troy that she didn't think they would ever need to set foot inside BRO to breach their system, that, logically, it would be connected to the rest of the system. Troy agreed.

"So, do you think we should tackle this now?" Troy asked.

"Yes. I mean, that's if you're up for it. I know it must be past your bedtime and all, so if you don't think you can manage…"

"I can manage. Don't worry about me. I'm used to it."

"Good to know," Destin replied in a flat tone.

"Okaaay," said Troy. Destin glanced at Troy, then back down at the computer, typing on the keypad.

"Okay. Let's see what we can do."

Troy bent over the computer with Destin. He watched what she was doing.

"This is as far as I've gotten. Any ideas?" she asked.

Troy moved his hands towards the keyboard and Destin slapped them away. "Tell me. Don't show me. We make no more moves until we agree on what's next."

"Alright. Good idea. Based on what you just did, what I think might work is this—" Troy went on to describe his thoughts on what was next, and Destin interjected with slight modifications. A couple of moves met with dead ends, and one frighteningly close call where they thought they lost their security wall. Some frantic moves reassured them that they were safe. At least as far as they could tell.

As they gained a level of comfort with working together, they began to move faster and with greater assurance in the other's skills, until…

"Whoa! Are we…?" Troy said as a screen opened with a list of files they hadn't seen before.

"YES!" Destin exclaimed, before adding, "Maybe. But we gotta open a file first."

"You can have the honors."

"You just wanting to blame me if something goes wrong?"

"Uh. No, just trying to be nice."

"Kidding, nerd. Just kidding."

"Oh. Okay." Troy gave a delayed, uneasy chuckle. And Destin jabbed his ribs lightly with her elbow. She clicked on a file.

"I'd say we're in," said Destin.

"It sure looks like it," Troy agreed. "What do we do now?"

"What do you want to do? No one knows we're in. They can't trace us."

"Are you sure?"

"Positive. Our system is designed specifically to prevent detection. It's better even than the one we just cracked into. Unbreakable, actually. Unless they've got someone smarter than me. And now you."

Troy's laughter was anything but uneasy this time. "Well, there's no way that's true. Before you, my dad was the smartest person I knew when it came to technology, and I'm better 'n him. A lot better."

"Okay, then, so what're we gonna do? We can't just close out of here without doing *something*."

"We have to figure out what these files are first, don't you think?" Troy said, stalling for time because making changes to the files was daunting. He was not as confident about the system's security. Even though he was completely confident in Destin's skills, he just wasn't completely willing to go so far as to say that no one could crack her code.

"Of course. But I can tell you right now from all the data I've been looking at, these have to do with the viruses. See this right here? It's the name they've given the virus. That's no different from the other areas of BRO. So, I think maybe this number here is something with the dosage because it's different for each data set."

"They don't provide names. We can't tell who's who. It's all just numbers."

"That's because they don't see them as people. Better that they don't, then they don't have to have any conscience about it."

"I wonder if we could figure it out," Troy mused.

"Do you really want to? I mean, does it matter who? It's all bad. Or would you just prefer to save the worthy people of Tier 3?" Destin said in a voice dripping with disgust. Her mask went on immediately.

"No. Of course not. Though I could probably think of a couple of people I might not care to help…" Troy added, only half kidding. "They're in Tier 3, by the way."

This time, Destin was the one laughing.

"Well, we can't change everything, but I say we lower the dosages of several of the people here. Randomly. I think they'd be less likely to notice if we just did a random few throughout. At least this time."

"Noooow your talkin'!" replied Destin. "I agree. We should lower the number. Not sure what the letter means. Maybe it has something to do with the formula they're using."

"Hey, wait. We just opened up the first thing we saw. How do we know these are new victims?"

"Good point. No sense in changing anything that's already happened. Can you see anything that might tell us?" Destin was looking through the information contained on the file.

"This looks like it might be a date. Maybe. It's formatted a little differently. Let's see if we can open something else, now that we're in, and compare them."

They looked for similar files in the system, and it didn't take long to find them.

"It looks like they've put their victims into batches, so that helps. Must be based on when they are dispensing the doses," said Destin.

"I think you're right. Let's open two and compare the information for what I think is the date."

They opened up two different files to discover that it appeared Troy was right. They also noted that the date was embedded in the batch name.

"Well, that makes this easier," Troy noted upon making the correlation.

"Sure does. Now all we have to do is find one that hasn't happened yet."

"Not as easy as you'd think since they're arranged by the batch name and not the date...wait, here, I think this looks like one!" Sure enough, they'd found one with numbers that would correspond to a date that had yet to happen. If they were correct in their interpretation of the numbers, this batch would be sent out the following week.

"I really wish we could see who was on here," Troy said again.

"Why?"

"If we knew, we could see if what we did worked. If those people didn't get sick, then we changed the right thing."

"Good point, nerd."

"Why are you calling me that?" Troy asked as she called him nerd for the second time. "What is it, even?"

"I'm calling you that because you *are* one. It's an old word my mom taught me when she found out how good I was at computers. It meant super smart, but in a way where you don't really fit in with others. It wasn't totally a nice thing to say. But I liked it when my mom said it. Made me feel like something more than a Tier 6 slave," Destin shut up quickly as it dawned on her that she'd become a little too unguarded with this kid. That could be dangerous.

But Troy didn't seem to notice the shut-down. He was too moved by her revelation.

"Well, then, call me nerd all you want. I like it, too. And I don't see anything wrong with it," he said. He wanted to say more but wasn't sure if he should. He risked it anyway. "And you *are* smarter than what Council has assigned your family to. It's a stupid system. The sooner we break it down, the better."

"So, let's get to work on changing some numbers, then," Destin replied, relaxing a little more again. But not completely. She'd have to be careful, she realized. It was too easy to relate to this kid, and she wasn't used to relating to many people. She never really could. For as far back as she could remember, she didn't get other people and they didn't get her. She had been an only child, but she wondered what it would have been like to grow up with a kid brother like Troy. *Probably would have killed him,* she thought, as they began the work of making changes to the BRO numbers in the Level 3 system.

CHAPTER 22

It had been a long night. Lucash made his way back to where he had left Juniper to find that she was burning up with fever and did not seem to recognize him. She kept mumbling his name, but no matter how much he told her he was there, she just kept saying his name over and over again. And then she'd fall into a fitful sleep for a while, before waking up and starting again with the mumbling. The only thing at all that seemed to help was his touch, but he couldn't hold her close. She was too feverish for that. When he tried, she started thrashing around, trying to get away. Instead, it was the light touches. His hand cupping her cheek or stroking her hair. These calmed her, quieted her movement, and seemed to help lure her into the times of sleep.

Lucash didn't sleep at all, but he was glad for the times Juniper did. Not only because he hoped the sleep would help her to get over this, but also because she was quieter when she slept. He was afraid her mumbling would be heard if someone came looking for them. He'd heard the passing sound of a vehicle on the road. Twice. He thought it was likely that the Guard were now retracing their route trying to locate them. His only option at the moment was to stay hidden with Juniper. Her condition was too bad to leave her. So far, it seemed the vehicle had only been searching from the road. He hoped it stayed that way.

Morning had dawned with still no improvements in Juniper's condition. They both needed water. He could use some food as well, but he doubted there would be anything edible in these woods. At least not anything he would recognize. He could go hungry, but neither of them could go without water. With Juniper's fever, she needed it even more. He hadn't heard a vehicle go by again since the last time one passed just as dawn was breaking.

"Lucash?"

Her voice brought his attention back to where Juniper lay curled up next to him. "Juniper? You awake?"

"Lucash…Lucash…"

No. Just more fevered mumblings. He sighed and began stroking her hair again. How to get water? And if he found it, how would he transport it back here for Juniper? Their packs hadn't made it onto the truck with them. Lucash had lost his when the Guard took him down, and Juniper's was taken from her when she was loaded in the truck. He looked around on the ground for something, picking up leaves and sticks, wondering if he could make something. If he could weave the sticks together…but then there were no large leaves to use to keep the water from seeping out.

Lucash wandered out of the hiding place, looking around on the ground until he found a hollowed-out piece of tree trunk that might work. It wouldn't carry a lot, but it would be something. He'd keep his eye out for another similar piece of wood while looking for water.

Still no sounds coming from the road. Looked like his best chance to go was now, while it was still early, and Juniper was still asleep. He checked on her once again, and again he covered his tracks and disguised the opening when he left. He couldn't be gone long. Lucash was not sure it was a good thing that he hadn't heard the truck again. Either they'd moved on from this area, perhaps looking towards Westlow, or, a not-so-pleasant thought, they had ditched the truck and were now conducting their search on foot. In which case, it would be more difficult to hear their approach, and they would likely wander this far back in the woods. The thought made his stomach churn, taking away any pangs of hunger he had been feeling.

No, he definitely couldn't be gone long.

Not sure where to begin, he made his way back towards the edge of the trees where he could see the surrounding terrain better. He knew that there was no water in the direction he'd walked the night before, but the road forked, with the one to the left heading towards what had appeared to be a town. Too dangerous. Behind him, the ground rose up. Not likely he'd find anything there unless he went over the mountain, and who knew what he'd find then. Out in front of him, there was no cover. He would be out in the wide open. Definitely not an option. So, back towards Westlow it was. He'd head that direction for a short time. If he didn't find a stream or puddle or something of the sort, he would rethink his options.

****

Lucash had been walking in a zig-zag pattern, covering as much ground as he could. He had not found a water source that was anything more than muddy sludge with a layer of brown water over the top. He'd actually contemplated drinking it, but when he tried to fill his cupped hand, he could not get just water. Mud oozed up over the top. When he bent down to try to slurp it off the ground, the smell of leaf rot and algae was too much.

He gagged. He stood up and moved on, getting discouraged and increasingly worried about being gone from Juniper.

His heart lurched and his stomach knotted up when he thought he heard the sound of voices. He stilled his movement and strained his ears. He heard it again. The words were indistinct, but there was no mistaking the rising and falling inflections for anything other than people speaking.

Without thinking, Lucash moved closer to the sounds. He had to see for himself. He had to *know* that it was the guards looking for them, to know what their current actions suggested about how much time he had before he and Juniper were discovered. They now had to be on foot. Otherwise, he would not have heard them speaking.

Lucash took a few careful steps, then stopped to listen, trying to judge how close he was getting. At the moment, they didn't appear to be moving because the sounds continued to come from the same direction.

The voices stopped. Lucash kept listening, feeling every bit as vulnerable as he had the night before. More, really. Whoever had been there on the mountainside the previous night had wanted to remain hidden as much as he did. Not so with the Guard. *Am I crazy? Just lookin' for trouble right now.* Still feeling the need to know, Lucash stayed put. The talking picked up again, so he moved closer. He was nearing a clearing in the trees. When he reached the edge, it wasn't the Guard he saw.

Three people stood among some boulders. They looked quite young. *Can't even be as old as me and Juniper. How'd they get out here?* This was definitely not what he'd expected to find, but it was still troubling. They didn't look distressed to him. Concerned maybe, but not distressed. He did not think it likely that they had escaped the same way he and Juniper had. That would be a crazy coincidence. None of them looked sick or injured. They kept looking at phones that did not look like his standard Council-issued phone.

Just then, he heard the sound of tires spinning over dirt and rock. He looked towards the road and back at the three standing by the rocks. The Guard. They'd catch these three if they saw them. But why weren't they moving to hide? They had large boulders right there, but they didn't make a move. Just looked towards the road, expectantly.

A truck came into view — different from the one he'd been put in the back of — and drove off the road and headed straight for the rocks where the three were standing. Now it was clear that whoever these three were, they were expecting this truck, and it had nothing to do with the Guard.

Lucash looked for a way to get closer. He wanted to be able to hear what they had to say, and the noise of the truck made it easier to move without being heard. He followed the trees around the clearing to where they grew closer to the fallen boulders. The truck was facing right in his direction. The people inside would be able to see him if he moved any more between trees. *This'll have to be close enough.*

He watched from behind the full branches of a pine tree as two people got out of the truck and headed towards the others. Of the two, one looked to be the same age as the others, while the second looked more like him and Juniper.

****

"How'd it go at BRO?" Rebecca asked as Remy and Selby approached.

"It was…interesting," Remy replied. "Karl was there still. Definitely in a panic. He looked rough."

"As rough as you're looking right now?" asked Cassidi. "Cuz you're looking pretty bad."

"Ha. Thanks, Cass. And you're looking quite spectacular yourself." Rebecca looked from Cassidi to Remy.

"And?" Rebecca asked to get them back on track.

"He came up on me and Bryn when we were talking, and I swear I've never seen him look so distraught. He looked like he was wanting to ask us something, but then he just turned around and walked away without saying a word. Very not like him."

"What did Bryn say about all this?" Rebecca had been a bit surprised that Bryn wasn't with Remy and Selby. She was almost certain Bryn would have demanded to come along. "I thought she'd come with you."

"She wanted to. But then we needed to see if those contacts had any more information for us. One of us had to stay and follow up on that. So. It had to be her. And, of course, she wasn't thrilled at the idea."

"She was really pretty *mad* at you. That's what you mean to say," Selby said as he stifled his laughter behind his hand.

"Was she mad that we're out here?" asked Rebecca.

"Well…she was mad that I brought *you all* out here. She told me I was being irresponsible."

"She called you an *idiot*, man!" Selby was quite enjoying this line of conversation.

"Did you tell her we are the ones who made the decision? She should know by now that we are quite capable of making up our own minds here," Rebecca found herself irritated at Bryn's insistence at treating them like they were incapable kids.

"I did. She can't help but still feel some responsibility for you. We both do, but Bryn is a little more stubborn than I am. I might feel responsible, but I know when to step down."

"Glad we don't have both of you harping on us all the time. It isn't like you guys are *that* much older than us. Just a few years…" said Cassidi. "So, did you find out anything useful?"

"Maybe. But we'll wait for Davi and Mel. They should be here any time now, shouldn't they?" Remy looked at his phone for any more messages and they all glanced around the clearing looking for signs of the last two of their little search party. They looked right past Lucash, who hadn't dared to move.

"Thought they'd have been here already," said Daniel. "Hey, Selby, how'd it go with the parents?"

"Better'n I'd a thought!" said Selby. "They were worried, I think, that I had gone so long without contacting them, but they tried not to show it."

"Unlike Bryn," said Cassidi.

"Right. They're pretty good about trustin' me. Thank god I didn't screw *that* up with all this. Anyways. They're actually glad we're lookin' for these two. Can you believe that? They wanted to help, too, but said maybe it'd be better if they stayed back. They've got my Colossus phone. If we get in trouble, we can message them from one of our other phones. Kinda feelin' naked without my phone," Selby laughed as he patted the pocket that normally held his phone within close reach.

****

Lucash was sure he'd just heard this last guy refer to a Colossus phone. He'd never heard of such a thing. They also seemed to be looking for someone, which at least said something about *what* they're doing out here, but it didn't really answer the question of *why?* Or *who?* Or *how?*

He hoped they kept talking. But fast. He had to get back to Juniper.

"Well, well, well…what have we got here?" came the voice from behind, as hands grabbed one shoulder and twisted the other arm behind his back, making it impossible for Lucash to run.

CHAPTER 23

Bendi had awakened with her head cradled in her arms and leaning over the top of her desk. She didn't remember laying her head down. She looked at the book, notes, and computer still scattered across her desk. Her computer's screen had gone dark. It was still dark outside, though a faint glow was just visible over the ridges to the east. Bendi rubbed the sleep from her eyes and stretched her arms overhead in an effort to wake herself up more.

Looking at her Colossus phone, she could see that it had been quiet as well. She wondered how everyone was doing with their missions. Selby should have been out by now. Rebecca and Daniel, too, actually. Why had no one contacted her? *How did it go?* Bendi typed the message into her Colossus phone and waited for a response from Rebecca. None came immediately. This caused Bendi some concern since they all tended to keep their Colossus phones close. She hoped that the lack of communication did not mean trouble but decided that at the moment there was little she could do about it. If Rebecca didn't respond and no one else contacted her by full daylight, she would try to reach one of the others. Melody, even, if it came to that.

Bendi returned to her notes. There was something that she felt she was on the verge of figuring out. Some hints in the notes as to what they were doing with this virus. The testing they were doing suggested that there was more to it than simple interest in killing off the targets. Had that been the case, a simple high dose amount would have done it. They would not have to be making alterations based on the genetic profiles of each individual. The reason for this made no sense at all to Bendi. At least not yet.

But she felt like she was getting close. There had to be *something* she was missing. Bendi picked up the notes again and started flipping through them. Paper. Such an odd thing for the scientists to be using to record their data. Paper was still used, but not often. Writing in this old form had been completely replaced by computers. Children now did not grow up learning how to make letters and numbers on paper. Everything was electronic. Some parents taught their children how to write, but very few, as most children saw no use for the medium. The scientists who made these notes were definitely familiar and comfortable with writing.

Bendi went through the notes again, not really expecting to find anything. She flipped quickly through the pages, unsure of exactly what she was looking for. Then, she saw it. The number of survivors actually *increased* over time. They wanted these victims to *live*. That had to be it! She looked more closely at the trials and saw now the similarities between the trials where the victims lived. She didn't exactly know how to interpret it all. She didn't completely understand how the virus was altered, but she did know the scientists were interested in one gene in particular and in injecting a dose that would not kill the victim.

But why? What would be the point of that?

Bendi picked up her Colossus phone again, though there had been no incoming message. What she knew was confirmed with a quick glance at the screen. Bendi's eyebrows knitted in concern. She sent a message to Selby, Troy, and Cassidi to see if any of them would respond. When none of them did, she grew even more worried. Troy wasn't even with the groups going into BRO. Why wasn't he responding?

Looking through the notes again, Bendi typed up what she was thinking on her computer. She didn't want to lose the connections she'd threaded together. Typing them up was also a good distraction.

Her phone buzzed. It was Troy.

Sorry. Busy with Destin. Not paying attention to the phone. Nope. No word from anyone. You neither?

No. Still nothing. Getting worried. Not like Becs.

No it isn't. Try Remy or Bryn.

I don't want to bother them, but if I don't hear from Becs soon, I will message Bryn. Have to discuss something with her anyway.

What?

Can't say now. Too much for a message. And I want to check with her first. It might be nothing.

Coming from you, I doubt it.

Thanks. If I am right, I'm sure we will meet up soon enough. How did it go with Destin?

Good.

Good? Really?

Yep. Really.

Bendi was happy to hear that. She knew the tension had been high between those two. Whatever changed it for them, she was glad of it. *Good. Anything important I should know about?*

There was a long pause. Either Troy was still busy, or he was trying to think of what to say.

No. Nothing important. But we did get the key cards completely finished.

Good. Destin was helpful then. Bendi wasn't sure she quite believed Troy, but she let it go, as was her nature. He would tell her when he was ready. She wasn't one to push.

Yes. Very.

Good to hear. In the middle of something. I have to go. Will message you if Becs gets back to me.

Ok. But I think you should message Remy or Bryn.

Will do. If I don't hear from Becs soon.

Keep me posted. Later.

I will. Bye, Troy.

Bendi returned to the notes and her computer. She still could not figure out why anyone would be interested in creating a virus that would make people so sick but not kill them. Yet, they were telling everyone that there were no survivors. There were so many questions, too. If these people survived the virus, where were they now? Anyone she knew of that had gotten sick had died and been carried away after the final ceremonial farewells. Like Jonathan. He was gone. Bendi was certain of that. But, if one of the targets were among the survivors, did that mean that they never got sick? Or did they only get a little sick, so their illness was thought to be a normal virus.

So many questions. Bendi's head was starting to swim. She closed the notebook and rested her head on the tips of her fingers, elbows propped on the desk. Lifting her head, she reached again for her Colossus phone and messaged Bryn.

Bryn's message came back immediately. *I have heard from them. All are okay, but things did not go as planned last night. We should meet to discuss. But don't worry.*

When can we meet? Where? I have something I need to tell you, too.

I can be free in an hour. Can you meet me at the ranch? Where Remy parks the truck.

Sure. See you in an hour.

See you then.

Bryn gathered up the notebooks. She transferred her own notes from her computer to a data storage device. She shoved everything in her pack and left her house without being noticed by the chattering group of siblings sitting in the living room. They were too engrossed in their conversation to see her slip by. Good thing, since it would probably take her nearly an hour to reach the ranch.

CHAPTER 24

CA 5349 opened his eyes. He was lying on a platform made from metal. He still wore the same uniform he had had on the day before. And the day before that. And the day before that. Though CA 5349 was completely unaware of this fact. His eyes opened to a view of the gray planks above him that made up the ceiling of the temporary barracks where he and the 299 others just like him stayed. The cold metal of the platform caused the physiological response of goosebumps on his skin, but CA 5349 did not feel the cold, just as he had not felt the warmth of the sun on previous days. The unit sat up in unison. CA 5349 was facing the CA Individual just in front of him. A flicker of recognition flashed in his eyes. And then it was gone.

CHAPTER 25

Davi held Lucash firmly while walking him towards the group. Lucash knew better than to fight against Davi; 7 against 1 were not good odds. Davi was not rough with Lucash. Not like the guard. But still Lucash stumbled over the uneven surface, as Davi's hold kept him just a little off balance. The group stood staring at him, bodies tense, eyes alert to any move he might make.

"Who are you?" asked the one who had been driving the truck.

"I could ask you the same."

"You could, but you won't get an answer. You, on the other hand, might not like it if you don't provide us with an answer."

"What are you doing out here?" asked Rebecca, more gently than Remy. "By yourself," she added. They were looking for two people, not one, and two people who had been injected with the virus. This was one guy, and he looked perfectly healthy.

"Who says I'm alone? Maybe I'm with the Guard," Lucash knew that was a stupid response as soon as the words left his mouth. Of course, he wasn't the Guard. A member of the Guard would be wearing a uniform.

Cassidi laughed, "Yeah, right. If you aren't alone, your...uh...friends...must not care too much what happens to you."

"I didn't say they were right here *with* me, now did I?" Lucash replied, buying a little time.

"Well, then, I'd say they aren't doing you much good, now, are they?" Cassidi shot back.

"We all split up," Lucash said.

"Why would you do that?" Rebecca asked.

"That still doesn't tell us what you're doing out here," Remy said at the same time.

"We're lookin' for someone. Two people, actually. Told you I'm with the Guard," Lucash added, trying to sound confident.

The others all looked at one another. Could he be telling the truth? Was it possible he was with the Guard?

Remy opened his mouth to say something, just as a vehicle came into view on the road, heading in the direction of BRO.

One look at Lucash's face told the others what they needed to know as they all scurried for cover, Davi keeping a tight hold on Lucash. There was no need. Lucash was just as eager as the others to be behind the boulders.

They all heard the vehicle come to a stop on the road. Doors opened.

"They saw us! I think they saw us. What do we do?" asked Mel.

"We have to make a run for it. Now." Selby said. "We gotta head right up this mountain and hope they can't climb as fast as us."

"He's right. Stay low. Go up as quickly as possible," Remy added.

"And spread out. It's what my folks taught me. If someone's after you, ya gotta spread out. Makes it harder for them to catch everyone."

"We have to go. NOW!" Remy said in a low and urgent voice. "I'm sticking with you, so don't get any ideas," he said to Lucash, pulling him from Davi's grasp and giving him a nudge in the direction he expected Lucash to go. Lucash's response was to take off through the boulders, looking back once to be sure Remy was with him, though it was unnecessary since Remy was right on his heels. The only thoughts running through Lucash's mind right then were that these guys were all as afraid of the Guard as he was and sticking with them was his best chance in leading the Guard away from Juniper. Rather than feeling threatened by Remy's presence at his back, he felt a little reassured. Just a little.

Rebecca dashed low through the boulders, unaware of any more than getting away from the men now heading in their direction. They would be across the distance between the road and the boulder field in no time. She was not about to get caught. Not now. Weaving her way at an angle she hoped was out of their direct line of site, she glanced behind her to see if she could see them. Instead, she saw Daniel rounding the boulder just behind her.

"Keep moving," he whispered. "We'll stick together. You lead the way."

Rebecca gave a nod as she turned around and started moving again. The boulders would provide cover until partway up the slope. From there, they'd be in the trees for at least a little while, before trees gave way to rocky terrain once again.

Selby waited for the others to disperse. He had a single taser on him. He'd brought it just in case. His parents had insisted. No doubt the four men heading in their direction were armed with something, but at least with the taser, Selby had some chance of holding them off if they got too close to the group. Selby had no intention of waiting around for them to reach him, but he did want to be sure everyone else was on their way and that he was bringing up the rear.

Cassidi turned to make her run for it, hoping she would see Rebecca, but she was already out of sight. She did see Selby, but when she started heading in his direction, he motioned her on, showing her his taser as he did so. Cassidi understood that he meant to stay behind until he knew the others were safe. She shook her head no with a scowl of disapproval and headed towards him anyway. If he was staying behind, so was she.

"Cass, you have to *go. Run.*"

"No. I'm sticking with you."

"You're wastin' time, man. I'm comin' right behind you, but you gotta go. Can't keep an eye on you and these guys. *Now go.* They're gonna be here any minute now."

"Selby, I'm not going. You need me here. You don't have a phone." Cassidi saw the realization hit him and smiled triumphantly.

"Seriously? You're *smilin'* right now?"

"Yep."

Selby rolled his eyes. "Stay quiet and stay behind me. Everyone else is gone. I'm gonna peak around the boulder one last time to see where they are, then we're gonna start making our way slowly up the hill."

Mel headed straight for the trees running up the column of boulders, wanting the cover of the forest, even if it meant that she wouldn't climb upwards as quickly. She felt safer there, like there were more places to hide. Davi followed her.

****

Once Rebecca started moving again through the boulders, she didn't look back to see if Daniel was still with her. She knew he was. She was afraid to stop, afraid that if she slowed down at all, they'd lose the distance between them and the men now hunting them down. The Guard would have no idea who they were, but a group of people out in the Borderlands would be sufficient cause for pursuit, regardless of the orders they'd been given. They had to get clear of the danger, and then find out who it was they had picked up along the way.

The slope was growing steeper, but the boulders provided the leverage needed to climb quickly. They were still large enough that they could weave their way in between them and remain hidden as long as they kept low. Now, however, the danger came in the possibility of loose boulders that could be sent crashing down from the weight of a person. Rebecca looked up above her at the distance she still had to cover. The image of the tremendous rock fall that had to have occurred to create this boulder field flashed through her mind. Her heart skipped a beat. Or two. And she felt her stomach drop as heavily as one of these giant rocks would if she sent it, and herself, sliding even further down the mountain.

Rebecca stopped moving.

"You okay?" asked Daniel, his hand on her back to steady her.

"Yeah. I'm good." Rebecca shook her head to clear it and started moving. She determined she would not look up again.

They reached the trees with no indication that anyone was right behind them. With 8 of them out there, they had a better chance of confusing the Guard and eluding them, but any one of them could end up with the Guard at their heels, too. She darted into the trees and onto the backside of a large oak. Rebecca stopped and leaned back against the tree, catching her breath.

"Let's just stop a sec. See if we can hear anything," Rebecca said.

"And catch our breath," Daniel added, gasping for air.

"Right."

Rebecca looked around the tree to see if she could catch sight of any movement below.

Nothing.

Except the sound of some small rocks being sent downhill.

"How far away do you think that was?" Rebecca asked.

"Not far enough, if it's the Guard. Too far, if it's one of us," Daniel replied.

"Nice answer."

"Thanks."

"Any time. Ready to go again?"

"Yeah. I don't think we should stop for long. I don't know how long these guys will chase us, but I bet they won't be stopping any time soon," said Rebecca.

"I bet you're right. Which way?"

Rebecca looked at the terrain and the trees. The terrain was rugged, and the trees were growing sparse up here. It wouldn't take much to get through them. She wanted their protection for as long as possible. She pointed a path up through the trees.

"Let's go that way. Angle away from the rocks."

"Good plan. After you."

Rebecca led the way, moving quickly but quietly. They'd been moving for a few minutes when the sound of a breaking branch and a flash of movement caught their attention. Daniel grabbed her arm to stop her, though it was unnecessary. They looked in the direction of the sound and the movement. In between the trees, a man in a guard uniform was moving in their direction. He was downslope a good distance, but moving fast, and with a purpose that suggested that even though they could not tell if he was looking at them, they had a feeling he knew they were there.

No words were necessary, Rebecca and Daniel took off at a run, no longer trying to be quiet. Just fast. Branches hit Rebecca in the face, but she paid no attention to the blood running down her forehead. She could not hear the footsteps of the guard downhill from them, but she knew that he would have picked up his pace as well. She hoped that he was not used to climbing on this terrain.

Daniel was right on her heels, making sure that there was no chance they'd be separated. She heard him slip on a loose pile of leaves and turned back to make sure he was alright. He was already up and running again, like nothing happened.

"I'm okay," he said, "Just keep moving. Don't worry about me, I'll keep up."

She paused for the briefest moment to see if she could catch sight of the guard. Yep. He was still there and seeming to have little trouble climbing this hill.

"He's closing in," she said as she turned and started running.

"I know. We can't slow down."

Rebecca's lungs were burning with the effort and the thin air, and her muscles were aching, but she picked up her pace. They scrambled over roots and rocks until the trees dwindled to granite and tundra. Sticking to the rocks as much as possible, the two of them climbed higher. The guard was still behind them. They could now hear his movements as he sent loose rocks tumbling down the mountain and slipped over the surface of moss and lichen. Still they did not slow or turn around.

Pure adrenaline fueled Rebecca's movements, just as it had on her first climb up the mountain at the edge of Daniel's family's ranch so many months ago. A lifetime ago. There was no room in her thoughts to notice the heights she was climbing, no chance to look either down or up. Just moving on instinct and fear with no choice but to trust her footing.

Until they reached the top.

Suddenly, the world opened up in front of her eyes. The great expanse laid out in every direction, with no place to avert her eyes from the abyss just a few feet in front of her. She pulled up short and swayed from the immediate wave of dizziness that engulfed her head, causing the world two swirl and tilt. Daniel was right there. He caught her in his arms as her knees began to buckle underneath her.

"Becs, look at me. Look right at me. Nowhere else," he panted out the words as he turned her towards him. "You can do this. We have to keep moving."

"I...I don't know if I *can*. Everything is spinning. You go. I'll...I'll hide...somewhere..." She replied, not sure where she could hide, and not even wanting to look away from Daniel to find a spot.

"No. No way. We're in this together. I won't let anything happen to you. I *know* you can do this. I'll go in front; you hold onto me...keep your eyes on the back of my head. Do *not* look away. Okay?"

Rebecca didn't respond, feeling frozen to the spot where she now stood, unsure if her feet would move, no matter how much she wanted them to.

"Rebecca. Listen to me. We. Have. To. Move. You don't have any other choice now. Jonathan is counting on you. So am I. So is everyone in this town. You are the strongest and bravest person I know." He leaned in just then and gently placed his lips against hers. Briefly. Lightly. When he pulled back, his eyes were locked on hers so that she knew how he felt. He believed everything he had just said.

The guard could be heard again below, getting ever closer, though not as quickly as he had in the trees. Apparently, his skill in climbing through forests did not translate to this new terrain. It had bought them a little bit of much needed time, but that time was now running out.

"Now," Daniel said, without looking away. Rebecca nodded her head. Just barely. But when Daniel turned, she grabbed his pack and found her feet moving forward, matching his every step.

****

Selby and Cassidi had watched as the four men heading in their direction split off in four different directions. They were now helpless in being able to protect the gang. Without knowing which direction everyone went, there was no way of being able to determine where they would be most useful.

"What should we do?" asked Cassidi. "Call your parents? Would they be able to help?"

"No. Nothin' they could do now. It'd take 'em forever to get here, first of all. An' we have no way of knowin' where anyone will end up. Nope. Best thing we can do is get movin' ourselves."

"Guess so. Okay."

"You lead the way…I'll be right behind. You know, just in case someone sneaks up behind us. I got your back."

"Haha."

"Seriously. Least there's someone I can make sure doesn't get hurt in all this."

"Well. Thanks, then," Cassidi said, taken aback a little at Selby's protectiveness. This wasn't bravado. He was really serious about it. And she believed he *would* protect her, if the need arose. This wasn't a drill. This was the real thing. And Selby was willing to do what no one else she knew would do for her. *Besides Becs, of course.* Before now, Rebecca had been the only person in her world she thought she could count on. Really count on. She felt suddenly lighter than she had felt for a long time. Selby. Huh. Who'd have thought?

Cassidi smiled, in spite of their current predicament, and the very real danger they were in.

"Uh. Cass? What's the grin about?"

Cassidi's face grew serious as she erased the smile, self-conscious now. Her face grew a little warm, so she turned from him quickly to avoid him noticing that too. *Geez, Cassidi, what's gotten into you? You really that desperate for someone to care about you?*

Aloud she stuttered, "Um, nothing. Just picturing you trying to defend me against four men. We'd both be dead."

Maybe not desperate, but still...

"Wouldn't be all four, but even if it were, I'm better at this than you think," Selby said, his tone indicated that her comment had hurt.

Cassidi then stopped moving and turned around to look at Selby, who'd almost bumped into her because he'd been watching his step rather than her.

Cassidi, regretting her words, reached a hand out and placed it on his arm, "Sorry, Selby. Just not used to anyone sticking up for me beside Becs. Thanks. And I know you're good. I've seen you in training, remember?"

Selby's face transformed. He grew serious. Stood a little taller. Ready to follow through on his promise. Cassidi shot him a wide, disarming grin, before turning back up the mountain and heading through the boulder field, veering to the right at an angle that would keep them in the boulders for as long as possible.

They'd reached the trees and then the top without seeing any trace of any of the men hunting all of them down. They stopped then, taking a look around for signs of any of the others or of the men. Cassidi couldn't help but feel exhilarated by the view. She could see forever up here! Mountains to the north, south, and west. To the east, she could see to where the land flattened out into the plains. This was a view she'd never seen before. She had had no idea, actually, exactly what lay east of Montrose. They were surrounded by mountains in their little valley. Even hiking at the outskirts of the recreational areas did not afford her these views. None of the trails went up high enough to see. But here? Here they were obviously on the edge of it all, and it made Cassidi feel a freedom she didn't know she could feel.

"Wish I could fly," she said, without realizing she'd actually spoken the words aloud.

"What? *Fly*?" asked Selby, confused at a comment that seemed out of place, given their circumstances.

Cassidi snapped her head around to Selby, just then figuring out that he'd heard her. She looked back out over the plains and shrugged. "Yeah. You know. Like the birds. I'd soar over those lands out that way. See what all is out there. Out past all these mountains."

"Well, guess that's one way to get away from the Guard," Selby chuckled.

"You're a funny guy," Cassidi said, pulling her attention back to their current situation.

"Yep, I try…I try."

"So, what now? Don't see a soul around us."

"Nope. Me neither. And it's quiet. Which makes me think that the others are a long ways off. Sound travels far up in these high places," Selby said.

"Really? How'd you know that?"

"Another of the *many* lessons my parents pounded into my head all my life. When you got someone teachin' you all they know from the time you can sit still long enough to listen, then you soak up a whole lotta information. Never thought it'd actually be something I'd ever have to use. Kinda thought my folks were a little nuts, to be honest."

Cassidi burst out with a laugh that was louder than she'd intended. She sucked in the laugh to quiet it, but her voice still carried the sound when she said, "I'm surprised they ever got a chance to teach you. When have you ever sat still for even a minute?"

"Heeeey…I resemble that remark," Selby said, winking in Cassidi's direction.

Just then, they heard a sound that made their skin crawl.

A scream, short and surprised, and quickly drawn out into silence.

They stared at one another with a look of horror.

"Who was that? Could you tell?" Cassidi asked.

"No. It was a guy. That's all could tell. Never heard any of us scream before."

"Maybe it wasn't one of us. Maybe it was one of *them*."

"Yeah, maybe. It came from that way," Selby said, pointing along the ridge.

"Wonder how far away. Can you tell?"

"No. Probably further than we think, but we gotta go check it out. If it's one of us, I'm guessin' soemone's gonna need some help. If it's one of them, then at least we have some good news to tell the others when we see them again."

"Well, what are we waiting for?"

"You to get movin'. I'm followin' you, remember?"

"Right," and Cassidi started jogging along the ridge, deftly managing the rough ground and not seeming to notice the sheer drop to her right. Selby's long legs moved easily over the ground as well but covering about twice the distance with one step.

There were no further screams, nor any other sounds that might give away exactly where the person was. Or who it was, for that matter. Their eyes scanned the ground on every side as they ran. The ridge was narrowing, slowing them down to a more cautious stride. One slip would mean the end of them. It would widen out again just ahead, but until then, it was better to tread with care. Concentration shifted to their footing. Doubtful that anyone would have been able to make it up the slope heading down in the direction of the road. Even an experienced rock climber would have found it difficult.

As they reached the end of the narrow section, their pace quickened again. But it only lasted a minute when Cassidi skidded to a stop. A section of the ground in front of them had been peeled away. Their eyes followed the path the loose rock would have taken downhill and came to a stop on the form of a crumpled body below.

"Oh my god," Cassidi gasped, grabbing Selby's arm tightly as they looked down at the scene below.

CHAPTER 26

Manglebee was there. At the BRO facility. Trevor had just received word. Trevor broke out into a cold sweat. He knew *why* he was there. Or at least he could guess. It wasn't because of the work he'd sent Trevor to do. No, he wouldn't have come for that. At least not so soon. Trevor was certain that he'd been called in because of the conversation he'd overheard in the garage. Apparently, they hadn't found the two escapees yet. That should have comforted Trevor, except that he somehow knew that since Manglebee was here, he'd take the opportunity to check up on Trevor. Not to mention the fact that it was Trevor who was in charge of this entire Bio-Programming operation. Whatever happened here at BRO was ultimately his responsibility, even though he really had no direct involvement in much of it. Regardless, this mishap was something else Manglebee could heave onto Trevor's shoulders, placing the blame on Trevor, though Trevor really had nothing to do with the escaped prisoners.

Trevor and his team had gotten no further on the task that they were sent here to do. They were still trying to figure out who it was that had broken into the computer system and changed the files so that the upcoming dosages would be programmed incorrectly for the intended targets. The team had been at it for hours. It was now well past daylight, and they had long forgotten their original assignment, so engrossed were they in the current crisis.

Until now. At least for Trevor. He hadn't told the others in the room yet. He still wasn't sure what he should do right now. They never would have guessed someone had changed the data if they hadn't witnessed it themselves. None of them, including Trevor, were very knowledgeable about the specifics on the virus. This team was simply responsible for the programming of the robots, using the data given them by the scientists who *did* work with the virus. They were looking for a malfunction in the program. Not in the data the scientists gave them.

While it was possible that the cases of immunity were due to an experiment by the individual who had infiltrated their system, they doubted it. This crisis took precedence. Someone managed to break into their system. So much more damage could be done than what had happened this morning. Their hope was that they could discover who it was and take care of it, without Manglebee's knowledge. Trevor wasn't entirely certain how he would pull that off. What, exactly, did he plan to *do* if they discovered where the intruder was located? Trevor had no idea. He would never be able to resort to Manglebee's methods. There was little he could threaten the person with other than turning them over to Manglebee. Meaning, of course, that he'd have to tell Manglebee. And then it would also be his neck on the line.

Trevor shuddered, as now it seemed he would not have the opportunity to figure it out.

Manglebee is demanding your presence down here. Henderson. Of course, he'd be here too. Trevor wondered how many of the Advisors came along for the ride.

Trevor's fingers paused over his phone. Maybe he should ignore it. Pretend he hadn't seen the message.

No. That would be the best way to raise Manglebee's suspicion, and perhaps even ensure a visit from him to the lab. At least this way, he'd have the advantage of being able to stall. He'd have the walk down the corridors to figure out exactly what he'd say to Manglebee that would satisfy the Head Councilor and keep him from finding out what was really happening. Trevor wasn't a good liar. That much had been made dreadfully clear by the state of his marriage.

Heading that way now, he replied, heaving a great sigh and bracing himself for what was to come.

Trevor arrived in time to witness the sight of Manglebee interrogating Karl. Manglebee looked like a time bomb ready to explode. It was a controlled pressure, but there was no denying the extent of his fury. Trevor did not have much experience with Manglebee. He hadn't been at this long. In the interactions he had had with him, Manglebee was more often than not exhibiting some level of irritation. His every interaction was laced with condescension. Trevor had been the target of his anger recently. He knew what that felt like. How that looked. But, up until now, he'd never seen Manglebee look as he did now. Trevor felt sorry for Karl. Trevor also felt relief that, for the moment, it was Karl and not him.

"…have four men out looking now, Head Councilor. They've been at it since last night."

"Why, then, was I not informed of this situation *last night?*" Manglebee said through a clenched jaw. Trevor wasn't close enough to see, but from Manglebee's tone, he was sure that the vein in Manglebee's temple would look ready to burst.

"I—didn't want to trouble you, sir. I thought if I sent two more competent individuals out with the guards who failed to secure the prisoners then you would not have to take time out of your busy schedule to deal with the situation," Karl responded in a meek voice. At least, meek for Karl. It was a strange sight to see. This Karl did not match the Karl of Trevor's experiences. It made him uncomfortable to watch.

"Do *not* attempt to flatter me, Karl. Your real goal was to save your own skin. And now, because of *your* incompetence, there are four men out there searching for two prisoners who could be anywhere. Does this about sum it up?"

At this, Karl actually sputtered. Trevor could see that he was not certain if Manglebee actually expected a response, but, after a slight pause, Karl replied in the affirmative. "The prisoners were injected with the experimental virus, sir. They should not have been difficult to locate. They should have been too ill to go far. They might even be dead by now."

"Or. They might not. Either way, we will need these prisoners to be recovered. Your stupidity has not only wasted valuable time, but it has also put this entire operation in jeopardy. If those two are not dead—and you should hope for your own sake that they are—and any sort of information about this leaks out to the citizens of Anecor, it will be the last mistake you ever make. Am I clear on this?" The blood drained from Karl's face. He nodded his head in response, words failing him in that moment.

"What is the current status of the search?" Manglebee asked.

"The men messaged a couple of hours ago to say that they had searched a wide area heading back towards Westlow, and they were now going to search the area between the location where they injected the prisoners and here."

"That is the last you have heard? In two hours, you have made no further attempt to contact them?"

"I have attempted to contact them, Head Councilor. I have not received a response."

"I suggest you try again." This was, of course, an order. Not a suggestion.

"Yes, sir," Karl replied, already beginning to type a message into his phone.

Manglebee turned his attention to Henderson, who appeared to be the only Advisor present, "Where is Trevor?"

"On his way, according to his message."

Trevor pushed the door the rest of the way open and walked through on trembling legs.

"Uh…here…I'm here, sir."

"Did you know about this?" His tone told Trevor that there was no right answer to this question.

"Well, not really. Sir."

"Not *really?*" Manglebee leveled his glare on Trevor.

"Well…uh…what I mean is that I…I didn't have direct knowledge of the situation. No one informed me. I overheard part of a conversation earlier when I came back to the vehicle for my phone, but I didn't hear the whole story. Sir."

"You did not bother to ask? Are you not in charge of this operation?"

Here we go, thought Trevor. *Why can't I just have my life back?*

"I didn't think that it concerned me, sir, and Karl seemed to be handling it, so I continued with what I was doing." Trevor knew it was coming now. There was no way to avoid Manglebee's questions about what it was he was doing. Trevor had tried to rehearse the lines in his head on the walk down the hall. He wouldn't tell him. He wouldn't lie, exactly, but he wouldn't tell him either.

"Tell me you have at least solved the problem you were sent here to fix."

"Uh, no. We haven't found anything yet, but the team is still working on it. They have not stopped since they started. They, uh, they'll keep working on it until they know one way or the other. Um, me, too. I am working with them, sir." *Please let that be good enough. Please don't want to see the lab.*

Please.

"What is the holdup? Is your team that incompetent?"

"No, sir. The team is the top of their field."

"So, the issue must lie with your own ineptitudes."

Trevor was shocked into silence. He couldn't find the words to respond to the last statement.

Manglebee's look was one of contempt. "I expect a full report the minute you finish. No one is to leave until you have done your job to my satisfaction. It looks like *I* will be here cleaning up this mess. Doing Karl's job and yours. Leave now."

"Yes, Head Councilor." Trevor didn't not hesitate even for a moment. He spun around and walked quickly to the door before Manglebee had time to think of anything else to harass him about.

Once through the door and around the first corner, Trevor stopped, leaned back against the wall, and slid to the floor. He removed his glasses and wiped the sweat from his forehead and eyes and buried his face in his hands. This was too much. The weight of it bore down on him to the point of breaking. He had no idea how he would survive all this. And if he did, what was it all for? Mica would never forgive him if she knew the truth. He was sure she would despise him for what he was doing now. And his son? He couldn't even bear the thought of what this would do to his son.

Not knowing what else to do at the moment, Trevor put his glasses back on and lifted himself from the floor. He ran his fingers through his hair and tugged at his shirt, hoping he was making himself look like the man his team expected to see walk back through the lab door.

CHAPTER 27

Bendi watched Bryn park her car in the place where Remy normally kept the truck. When she got out, Bendi could see that her face was strained, and she had the look of a person who had not gotten any sleep. Not that Bendi looked any better. Her hour or two of sleep hunched over her desk was not exactly restful. But Bryn was worried about something. That was clear. She had told Bendi that everyone was okay. Had something changed? Bendi, who was normally calm and not easily shaken, was now a worried. She felt an unusual sensation of butterflies in her stomach.

"Is everything okay? Is Becs and everyone else alright?" she asked as Bryn got closer.

"What? Oh, I think so. I haven't heard from them in a while, so I'm not exactly sure what's going on."

That response did not help calm the fluttering in Bendi's stomach. "I'm sorry, but you don't look good, Bryn, and it's making me nervous."

"Yes. Well. It's been a long night. Let me catch you up to speed."

"Please."

Bryn filled Bendi in on the aborted attempt to enter the BRO facility, the meeting afterwards, and the decision Remy and the others had made to go against Melody's orders and look for the escapees.

"Why?" asked Bendi when Bryn told her of the gang's plans.

"Remy's reasoning was that perhaps we could get some insight into the virus if we had two people who had been injected with it. He also thought we might learn something from them about The Disappeared and maybe the Resistance, if they were a part of that group. Melody does not mind those individuals taking the fall so long as her crew is safe. She doesn't agree with what they do, so, to her, there is no sense in us risking our own safety for theirs."

"They are still people," Bendi said quietly. "That should be reason enough to try to save them."

"I agree."

"But you haven't heard from Remy or anyone else since they went out to look?"

"No. Remy left me at BRO to go pick up Selby. Oh. That's something else I need to tell you. I forgot. You weren't there. I just found out from Remy."

"What?"

"Selby's parents know."

"They *do*?" This was truly a surprise to Bendi. She couldn't imagine Selby betraying Rebecca or Colossus. *Then again, he had already betrayed his parents trust. He had to have had a good reason.*

"Yes. Shocked me too. And everyone else, apparently." Bryn then gave Bendi the details as she understood them from Remy's recounting of what Selby had told the group.

"Wow. So, they really want to join us? I guess Selby's parents are the only ones I can imagine who would."

"From what I heard of their background, it seems we could use them. But after today, I'm not sure anymore what is going to happen. Selby was telling his parents about what the group's decision was. I don't know how that turned out. I assume he's with the group, but I really don't know. They thought it best if his parents didn't join them because there would already be 7 of us out there."

"I hope everything went well for them," Bendi said.

Bryn sighed. "I do too, Bendi."

Bryn looked troubled again.

"You said you had something that you wanted to talk to me about too?" Bryn asked, shaking off whatever thoughts had crept in at that moment.

"Oh. I do. I think I figured something out from the scientists' notes. I can't be sure, but if I'm right, it's very important information. Though I don't exactly know why."

"Okay, Bendi, you have me very curious. What did you discover?"

"Well, I've been going through the scientists' notes for a while now. I don't understand them all, but I've been learning more about human genes and viruses, too. I've been thinking there has to be something I'm missing. I could tell they were altering something with the virus structure, but I wasn't sure why. We know they are altering the dosage based on the individual's health and genetic profile, but they've been altering the virus's structure as well."

"That make sense, and I am not entirely surprised by this. Though I thought they'd already had the structure they wanted sorted out. They wanted to create a virus that was lethal, but not contagious," Bryn said.

"That's just it," Bendi said, "I don't think they want it to be lethal."

Bryn sat looking at Bendi as if she wasn't quite comprehending what she was saying. Bendi took the notes out of her bag and started flipping through the pages.

"Look. If we look at the beginning of these tests, you can see these diagrams for the virus structure and the data for the victim. They all show that the victim died."

"Okaaay."

"But, if we look further along in the notes, at later dates, we see that there are some who have survived. And the further along we go…" Bendi was now flipping quickly through the pages and pointing at the diagrams and the notes on the victims.

"More and more people are being listed as surviving…" Bryn finished Bendi's sentence.

"Yes!"

"But why?" Bryn said, shaking her head.

"I don't know. I have been trying to imagine the reason for it myself, but nothing makes sense. And another thing—who are these survivors? I know of no one who has gotten sick and survived. Do you?"

"No. I don't. But maybe…just maybe…"

"The bodies? The ones inside the BRO facility."

"Exactly. Maybe there is a connection. Are these the survivors? And, if so, then what are they doing with them?"

"And do their families, friends still believe them to be dead?" This last voiced thought was horrifying to Bendi, but even as the words left her mouth, she knew them to be true. "There were a lot of bodies in there. If they all survived, then that is a lot of people who are believed to be dead that aren't," she added.

"If those are all the survivors. Judging from the numbers in that notebook, that wouldn't seem to be the case. Even if there are more scientists working on the same thing. So, perhaps not all of them survive after they are delivered to the facility," Bryn said.

"That's a good point. I'm not sure what to do with all this information. How do we find out what they are doing? Should we go to Melody?"

"No. At least not yet. We might need to, but I want to wait until we find out what has happened today. Until we know what we're dealing with there. And—" Bryn stopped short, the troubled look coming to her again.

"What is it, Bryn? What have you not told me?"

Bryn sat quietly, contemplating whether or not to divulge the information she had received from one of the contact Melody had wanted she and Remy to talk to. Remy didn't know yet, and she hadn't told Melody either. She stared hard at Bendi, thinking about how young she was, and how sad it was that she and her friends had become caught up in such a dangerous game. Bryn wasn't too far away from being 15, but far enough to realize that once you lost your youth, you didn't get to just get it back. At least not now. Not the way their world worked now. So, she wished for Bendi that she could just be 15, even though Bendi had probably always seemed wiser than her years.

"Well," Bryn said, making the decision to tell Bendi, "it does have to do with what the gang is out there doing right now. These two might have been part of the Resistance. We know that they have become two of the Disappeared. But it seems that the Disappeared are actually being kept in facilities in the Borderlands. In horrible conditions. The contact today had been there. He was very afraid to talk to me. He had been threatened, as you can imagine, with his life if he told anyone what he saw."

"Those poor people. Just for disagreeing with Council. There has to be something we can do, doesn't there?"

"I don't know. This just adds another layer to what we're already dealing with. The contact also said that during his visit, there had been a conversation that he was sure he wasn't supposed to hear. In this conversation, there was talk of new facilities being constructed in the Borderlands and that some of the Disappeared would eventually be joining the others in the new facilities."

"What other?"

"He didn't know. The person talking had said just that: 'the others.' But it seemed to this contact that they were military facilities. Manglebee seems to be building an army again, and it appears that he wants to force the Disappeared into being part of it."

"He's attacking his own country again. Just like in The Reckoning! Only this time he's also using a virus. And an army."

"It would seem so. Really, a lot of this is speculation until we have more information. This contact was only there the one time, on BRO business. What he saw, and heard, terrified him. He doesn't want to join Colossus, but he wanted us to know. In case we could do something with the information," Bryn said.

"How did he know about Colossus?"

"He knew Manuel. They had been close. But he'd only learned about Manuel's involvement in Colossus just before he died. After what happened to Manuel, he didn't want to be a part of it, though he had been considering it before."

"Manuel is the man who Remy came to replace, right?" Bendi asked.

"Right. Karl caught on to his work with Colossus, except that he was never able to figure out exactly who it was Manuel was working for. Manuel never betrayed his loyalty to us, even though it cost him his life. I'm sure he knew it wouldn't have mattered. It's highly unlikely he would have been allowed to live even if he had divulged everything. Still. He was a brave man." Bryn's eyes glistened with unshed tears before she blinked them back and returned to the present.

"What do we do now?" asked Bendi.

"Now? Well, right now, we wait. We can't do anything else until Remy and the others have returned."

"Shouldn't we send them a message? To find out how it's going?"

"I've done that. I still haven't heard. Depending on where they are, my message might not get through to them. They should return by sundown. If not—"

"Do we go out and find them?" Bendi asked.

"I don't know. We'll cross that bridge when we get to it. For now, let's have a look at those notes again."

CHAPTER 28

Troy and Destin were exhilarated by their secret workings in the BRO system. They felt empowered and grew more confident by the moment.

"Now *this* is taking action. You know, we're doing more right now to help Colossus than anyone else," Troy mused.

"Yep. That we are. Wish we could tell them."

"We can't?"

"Not sure we should. Yet. I mean, you probably have seen enough of Melody by now to know she like to have control. Sure, she trusts us to make the decisions we have to when we are fulfilling her orders. She has to let us do that. It's all about safety for her. If we're gonna stay safe, then we have to be able to make judgement calls sometimes. But. This right here? This wouldn't qualify as 'keeping safe' exactly."

"Ha! Quite the opposite, actually," said Troy. "You're right. Guessing she wouldn't really be happy with us doing this without her knowing, huh?"

"Nope."

"So. What else are we gonna do? Maybe we can smooth the way by discovering something that she *would* approve of before telling her what we actually *did*."

"Good idea. I'm sure she'll be thrilled to know that we got through Level 3 Security. Overjoyed, actually. And we can tell her about these files. We just don't have to tell her we altered them," Destin said.

"We *can't* stop now! I think we should at least see what else we can find out. There are more files than this in here."

Destin looked sideways at him and shot him a quick grin, "You really are alright, nerd."

Troy returned the grin. "Thanks. So?"

"So? What are we waiting for? Sun's coming up and my dad will be home before too long, so if we're gonna do this—"

"Like you said...what are we waiting for?"

The file system followed some sort of order that was not obvious to Troy and Destin, so working their way through took time and patience. They both had the patience, but time was short, so they found their patience wearing a little thinner than it would if they did not feel up against a clock. Most of the files were the same kinds of records that they had already been looking at. Without any more information than what was recorded on those files, they weren't learning anything new.

Destin glanced at her watch, "Argh! My dad's shift is done in 30 minutes, and this feels like we're getting nowhere!"

"When do we need to stop working? We aren't quitting today until we have to."

"I'd say we safely have less than an hour. It takes just over an hour to get back here from the plant when our shifts end."

"Then we've still got time."

****

Trevor made his way back to the lab, dragging his feet. He reached the door, put his hand on the handle, closed his eyes for a brief moment to regain his composure, and pushed on through. The team continued their work and did not even appear to notice he'd walked through the door. He wasn't even sure that they'd noticed he was gone in the first place. Good. Fewer questions then. He walked to his computer station and logged back on, resuming his work comparing old files to the ones that were just changed.

"Any luck so far for any of you?" he asked his team.

The responses ranged from a frustrated "no" to a groan that sounded anything but positive.

"Just keep at it. Something's bound to break at some point, right?" he said, trying what meager encouragement he could summons.

"Files aren't changing anymore, so whoever it is has stopped their work for the day," came a voice from one of the computers closest to the door.

"Well, that's something, anyways. I'll take any form of good news I can get right now." With that, he saw a couple of heads raise and look at him with a touch of concern. When he didn't say anything more, they bent back over their keyboards, eyes locked on the screens in front of them, and went back at it. Trevor did the same, working with one half of his brain on his task — comparing data from two different files did not require much attention — and the other half in musings over telling Manglebee exactly what he could do with this job and stomping out on him, never looking back, to return to his normal life with his wife and son.

After looking for a half hour, he was convinced that the individual who had somehow broken into their system today had *not* changed the files from earlier. The changes in the earlier files were far too random. Too few spaced too far apart. It just wasn't logical to think that someone who had made such random changes previously would suddenly make numerous changes all in one sitting. *Well, on a positive note, at least I won't have to report to Manglebee that someone's been infiltrating the system for weeks now.* He wondered again if he should even report today's fiasco at all. *He might never find out…but, then again, who has ever gotten anything past that man? If someone has, I'd like to know who they are so I can ask them for pointers.*

Trevor decided to turn his attention to the task they'd originally set out to do. It would take more of his concentration to look at the previous targets — *not targets, Trevor. These are people. Don't ever forget that* — who hadn't succumbed to the virus and examine the programming for the robots who delivered the virus on the nightly "flights" from the "hives." He really doubted he would find anything. It wasn't like his team to be careless. They were good at what they did. The best really. Or Manglebee wouldn't have them there.

"Whoa…whoa…whoa…YES!!" came a shout from one of the others.

Trevor bolted out of his chair and was at the side of the person who spoke the words in an instant.

"What? *What?* Did you find something?"

He glanced up at Trevor, a look of surprise on his face. "I can't believe it, but, *yes.* I think I broke through. I have a location. Or, at least I think I do. Unless it's another layer of security that's landed me at a false location."

"Okay. Well, that could be. I certainly wouldn't be surprised. So, show me what you've got." The young man zoomed in on his screen so Trevor could see more easily what was up there. Sure enough, it looked like he nailed a signal from the computer being used.

"It does look like you might have found a location. Pull it up on a map. Let's see where it lands us," Trevor said.

"Sure thing, boss."

By this time, the other team members had made their way over to the computer and were all squeezing around the single chair to witness what they had all thought to be the impossible. When the map popped up, there was a collective sharp intake of air. And then exhales of disappointment.

"Looks like you were duped," said one of the onlookers.

"Yeah. No way this came out of Quadrant 4. No one's even allowed computers out that way. Not to mention the training in computers a person would have to have to do what this person did today," another chimed in.

"Uh-uh. Not a chance," said a third.

"You're all probably right," Trevor said cautiously. "However, I think, given the circumstances, we should not dismiss this offhand." They all looked at him like he'd gone mad.

"Don't you think that's a waste of time when we should be looking for another layer of encryption?"

"I'm not saying we'll stop digging deeper. I'm just saying that I think we need to also investigate this further. See who lives at this location. Find out anything we can about them…without alerting anyone of what we're doing. This is to stay right here in this room for now. No one else is to know. I do not want to create chaos if we don't have to."

"Easy enough. We got access to anything we need right here anyway."

The team member who had originally cracked the security encryption volunteered to continue digging. He sent one other person the information she would need in order to get where he was, so now there'd still be two of them working to get past whatever security wall the clever hacker had erected to fool them into thinking he was located in Quadrant 4.

Trevor knew he should be happy that someone had broken through at least some part of the security put in place by the individual who had breached their system. He wasn't, of course. This new turn of events just directed his anxiety on another course. Now he really had to start considering what it was he would do if they did manage to pinpoint this person. Back at his computer, he found himself staring blankly at the screen, his mind entirely absorbed in how to handle this situation.

****

Time was clicking down to the last ten minutes for Troy and Destin when a file caught Troy's eye. MBD-v04.

"Hey. Hang on a sec," Troy said to Destin as she swiped by the file, not noticing at first that it was different than the others they'd seen so far.

"What?"

"Go back one. There! That file. It's different."

"Good eye, nerd. I didn't catch that."

"I'm sure I've seen that somewhere…can't have though, right? Weird."

"Yeah. Really weird. It doesn't look like anything we've seen so far, so there's no way you could have seen it before."

"Right. Let's see what we've got," Troy responded, still perplexed.

"Sure thing."

They opened the file and began sorting through its contents.

"Whoa. Would ya look at this? Now we're talkin'!" Destin said as they began to uncover a goldmine of information.

"This is *incredible*."

"And horrifying. Now we know for certain this was all Manglebee's idea. The man is a monster."

"That's no surprise."

They both fell silent for the time it took to read Manglebee's scheme to use the people of Montrose to test an experimental virus. The goal was to perfect it and then to use it on the

Disappeared. Not that the documents mentioned the Disappeared by name, but it was clear who they were talking about.

It was also clear that the goal wasn't death, as they had all assumed.

"Whoa," Troy said again. "They're killing all these people with this virus, but they aren't actually wanting to do that…why?"

"No idea. Doesn't make sense. Keep reading, maybe it'll say."

Another minute passed.

"Look. They're bringing everyone into BRO. So, it isn't the Disappeared we saw. Those bodies. They're from the virus." Troy grew very somber. "That means that when Becs, Selby, and Cass were inside with the bodies, it was people from right here in Montrose they saw. They could've seen someone they knew…" This thought made it all seem even more real to Troy than it had at any other time.

"I'm glad they didn't. I can't imagine what that would have been like. At least with my Mom, I was expecting it."

Troy stopped reading to look at Destin, "I can't imagine how that was for you."

"Yeah. Well. It was as hard as you can imagine."

"And Becs. She had to watch her own brother die from this—" Troy broke off as a thought struck him. "Wait. Maybe the bodies they saw are the ones who survived, since the goal was for them to live…for who knows what reason…and maybe…maybe that means Jonathan—"

"Didn't die," Destin finished for him.

They both turned back to the computer and started scanning the documents again, quickly this time, looking for clues as to what they were doing with the survivors. Looking for clues that might give them hope that Rebecca's brother might still be alive. And then, it was there, in front of them.

"This can't be. How could they be doing this? Is it even possible?" Destin asked, stunned. When Troy didn't answer, she glanced over at him to see where his eyes had landed, at the bottom of the screen on a list of the names of people on Manglebee's team. The look on his face flashed between anger and disbelief. Tears sprang up in his eyes. His neck and face turned red, and then he started heaving. Without food for hours, nothing came out except the awful retching sound. Troy scrambled to his feet and bolted for the door, swinging it open and rushing out without closing it behind him.

Destin was baffled. She did not understand Troy's reaction. She scanned the page again. The people identified seemed only to be Manglebee's Councilors and one other name she didn't recognize: Trevor Sullivan. Who was he? Why had Manglebee included him in his plans? This was something to bring to the attention of the rest of Colossus, but she still couldn't understand why Troy was so upset.

Destin looked at her watch and saw the time. They should have shut down several minutes ago. She backed out of the system quickly, then logged out of the computer and shut it down, stashing it in its hiding place just as she heard her dad coming up the walkway to the house. She hoped Troy was alright. She wouldn't be able to do anything about it immediately with her father walking through the door this moment.

And it was just then that realization slammed into Destin knocking the breath from her lungs. It was Bryn's introduction of Troy that first night she met him.

She had introduced him as Troy Sullivan.

CHAPTER 29

Lucash led the way up through the boulders, but his inexperience in this terrain made him too slow for Remy's liking. It was obvious to Remy at this point that Lucash's only desire at the moment was escaping the guard and surviving.

"Wait," he said to Lucash. Lucash stopped and turned to look at Remy, worry and fear etched in the lines on his face and the set of his mouth. "If we are going to make it here, we're going to have to move faster. I take it this is the first time you've been on a mountain?"

"Yes."

"Right. Well, it's clear we both want to put as much distance between ourselves and the guard as possible. We can only do that if we move quickly. Can you at least keep up if I take the lead?"

"Yes. I'll keep up."

"Okay. Do your best to follow where I step and what I grab onto. Way too easy to miscalculate how secure these boulders are unless you know what you're doing. Even then, avalanches happen all the time."

Lucash nodded, and then he turned his body sideways so that Remy could move past him.

"One other thing. Don't even think about trying anything. It wouldn't take much to ensure that you landed at the bottom of this pile of rocks…"

"Wouldn't dream of it. Can we just get outta here?" Lucash said, glancing back down towards the bottom of the slope, fearing he'd see the men coming up just behind them. He didn't. And felt relief as well as apprehension. At least if he saw them, he'd know for sure they hadn't discovered Juniper. *Please, Juniper, just stay asleep, or, at least, just stay put.*

Remy started up at a much quicker pace. Lucash struggled to keep up with him but wasn't about to let him get too far ahead. He couldn't afford to get lost out here. Or caught by the Guard. Or piled up as a heap of bones at the foot of the mountain. Remy was now his most likely chance to survive all this and get back to Juniper. *But, man, he moves fast.*

Remy could hear Lucash breathing heavy behind him. No need to turn around to check on him. He was surprised Lucash was able to keep up. Impressive for a guy who'd never done this before, though the adrenaline of fear can lead to amazing feats. And this guy is definitely afraid, thought Remy. *Who is he, and what is he doing out here?* These questions kept tumbling through Remy's mind, intertwined with his own thoughts on survival. It would be the worst thing for himself and all of Colossus if he got caught. He still couldn't bring himself to regret the decision to come out and look for the two escapees.

Now, he was determined to lose the Guard. Even if it meant another trip out here. His priorities had just shifted in the past hour. First priority: survival. Second: find out the story on this guy who was now following him up the mountain. Only then could he conceivably turn his mind back to the search for the two escapees.

Remy stopped suddenly at a sound that came from beyond their immediate vicinity. Lucash followed suit, though he hadn't heard the sound over his own heavy breathing and his just as heavy thoughts. He looked questioningly at Remy, who simply held a finger to his lips to indicate that Lucash should not talk or make any other sound. They both shrank behind a very large boulder, squeezing in the space between a crack in the rock and the ground.

Remy caught movement. The person was not being overly cautious and seemed to be struggling with the climb given the sounds his movements were making. He doubted it was any in their group, as the only one without experience was the guy currently hiding with him. Remy could only assume it was one of the four men who had come up after them. Though the orientation of sound could be difficult in these areas, Remy was able to determine from the glimpse of movement he'd caught earlier that the person was passing them up at a good distance away. The individual had not seen them.

They'd just wait this out. It was unlikely this person would backtrack. When it was clear to move again, they would make for the trees to regroup. It was no use following the person up the boulders and risk meeting up with him at the top. They weren't completely out of danger yet, either, since it seemed there was only one person near them. That means the four men split up. A logical move that would make it more likely that one of them would catch up with *someone* from the group, just as they'd all split up to make it less likely that any of them would be caught.

The sounds of the man climbing grew quieter, until they sounded far enough up the hill to make it safe for Remy and Lucash to move again.

"We're changing course," Remy whispered, pointing in the direction of the trees. "We'll go slower now so that we can make sure we make as little sound as possible."

"Works for me. Ready when you are," Lucash whispered back.

They arrived at the forest. A still stand of trees with a blanket of needles laying underneath. They found themselves in a patch of more densely populated fir and spruce trees. A good place to stop. These trees grew tall and wide enough to provide cover under the low branches. Sound was absorbed better in the forest, which meant that they'd have a harder time hearing someone approach than out on the rocks, but they'd still likely know well before anyone was right on top of them.

Remy guided them into the thick of the forest and stopped.

"We have to decide what our next move is, but, before we do, I need some answers."

Lucash leaned back against the trees, a pained look on his face as he closed his eyes and inhaled deeply, then exhaled. The sounds of the forest were still wholly unfamiliar to him. Westlow had prairies and fields surrounding it. No trees at all except for the ones on the tree farms that supplied the area with any wood it needed. He'd never been on one of those farms. His family were Tier 5 laborers. He worked on the road crews. Not on the farms, which was a Tier 4 designation. Lucash had little familiarity of what was normal for a forest other than his experiences up to this point after jumping from the truck.

Right now, he let the quiet of the forest envelop him and comfort him for just a moment. He felt safe. Sort of. Much more so than he did out on the rocks, for certain. Lucash realized he'd been silent for longer than he'd intended. He heard Remy shifting uncomfortably. Lucash knew he would tell Remy everything. He was just…waiting out these last moments of anonymity, knowing that revealing who he was was a risk he had to take.

"Name's Lucash. I'm from a town called Westlow. Don't really know where that is from here, except that it's east. No mountains there."

"How'd you get here?" Remy asked, though he'd already guessed the answer. Lucash didn't know Remy knew who he was, so Remy wanted to hear it from him.

"On the back of a Guard truck."

"Explains why you're running from the Guard down there. And who is it you are looking for?"

"Nobody. Just told you that hoping you'd think I wasn't outnumbered so badly. But—" Lucash trailed off.

"But, what?"

"The Guard are looking for me. And Juniper. Both of us were on that truck, and we both got off of it."

"So, where is she now? This Juniper who got off the truck with you?"

"I'd have to show you. Can't tell you."

"Is she…is she alive?"

Lucash's breath caught in his throat. Remy saying those words aloud made the possibility that they weren't true more real than he'd allowed himself to acknowledge up to now. In spite of himself, he felt the tightening behind his eyes that threatened tears, though he managed to keep them from springing forth. Somehow.

"I think so. I sure hope so," he replied, voice hoarser than normal.

"Why do you say that? Is she hurt?"

"No. Really sick," Lucash said, staring off in the distance, recalling those last minutes in the truck. "On our way here, the two guards stopped the truck, came in back, and stuck us both with something. Don't have a clue what it was. Thought it'd kill us, but it didn't. Juniper started gettin' sick after a while, though. But not me. So, I guess it wasn't cuz of whatever they put inside us."

"I know what it was. Or, at least I thought I did. But I would have thought you'd be sick too. Actually, I would have thought you both might be dead. So, there's a chance my information is not accurate," Remy said. They had their escapees, or at least one of them. Somehow, this one in front of him seemed perfectly healthy, while the other was apparently really sick. That didn't seem like the virus, even though the tirade between Karl and the guard indicated that they'd been injected. To Remy's knowledge, no one had survived the normal virus. Even if this test strain was weaker, he couldn't imagine how Lucash would not be showing any symptoms. Maybe something was wrong with one of the serums. *Or, maybe…now, don't get ahead of yourself, there, Remy.*

Lucash's head snapped up at Remy's words, "How might you know what it is?"

"Phew…well, it's a long, long story that we don't have time for now. But we suspect you were injected with a synthetic strain of a virus that has been designed to be deadly, but not contagious. We were out here looking for you two."

"You *were*? Who are *you*, then?

"I'm Remy. That's all I can say for now. Other than we want to help. Anything I say beyond that will take too much explaining, so it'll have to wait until a later time. And now that I know your friend is sick, I think we need to get to her, right away."

"How do I know I can trust you?" The idea of showing Remy where Juniper was hiding terrified him. He knew nothing of this guy, so he had no reason to believe him other than the fact that he'd not done any harm so far, and he was also wanting to stay clear from the men hunting them down.

"You really don't know, do you? But I don't see you having many other options right now. And, Lucash? If this is the virus I'm talking about, it's deadly. No one here has survived it. So, you standing here in front of me after being injected is perplexing. That's why I'm wondering if we got the wrong information. If I'm right though, you might have very little hope of helping Juniper unless you trust me. Even then, depending on what we're dealing with…well, I can't guarantee anything other than that we'll try."

"Why would you do that?"

"Lots of reasons. Most importantly, though, is that we are trying to find a way to stop what is happening here, which seems to have just gotten bigger than we realized. But first, we need to get to your friend as quickly as possible."

"My girlfriend."

"What?"

"Juniper. She more than my friend. She's my girlfriend."

"Right. Then I imagine you'll really want us to do everything we can. So, if I get us back down, can you lead me back to where she is?" asked Remy.

"Yes. I know the way."

"Okay. When we get to the boulders, watch yourself going down. It's much harder than the way up."

"Harder?"

"Yeah. Counterintuitive, I know. It's more dangerous. Gravity gains momentum on the way down. Oh, and we still have to watch our step. We have no idea where the other three men are, though I assume they all went up, we don't want to be caught off guard."

"Got it."

Remy led the way again, and the two of them made a careful path down towards the base of the mountain, cutting a path just above the place where the truck was hidden toward a thin stand of trees. Once there, they were able to keep up a faster pace to the bottom, at which point Lucash took over the lead.

Twilight was upon them as Lucash guided Remy quickly along the edge of trees that paralleled the road until he found his way back to the spot where he had led Juniper into the forest. There, he hesitated, knowing that to take Remy deeper into the forest to where he hoped Juniper still slept was a point of no return.

Remy looked at him questioningly, but with concern as well. "Lucash, we're wasting valuable time here. Where is she?"

Lucash shook off his fear, "This way. Right in here a ways…not too far." He charged in then before he lost the courage to do so.

Remy felt his Colossus phone buzz.

CHAPTER 30

Bryn looked down at the message that just came in on her Colossus phone.

"What is it?" Bendi asked when she saw the look on Bryn's face.

"Destin. She said she needs to see me right away," Bryn said as she typed in a reply.

"Did she say anything about why?"

"No. That's what I just asked her."

They both waited expectantly for another message from Destin, more curious than concerned.

"Oh. Oh no," Bryn said, reading the reply. Bendi was patient. When Bryn finished reading, she continued, "Well. It seems she can't tell me everything in a message. There's a lot of that going around today! But, it's something to do with information she and Troy discovered, and…something about Troy, himself. She says it can't wait."

"That doesn't sound good."

"No, Bendi. It doesn't." Bryn looked at her watch, then took note of her surroundings for the first time in a while, so consumed had she and Bendi been in the notes from BRO. "The sun will be setting soon."

"And still no word from Rebecca or Remy," Bendi added, a small frown turning down the ends of her mouth and her brow. "What are we going to do? Should I message Becs?"

"Let me think a minute."

Bendi pulled out her own phone while she waited, just to make sure she hadn't missed a message. She hadn't. She returned it to her pocket and started putting away the notes she and Bryn had been pouring over. Whatever Bryn decided, they wouldn't be continuing that task. They hadn't really gotten much further anyway, though Bryn was now even more certain that Bendi's assessment of the notes had been correct. She was also able to discern which component of the virus they were changing in order to try to prevent the targeted individual from dying. That could be important, though Bendi was not sure how, unless they were going to actively prevent successful injections. It might help them save the two escapees. At least that would be something, she thought.

"Okay. Here's what I think we should do. You go ahead and message Rebecca. I'll shoot a message to Remy. Then I'll let Destin know that we are on our way to pick her up, but that she should go to the central transit station, just so that we don't draw any attention. It's getting dark, but it's still early enough."

"What about the others?"

"If we don't hear back from either of them by the time we get Destin, we'll go look for them. We can fill her in on the way out there, and she can tell us whatever it is she needs to tell us. Would you prefer to go home instead? You don't have to come, you know. I'll keep you posted."

"Yes. I *do* have to come. It's Becs. And Selby and Cass, too. I can't do nothing."

"Okay. Well, the sooner we go the better," Bryn said, and then noticed that Bendi was already one step ahead of her, with everything packed up and her bag slung over her shoulder. Bryn gave Bendi a tired smile, "And it seems you're already there."

They both sent their messages and then walked through the fading light to where Bryn had parked her car. "Destin's leaving now. She said she should be there in 20 minutes or so, which should be about right for us, too."

"Good."

"Food. Are you hungry? I don't have much in my bag, but you can check for a meal bar in there. Who knows when we'll finish up?"

"No. I'm alright for now, thank you. I have a few bars in my bag, too. I've learned to keep something in there. Seems we're always missing meals when it comes to work with Colossus."

Bryn laughed, "Yeah, I guess that's one of the hazards of this work. Won't your family wonder where you are? Why you aren't home for dinner? I've wondered about that with all of you. How are you getting away with being gone so much?"

"My house is crazy. I'm from a big family, and we have all always had different schedules and things we like to do. We haven't had a family meal in years. Usually, there are a few people eating together, but never the whole family. Even now. Probably more now. I have a sister and two brothers who should also still be in school. Since we aren't, we find other ways to stay busy. None of us is really the kind to get into trouble—except me now, I guess—so I don't think my parents think anything of it, really."

"That's fascinating. I've always wondered what it would be like to have brothers and sisters. It was always just me and my parents. Now it's just me and my cat. Must be nice to have such a full house."

"Sometimes. Yes. But it's also loud sometimes. We all get along for the most part, though, so I guess that's lucky. Cass doesn't get along with her family."

"Really?"

"Yes. I don't know much about it. She isn't one to say a whole lot, but I think her parents are probably happy that she isn't around. I know she's happy that she isn't around them."

Bryn looked over at Bendi with astonishment. "Wow. That's sad."

"I think so, too. Cass doesn't act like it bothers her, but I'm sure it does."

Bryn nodded, turning the car down a thoroughfare that would lead to the main transit station. Few other vehicles were on the road. Few people had permission to drive other than for work, and with much of the work at a standstill due to the lockdown because of the virus, hardly anyone would have reason to be in a car. With Bryn's connection to BRO, she'd have the correct permissions available to show the Guard or Citizen Patrol if she got stopped. It was still risky, especially with passengers, but it was a necessary risk. She just hoped she didn't ever get stopped.

"What about the others?" Bryn asked, checking her mirrors to be sure there was no patrol vehicle behind them.

"I'm surprised Troy gets away as much as he does. It's just him and his parents. Just like Selby. Cassidi has two siblings, I think. Like I said, she doesn't say much, and I've never been to her house. But Troy and Selby are both the only child their parents had. Now Selby's family knows. I'm not surprised. And I won't be surprised if Troy's parents find out either."

"And Rebecca?"

Bendi was quiet for a moment before responding, "Well, I guess Becs is an only child, too, now. She said once that her parents were having such a hard time with Jonathan being gone that they seemed lost in their own world. I think they just don't notice. It must be so hard for Becs. They were all so close. We *have* to end all this, Bryn. We have to find a way." Bendi said this last with a passionate intensity that she rarely showed, as she blinked back the tears welling up in her eyes.

Bryn's heart ached for this girl who felt everyone else's pain. Yet she was also starting to see that Bendi had a strength that belied her gentle nature. Not for the first time, Bryn found herself entirely impressed with this group of kids. She did not think that 5 or 6 years ago she would have had the same courage they all displayed, not even in these same circumstances. *Was it really only 5 or 6 years ago that I was their age? It feels like a lifetime.*

"We will, Bendi. We seem to be getting closer now. You guys joining us? Well, it seems to have sparked progress, even if Melody isn't open to it. We'll do what we have to."

They were now pulling up to the transit station. Destin was already there, waiting in the shadows of the platform so that she wouldn't be easily seen by anyone coming and going from transit. At this time of the evening, there were still enough people making their way between the center of town and each of the quadrants that the transit center was far from vacant, though only two other vehicles could be seen in the area. Destin stepped out from the shadows as she saw Bryn's car approach.

Bryn's concerned heightened when she saw Destin's look of fear and despair. She could feel Bendi tense up beside her, as well. Bryn couldn't imagine what could possibly cause this sort of reaction in Destin.

"We drivin' out to look for the others?" she asked as she climbed in the back seat. Bryn and Bendi looked at their phones to see if they'd received messages from Remy or Rebecca. Bendi looked at Bryn and shook her head no, indicating that she hadn't received a response.

"Looks like it," Bryn replied.

"Cuz we're going to have to look for Troy, too."

CHAPTER 31

"Not one of us."

"No. But, I still can't breathe. You think he's—"

"Oh, yeah. No *way* he survived that fall."

"It's one of the guys from BRO. No Guard uniform."

"Yeah…wishin' it had been a guard, though."

"Why?"

"Cuz you can bet they have more skills at huntin' down folks than the guys from BRO who got sent out with them."

"Good point. Probably why he's down there, though, and not still up here. At least it wasn't one of us."

"Yeah. And our odds just got a little better," Selby shot a grin in Cassidi's direction.

"You're a strange one, Selby." Cassidi looked back down at the body crumpled below, "I've never seen a dead person before."

"Me neither, man. The bodies at BRO were the closest thing. They *looked* dead, but I know they weren't *really* dead, so that doesn't count."

"Becs saw Jonathan after he died. I don't think I could have handled that."

"Can't imagine how that musta been."

Cassidi and Selby stared down in silence for a moment before turning, without words, and continuing along the ridge to where it widened. They scanned the area below, looking for signs of the other three men, but seeing nothing. They walked on a little further, reaching a place where the ground rose up again in front of them.

"Looks like we got a choice here. Goin' up wouldn't be smart," Selby said, surveying the situation before them and the steep, shear slab of rock rising up quickly from where they stood.

"Nope. Forgot my climbing gear today," Cassidi replied. "So, it's right or left."

"Yep. Goin' right takes us into new territory. Going left will take us back towards Montrose, or back down to the road. I vote right."

"You do? Why?"

"Cuz we've never been there before." Cassidi rolled her eyes at this comment. Selby added, "And, besides, it looks like two people already went that way."

"Seriously? How can you tell?" Cassidi asked looking in the direction to the right of the rock face.

"Not hard when you look down," said Selby, pointing at the ground a short distance off where two sets of scuff marks were evident in the sandy surface. "You can see that these marks are too big to be anything but people. And it's probably two of us."

"Since it looks like the four men broke off from one another. And now there are only three."

"Yep. Exactly."

Cassidi turned and led the way to where they hoped they'd meet up with two from their own gang. The route was slow going as they continued to look for signs of the other two passing through. Periodically, they called out Rebecca's name and Remy's. Barely above the sound of their speaking voice, just in case another of the men found his way down this side of the mountain.

Their phones had no signal here, so messaging was pointless. Their best bet was to catch up with whomever went this way, tell them the news of the fallen man, and attempt to make their way back towards Montrose. It would be getting dark very quickly. Once darkness fell, movement in this unfamiliar terrain would be slow, but they'd have the benefit of the cover of night to hide in. At the very least, they would be able to retrace their steps and head back down to the road with much less fear of being spotted in the forest.

"Becs?" Cassidi called into the trees again. Silence followed.

And then, "*Cass?*"

"Yes! Where are you?" Cassidi answered back, trying not to shout out loud in her excitement.

Rebecca and Daniel came through a thickness of undergrowth. Cassidi broke into a run and caught Rebecca in a hug, then held her away from her, observing the strain on her face.

"You okay?"

"Yeah. One of the guys was chasing us. He fell."

"I know. We heard the scream and went to investigate. I was *so* scared of what I might find, but we had to know."

"I thought for sure he'd catch us. It would have been my fault. I slowed us down," Rebecca said in a stricken voice.

Daniel came up behind her and put an arm around her. "No. It would *not* have been your fault. You did great, Becs."

Cassidi looked questioningly from Rebecca to Daniel.

"I froze, Cass. I did fine climbing up the rocks, but then we got to the top. And the world just started spinning. I couldn't move. And I wouldn't have without Daniel. I'd have stayed right there, like I was waiting to be captured!" Now Rebecca sounded angry. Angry with herself for a fear she'd had since early childhood. A fear that gripped her. A weakness in herself she hated.

"But you moved past it, Becs. You overcame it! You ended up doing it on your own. Without my help. I just got you started. You did the rest. Don't blame yourself for any of it. I'm not sure I could've done what you did," Daniel said.

"What was that?" Selby asked.

"I had Becs get behind me and hold on to me, so that she would have something to look at, you know, to keep her from looking around. Well, the guy who was following us was getting closer. She saw that, and…well…she just, I don't know, shoved the fear aside, pushed me ahead, and told me to move faster or we'd get caught. She let go, and we sped up. Even I was nervous up there. It got real narrow. But Becs just kept going, not letting me slow down or help her. Of course, that made the guy speed up, and he obviously didn't do so hot on getting across. Even when that happened, she wouldn't stop."

"No. I couldn't think about it. There was no way I was going to turn around to see what happened. Even though I knew. The only thing I was thinking about was getting to where the ground got wider and there was more around me."

"Yoooo…Becs! That's somethin' else, man!" Selby went up to her and picked her up in an exuberant hug, then plopped her back down in front of Daniel. "Oh, sorry, man. Didn't mean to take her outta your arms or anything."

Daniel laughed, "Think nothing of it, Selby."

"Becs, you're amazing. You've had that fear for as long as I've known you, which is pretty much forever. Never mattered to me. It was just a part of you, but I totally thought you'd never get over it," Cassidi said, voice filled with pride.

"Thanks, guys. But it could have turned out really bad, if Daniel weren't there. I just wasn't about to put any of us in any more danger. I had to do what I did. Maybe now I won't freeze the next time. I hope not, anyway."

"I hope there *isn't* a next time," Cassidi said.

By now, twilight had fallen over the forest. It was quiet, other than their voices.

"Guys, I think we oughta head back. It's gettin' dark. Hopin' that means the three guys left will give up the hunt. But I have to let my folks know we're alright before they decide to take matters in their own hands."

"Don't think Remy would be too happy about that," Daniel said. "Especially since he hasn't even told Melody yet about them."

"Yep, so let's start headin' back," Selby said as he turned to head back in the direction they'd come.

"Wait, Selby. Daniel and I came this way because we can get back to the ranch from here."

"Really? How do ya know that? You been out here before?" asked Selby.

"Nope. But I've been on the peaks all around the ranch, and I can see out this way from the opposite side of the ranch from where BRO is. That peak right up there is the next one over from the lower ones around the ranch. We don't want to go all the way down this mountain, because then we'd have to climb back up. But if we can traverse it, we can climb over and down onto the ranch after we get past that," Daniel pointed to the silhouetted peak above them.

"I'm all for not backtracking," said Cassidi, "especially since there are still three men who might be looking for us. Or waiting for us anywhere along the road back."

"I hope the others are alright," Rebecca added.

"Well, we aren't gonna find out just standin' here." Ever eager to be making forward progress, Selby was getting antsy now with the chatting. "Daniel?"

"Right. This way," Daniel replied, leading the group in the direction that he was fairly certain would take them to the ranch. He hoped so. He'd seen that jagged peak above them countless times, seen all the intervening space between the ranch and the peak. He just hoped that memory would serve him well down here on the ground. He wasn't about to let the others know of his doubts, though. Not with Rebecca counting on him to get them to safety.

CHAPTER 32

Remy looked down at his phone, surprised to see that a message had come through. It was from Bryn.

"Lucash, wait." Lucash stopped and Remy opened the message, typed a quick response, and then gestured to Lucash to keep going.

"Something wrong?" Lucash asked.

"Maybe. Why?"

"Just looked like it when you read the message."

"Yeah. Not sure yet. But we need to get to your girlfriend and get back out here by the road. Someone's coming to get us. Don't worry, it's someone you can trust. She's in on all this too."

"What about the Guard and the other two men? What if they come back this way? It's gettin' pretty dark and I'm not thinking they'll continue up on the mountains."

"No. Probably not. That's a risk we have to take. I'll warn Bryn if they pass by us on the road. She can pull off and hide. Doubtful they'll be looking for a car on the side of the road. But we need to get back there fast, so they don't go by without us knowing."

In the growing darkness, Lucash was having to find his way by the light of Remy's headlamp from behind. He still moved quickly. By now, he knew this trip in from the roadside well enough. He was holding his breath the entire time, afraid he'd get there to discover Juniper gone. Or worse.

As they reached the hiding spot, it seemed to Lucash in the dim light that it was undisturbed. Unless Juniper left and covered her tracks. He halted at the entrance.

"This it?" asked Remy.

"Yes."

"Why are you standing there, then?"

"Just trying to be prepared for what I might find," Lucash said in a voice almost too quiet to hear.

"Oh. Of course. Sorry, Lucash."

Lucash took a deep breath, and then quickly pushed aside the brush at the entrance.

****

Bryn unlocked her phone with a touch, then handed it to Bendi, "There's a message. From Remy. Can you read it? I don't want to pull over." They had just picked up Destin and were beginning to make their way to the edge of town and out to the area where Bryn knew Remy and the others had gone to look for the escapees.

"Sure," Bendi said, taking the phone from Bryn's hand and opened the message. "'*Got one of the escapees, on the way to get the other. Guard found us. We all ran. Different directions. Meet us on the road out. We will wait for you. Three of us. One is very sick.*' Oh! Oh, no. I wonder why just one? That doesn't make any sense."

"No. But...this *is* likely a milder version since it isn't programmed specifically for the targeted person," Bryn said, mulling this new information over as she spoke.

"It's going to be a tight fit in here with three more people. Didn't Remy have his truck?" Destin interjected.

"He did," Bryn said. "Not sure why he doesn't have it, but it might have to do with the Guard. We'll find out when we get there, I suppose." Bryn picked up speed as much as she dared. The city streets were becoming less and less occupied by people, but one never knew when either the Guard or Citizen Patrol would show up in the area. They had their regular rounds, but a lot of ground to cover. Once they got to the edge of town, their biggest concern would be the guards who went in search of the escapees.

Bendi checked her own phone again. Still no message from Rebecca. Now she was growing very alarmed. After reading Remy's message, she had to acknowledge the possibility that something could have happened to any of the others. They knew Remy was okay, but that still left Rebecca, Selby, Cassidi, and Daniel to worry about. And Davi and Mel, too. She didn't really know them, but she was concerned for their safety as well.

"Destin, we'll be driving for a bit, so how about you tell us what you meant when you said we had to now find Troy, too? What happened? What did you do?"

"*Me?* Why do you assume *I'm* the reason he's gone?" Destin asked, truly offended.

"You really have to ask, Destin?"

"Well, for your information, me and Troy were doin' just *fine.*"

"Really?" the surprise was evident in Bryn's tone.

"Yes. Really."

"Okaaay. So, what happened then?"

"Well...I'm a little afraid to say, honestly."

"Why?"

"Two reasons. First, you're probably gonna be mad, and I really don't want to deal with that right now. Second, this one's here," Destin jabbed a thumb in Bendi's direction, "and I know she's Troy's friend, and I don't want to upset her. It's…um…pretty disturbing…"

"Please don't worry about me. I want to know," Bendi said.

Destin hesitated, doubtful of the truth of that statement given what it was she knew about Troy now. And that was just scratching the surface of the nightmare they'd discovered in the files. It was almost too much for Destin to process, and she wasn't a kid anymore. She quit being a kid years before she was Bendi's age. Destin could not understand what Bendi was doing here, mixed up in Colossus. She seemed so naïve. So…sheltered. Even more than her other Tier 3 friends were.

"Destin, you don't have to worry about Bendi," Bryn said when Destin still hadn't started talking. "She can handle it. Whatever it is. She's a lot tougher than you think. And I promise I won't get mad," Destin reacted with a grunt of disbelief. "I mean, seriously, look at us right now. Do you think that this doesn't fly in the face of Melody's orders?"

"Oh. Alright. But you asked for it. And don't say I didn't warn you." She was quiet again, this time, gathering her thoughts. "Hard to know where to start."

"Start with Troy. If he's disappeared, we need to know why so we can figure out what to do about it. After we deal with our current crisis."

"Troy's dad is working with Manglebee and BRO," Destin blurted out, then fell back against the back seat, as if exhausted.

And that wasn't far from the truth. This evening had taken its toll, and the information she and Troy had discovered, as well as Troy's disappearance, left her feeling like all she wanted to do was go home and sleep for days.

"*What?* Are you *sure?*" Bryn asked? Bendi didn't respond.

"Well, I am almost positive. You said his last name was Sullivan, right? When you introduced us the other day, I thought that's what you said."

"Yes. That's right."

"Yeah, then if it isn't his dad, it's someone else close to him. Last name Sullivan. That's what I saw."

"Did you see the first name? Was it Trevor?" Bendi asked.

"Yep, that was it! I'm right, then, aren't I? It's his dad."

"Yes, his dad's name is Trevor. He works on AI with the Security Division. Both his parents work in the Security Division, but different jobs," Bendi said, with a calm that surprised Destin. Bryn, too. "Are you sure that what you saw didn't have something to do with his normal job?"

"Well, I'm sure that it has to do with BRO and this virus, so unless that's a part of his normal job, then I'd say what we saw was something else entirely. And when Troy saw it, he bolted for the door without a word. Almost fell out of his chair in his hurry to get up and away from there. I had too much sensitive information open on the computer to chase him down before I shut everything down. Then Dad showed up right after I got it all put away safely. Tried messaging Troy, but he didn't answer, so I contacted you because I didn't know what else to do. Didn't think I should go to Melody with this."

They were at the edge of town now, moving from the pavement to dirt. Bryn turned off her headlights and slowed her speed down while her eyes adjusted to the darkening light. No need to give the Guard notice of their approach if they happened to be coming this direction on the road. She only hoped they had their lights on. She exhaled a large breath of air, trying to calm nerves that were beginning to fray. So much was happening so quickly. And after months of nothing. It was hard to know what was coming from one minute to the next.

"No. You did the right thing, Destin. I'm glad you came to me first. I'm not sure what to make of it yet. I hope Troy comes around quickly. I know that this had to be a shock. Sounds like he had no idea."

"No way. Totally a surprise to him."

"Are you okay, Bendi?" Bryn asked.

"I'm okay. I'm a little shocked myself. I would not have imagined that someone I know could be involved, and I really can't imagine how Troy must feel right now. This has to be awful for him. I am going to message him to see if he responds."

"Good idea. You might not want to mention that you know anything, though," Bryn suggested.

"No. I agree. He definitely would not answer if he thought I knew. I just want to see if he answers. If he does, I might be able to find out where he is."

"Good idea. So, Destin, what were you guys doing that you were able to see Troy's dad's name linked to Manglebee and BRO?"

"We breached their security system and broke into their files."

****

She was there. Juniper was still there. Lucash exhaled a breath he didn't know he was holding, tears springing to his eyes. He quickly jabbed his palms against his eyes to rub them away. Then he knelt down beside her.

"Juniper?" There was no reply, but her labored breathing assured Lucash that she was at least still alive. For now. He rested his forehead against his arm, just for a moment. A moment to recognize that he'd made it back to her. A moment to hope that this man behind them might be someone who could help them. Someone who could help Juniper come back to him.

He lifted his head, and brushed her hair back from her face, where it had fallen again and stuck with the moisture of her fevered sweat. During this, he was grateful for Remy's respectful silence. He didn't rush Lucash, though they had a great need to get back out to the road in a hurry. Lucash cradled one arm under Juniper's neck and the other under her knees. He gathered her up in his arms and stood up, whispering reassurances to her as he did, though the words fell on unhearing ears. She'd stopped even mumbling his name.

Only after he'd stood up with Juniper in his arms and turned towards him did Remy approach to check on her condition. He placed a hand on her forehead then shined a light towards her eyes and peeled back her eyelids, to which there was no reaction. Her ragged breathing indicated the effort her body gave in bringing in much-needed oxygen.

"She doesn't look good, Lucash. I'm sorry. Has she been hallucinating?"

"I—I don't know. She's said my name over and over again but didn't respond when I answered her. Is that hallucinating?"

"Yeah, I'd guess she was, though that's not as bad as what some get. This could be a milder form of the virus, though if it is, you should have it, too," Remy said, hesitant to confirm the possibility that it was the virus when Lucash showed no symptoms.

"Can you guys help?"

"I sure hope so. Let's get her back out to the road. Can I help?"

"No. No, thanks. I got her."

They left the hiding spot and Remy took the time to cover the entrance and brush away evidence of their entry as a precaution, removing any sign that anyone had been there in the first place. The fewer clues they left behind of their whereabouts, the better. Remy led the way back out towards the road, where they waited, just inside the trees.

Within moments, headlights shown on the road, but from the wrong direction. The Guard. It had to be them, making their way back to BRO. Remy sent out a message to Bryn: *Guard truck headed your way. Get off the road now.*

Lucash shrank back further into the trees with Juniper at the sound of the truck, petrified. He held Juniper as close as possible, willing their invisibility in the dark.

****

"Another message from Remy," Bryn said, handing Bendi the phone again.

Bendi opened the message. "Pull over! Fast! Get off the road!"

Bryn was off the side of the road before Bendi got all the words out. She knew why she was being given the directive without even hearing the message. They bounded over the field a good distance, Bryn driving blind to the terrain they were crossing. Without headlights she had no ability to tell what they were driving into or over.

There was no place to take cover. They just had to hope the guards weren't looking off on the sides of the road, or, if they were, that the car was not visible in the dark. The field was grass. Soft enough that they'd likely leave some tracks there that might remain visible by morning. At least they didn't kick up a lot of dust. Dust would be visible in the headlights of the Guard truck as it passed.

All three waited in silence. Afraid to speak. Afraid to breathe too loud. They were all twisted in their seats, eyes piercing the night behind the back window, looking for the telltale headlights of the Guard truck headed their way.

****

Remy watched the Guard truck pass slowly by, while Lucash stayed put, back to the trunk of a tree, Juniper held tight in his arms.

CHAPTER 33

"Find anything yet?" Trevor called out, checking on the others without lifting his head up from the screen.

"We aren't finding another layer of encryption. Either this guy's really good—and we already know he is—or he's really in Quadrant 4."

"Two people live at that location. Father and daughter. Seems mom died not too long ago. Health file says she died of 'natural causes.' Doesn't say anything else about it, though. She was young when she died. Just 47. Whole family works at the nuclear waste treatment facility, including the daughter, who is 18," came the report from behind one of the other computers.

Yeah, right, natural causes…more like radiation toxicity. Trevor kept the words inside his head.

Out loud, he asked, "What are their names?"

"Dad's name is Sy; daughter is called Destin. Last name's Orr."

A father and daughter, who just lost their wife/mother. The one thing Trevor never thought about when he began his new life after The Reckoning was the impact this new way of living had on others. He had been too happy with his own change of circumstances to realize that it wasn't the same for a large number of people forced to do the dirty and dangerous work in the newly formed country and to live in barely survivable conditions. Now he was being confronted with yet another brutal reality in the world Manglebee created. *What am I supposed to do with all this?*

"That doesn't seem a likely pair to be breaking into our system," Trevor said.

"Not likely is right. Quadrant 4 is still working, right?"

"Yes. Just like us," grumbled one of the team members.

"Yes, they're working, but on reduced shifts," said Trevor.

Everyone grew quiet again, with only the sounds of occasionally whispered words against a backdrop of computers whirring. Trevor was finding no indication at all that there had been an error in the programming of the robots. All the codes looked as they should for the days he'd checked so far that had had an individual with no reaction to the virus.

Immunity. That was the only plausible answer. He saw no need to continue his efforts in looking for human error. He would have found it already. He would have to report this to Manglebee. The question was when? Before or after they solved this current problem?

"It was the daughter who was home."

"The daughter?" Trevor was a little confused by the statement.

"Yes. Dad was at work. If it was someone in this house, it would have been the daughter."

"An *18-year-old* broke into our system? This is growing more unbelievable by the minute."

"Not necessarily *impossible* to believe," said Trevor, thinking about his son. Trevor might not have been able to break into the system, but he recognized how much more talented his son was than him, even at 14. Someone with Troy's smarts could break into their system, though he highly doubted there were too many kids that smart out there. Still, he had to allow for that possibility. "What is *harder* to believe is that someone in Quadrant 4 would have the knowledge and the access."

"What do we do now?"

"Good question. I'd like to know we are right about this before reporting it. No sense getting Head Councilor involved until we are sure. And I don't know of any way to be sure other than to go to that location and see if we can find the computer."

"Okaaay. You sure that's a good idea? Shouldn't we just tell Head Councilor so the Guard can go looking?" The question came from the newest team member, but the others nodded in agreement.

"Tell Head Councilor *what*, exactly?" asked Manglebee himself, evidently having just entered the room without notice.

Trevor stiffened at the sound. He suddenly lost all feeling in his limbs, and the hair on the back of his neck stood on end. Now, he'd have to tell him. He'd have to tell him and put this family of two in danger. Trevor felt an odd connection to Sy and Devin, and the now dead wife. He suddenly wanted to know her name too. It was an irrational thought at that moment, he knew. Something that was keeping his brain from immediately registering what was happening right here, right now. He stole a glance around the room at the others, all of whom had bolted to their feet at Manglebee's entrance. There wasn't a one of them who looked anything less than terrified.

Including himself.

Trevor quickly ran through his mind the option of telling Manglebee about the lack of evidence for a programming error in the robots' delivery of the virus, but he quickly realized that was out of the question. Manglebee almost certainly heard their comments about the Guard. No. He wouldn't get away with it.

Manglebee stood in front of him now, flanked by Henderson and Witton. Witton hadn't been there earlier. He must have been ordered in to assist Trevor, which is probably why they were all there right now. Manglebee would want to coordinate between Witton and Trevor, as well as receive an update. Trevor noticed how uncomfortable everyone was starting to appear. All except Manglebee, of course. He wondered how long he had let the silence drag on.

"Sir, we have been working on two different issues."

Manglebee raised a single eyebrow.

Trevor heard someone clear his throat nervously, as it became apparent to the team that he was going to tell Manglebee everything. He could almost feel them bracing themselves for the outcome.

"Well…uh…first, the issue we originally came in for…it appears that it isn't a programming issue. I could find nothing wrong in the code on the days there were…uh…concerns."

"You are absolutely certain of this?" Manglebee asked in a too controlled voice.

"Yes. The code checks out." Trevor watched Manglebee's face visibly harden and felt like he always did in these situations. He felt like it was his fault, even when there was nothing wrong in what he did. It should have been a good thing that there were no issues with the coding. That meant his team was doing exactly what they should. But this was a no-win situation. There was really no good outcome. Either the team screwed up, or there were people who were immune to the effects of a virus that was designed to work specifically on that individual.

"The second issue?" Manglebee asked when Trevor hadn't continued to speak.

Trevor had been waiting for a response that was obviously not forthcoming.

"Yes. The second issue." Trevor took a deep breath. Embarrassingly, he felt his face growing flush. He felt a little light-headed, while the edges of his vision darkened. He realized with horror that he was close to passing out. *Get a grip, Trevor.* He took a second inhalation of air and willed his heart to slow down. He pushed his glasses up on his nose and wiped away the bead of sweat making its way down the side of his face.

"We were examining the files for coding errors when we noticed that data were being changed as we watched. The changes were being made to the doses." Trevor shot these words out in a blast, afraid to even stop for a breath. When he did stop to breathe, he waited for the wrath. As did everyone else in the room.

Witton and Henderson both took a step back and stood with feet shoulder width apart, as if they were actually bracing themselves for a physical combat. Manglebee's barometer was the vein at his temple. Trevor had grown used to watching that to gauge Manglebee's mood. Sure enough, the vein was pulsating and looked ready to burst.

"Your *team*," he spat, "assured me our system was impenetrable."

At this point, the members of his team looked ready to bolt for the door. Trevor understood the feeling.

"Yes. Sir. The system is…was…impenetrable. We aren't sure how this person was able to manage. Truly genius. Sir."

"Tell me you have at least tracked down the identity of this person."

"We aren't sure, sir…Maybe."

"Maybe? You seem to be uncertain about a lot these days," Manglebee's voice oozed disgust.

"Yes. Uh. The thing is, we broke the encryption and found a location. But…uh…it doesn't make sense…where the signal is coming from. We think maybe this person has another layer of encryption. That he put a false location signal up under the first layer. We can't find it, though."

"What is the reason you believe you have not found the actual location?" Despite himself, Manglebee seemed almost interested.

"It pings to a location in Quadrant 4 where a father and daughter live. During the time of the incident, the father would have been at work at the nuclear waste facility. Only the 18-year-old daughter would have been home."

Manglebee looked surprised. Trevor had never seen the look on his face prior to that moment. It felt like something of an accomplishment. Or it would have, if his heart still weren't pounding out of his chest from fear.

"It does not seem possible that your information is correct. I agree. However, I will not take chance that you are wrong. What is the location? I will have the Guard search the premises. In the meantime, I expect you to continue looking for the real intruder."

"Yes, sir."

"One other thing."

"Yes, sir?"

"Fix that security system. If your team continues to demonstrate this degree of incompetence, you will have a heavy price to pay. Do I make myself clear?"

"Yes, sir. We'll…we'll get right on it." Manglebee's eyes pierced his own. His threat was far from empty, Trevor knew. He also knew that the only reason he was still here right now, even after all this, was because there was no one else to replace him. Manglebee really couldn't get rid of him. But he could certainly replace his team. Their expressions said that they, too, understood this.

"I am still waiting on the location."

One of the team called out the coordinates in a quivering voice. Manglebee turned without saying another word and walked back out the door. The other two followed him out. Within minutes, Witton returned. Though he was one of Manglebee's 12 Councilors, Witton, like most of the others, was terrified of Manglebee. He seemed to covet his role a little less than the others, however. Rather than doing anything he could to keep it because he liked power, he did anything could to stay in Manglebee's good graces because he liked living.

Witton approached Trevor as Trevor was giving instructions to which of the team were to work on reprogramming the security system and which were to continue digging for their clever intruder.

"Head Councilor is sending the Guard to the location. He is not happy about this turn of events, especially on top of the escaped prisoners," Witton said to Trevor in a low voice so the others would not hear.

Trevor had an easier relationship with Witton than he did with any of the others. Without saying it, they both recognized in the other their similar positions on working for Manglebee. They did not, however, do anything that would reveal their friendship — of sorts — to the rest of Council.

"I know. I am surprised he remained as calm as he did."

"Yes, well, that's always the case in front of others. He was less calm when we walked out the door. Fuming, actually. Though this person who managed to break through our system intrigues him." Witton gave Trevor a long look before continuing, "He said something about using this person when they find him instead of you, if you can't get your act together. We both know Manglebee has no sense of humor. I just thought you should be warned."

"Thanks, Witton. I can't say I'm surprised. I'm more surprised that I'm still here, in all honesty."

"You and me, both. I think we are all still here because Manglebee won't trust anyone else. Not that he trusts us, but he feels he can predict and control us. Anyone else is an unknown. He really didn't even want to bring you on. Shocked all of us when he did."

"Wish he hadn't," Trevor said, shaking his head. "Any word yet on the escaped prisoners?" Trevor held off from expressing his desire that they didn't get caught. Witton likely felt the same, but it was a sentiment he didn't quite want to risk revealing.

"No. The Guard messaged in that they spotted several individuals out in the Borderlands while looking for the prisoners. Manglebee told them to pursue the group and search for the prisoners later. To my knowledge, he hasn't heard from them since."

Taken aback by this new information, Trevor felt like there were so many dangling ends out there right now. He wondered how much control Manglebee really had. A flicker of hope sparked in his chest. It was a tiny flicker, but it was the first real hope he'd had in weeks. He didn't relish the idea of everything falling apart again, but it would be worth it if Manglebee's power crumbled with it. The likelihood seemed a long way off and only the remotest of possibilities. *Still*, he thought…*what if?*

CHAPTER 34

Several tense minutes passed for Bryn, Bendi, and Destin. They saw the headlights approach slowly, lights shining on a path wider than the road. Bryn was glad she managed to get off the road as far as she did.

A third light swiped from side-to-side. It was brighter than the headlights.

"They're still looking," whispered Destin. "That's a search light."

The light made a sweep through the trees on the opposite side of the road.

"Remy said nothing about that," Bryn sounded slightly irritated. Now she wasn't at all sure she was far enough off the road. If they shined the light this way right now, it would have no trouble finding them.

The truck was taking an eternity to pass by them. The search light made a second pass in the trees and then disappeared, only to reappear a moment later on the other side of the road. Their side of the road. The bright beam lit up the field, just on the other side of their tracks leading right to where they now sat. The truck kept rolling forward. The light glided across the terrain, catching a corner of the car. All three gasped.

And waited.

But the beam started moving again, away from them, making its pass back towards town. The exhales were audible. Destin turned around and sunk low into the bench seat in the back.

"That was close," she said.

"Too close," Bendi agreed.

Bryn was already typing a message into her phone to Remy. When she'd finished, she turned her gaze again towards the truck still moving away from them, search light back on the forest. She watched the taillights grow smaller, until, at last, they made a curve to the right, towards the BRO facility. Only then did she speak.

"Well. Time to roll again. Just told Remy we were safe and headed his way."

Bryn cranked the engine and eased the car into gear. An idea occurred to her. There was no way to cover up the tracks they'd left on the ground, but if she made new tracks, leading away from town, then maybe…just maybe…anyone who discovered them would be uncertain as to which direction they were headed. Cutting a new set of tracks, Bryn angled the car back towards the road, driving as fast as she dared. Once back on dirt, she sped up, in a hurry to get to Remy.

"Keep your eyes peeled. They're by the trees and shouldn't be too far from here since it didn't take the Guard long to reach us after Remy messaged."

"Where we gonna go after we pick these guys up?" Destin asked, forehead pressed to the window, hands cupped around her eyes, for a better view into the trees.

"We should probably go back to the ranch. If one of the escapees is sick, we'll need to figure out what the problem quickly and see if we can help her."

"How are we going to do that? We can't get into BRO. Where else are we going to get the necessary medicines?" asked Bendi.

Bryn actually smiled, "I'll let you two in on a little secret."

"Tonight's a good night for that," Destin said.

"Yes, it sure is. Well, since Remy and I have been working on an anti-viral, we have been taking small amounts of promising versions of it and keeping the vials hidden in the storage building at the spot where Remy parks the truck. Like so much else on this sprawling ranch, it's a place rarely visited by anyone but us.

Not much useful in there. At least from his parents' perspective. Just like his truck. It was parked there because it wasn't running."

"Well, isn't that convenient?" Destin said, with a hint of sarcasm in her voice.

"Meaning?" asked Bryn.

"I just mean this girl is lucky, that's all."

"That isn't what it sounded like," Bryn replied tensely.

"Look, I know you guys say you can't help all these folks getting sick. I get it. I guess…well, no. I don't really get it. If you are hiding these medicines away, why can't you use them to help more people. Do they actually work? Or are you just saving them for people important enough to save?"

"Destin!"

"Look!" Bendi was pointing off on the side of the road, "It's them."

"We'll talk about this later, Destin." Bryn pulled the car over to the edge, but staying on the road, while Remy and another young man approached carrying a girl in his arms. Bendi hopped out of the car, and Destin followed her lead. The two girls did what they could to help Lucash get Juniper in the car, then got back in on the other side, while Remy joined Bryn in the front.

Bryn did not drive away immediately, asking instead, "Where's your truck?"

"Down the road a ways. Not too far."

Bryn looked back in the back seat at Juniper, gauging her condition. "I think we should get your truck. We don't want the Guard coming back to get it or anything."

"No. I agree. We need that truck, and I don't want to risk them even searching it for clues as to who they chased up that mountain. Not sure, but there could be something in there that they could link back to me."

"Right. We'll make it fast. I want to get her back to the ranch."

"*Her* is Juniper, by the way. And that's Lucash. Lucash, this is Bryn," Remy gestured to the driver's seat, "and in back with you is Bendi and Destin."

Lucash acknowledged everyone, though he hardly seemed to register what Remy had said. They quickly reached the place where Remy's truck was parked among the boulders.

"Remy, let me talk to you out here real quick," Bryn said as Remy jumped out of the car.

They met just in front of the car, where she could talk to him without Lucash hearing. Not that he would. He didn't seem to be attuned to much besides Juniper. Bryn had him fill her in quickly on what had happened, and then she told him about Troy.

"Troy's *dad*? Working with Manglebee?"

"Yeah. I know. Utter surprise. Obviously for him too. He's run off to who knows where. Bendi tried messaging him but hasn't gotten a response. What about the others? Hear anything from them yet?"

"Not yet. Signal isn't great out here. I was surprised your message came through."

"Just glad it did. Do you think we can trust these two?" Bryn asked, nodding her head slightly in the direction of the car.

"Well, Juniper we don't have to worry about at the moment. Sorry," he apologized, knowing he sounded callus, though that hadn't been his intention. "I think Lucash is alright. I mean, he isn't going to be on Manglebee's side or anything."

"Right. Okay. Well, there's a lot more to tell you, but, first things first. We have to get Juniper back and start treating her before I drop any more bombshells on you." Remy looked startled. How could there be any more bombshells than Troy's dad working with Manglebee and Troy running off? It dawned on him then that she hadn't mentioned how they found out.

"Trust me," Bryn said, reading his mind, "we don't have time to go into it now. And Destin hasn't even finished telling me everything, so there's more to it than I even know, at this point."

"Wow," Remy ran a hand through his hair. "Well, guess let's just head back to the ranch. One thing at a time, right?"

"Right," Bryn turned back to the car as Remy headed for his truck.

****

Daniel reached down for Rebecca's hand, giving her a lift up the steep rock face. Rebecca refused to give into her fear. She wouldn't look down. Just up at Daniel's reassuring smile. She was thankful for the darkness. She could just make out that smile, while the mountain they were climbing fell away into the dark. *I will not give into this fear. I will not let myself be overcome again. I. Will. Not.* Indeed, she found that the more she attacked her fear of heights, the less afraid she felt. It hadn't disappeared, but she dealt with the waves of nausea as they struck and found a focal point to keep the dizziness at bay.

Cassidi followed closely behind. Rebecca knew it was because she was worried about Rebecca and wanted to make sure she was in close proximity. Rebecca was grateful but wanted to reassure Cassidi that she was fine.

"I got this," she whispered in Cassidi's direction.

"I know you do," she whispered back, making no move to back away. Rebecca smiled.

Selby trailed the others, wanting to make sure he had them all in his sight. He knew it was unlikely that anyone would have followed them this far and in the dark. Even so, he felt the need to be the lookout. It was his job to watch out for his friends. He was the only one here who would have any idea what to do if someone came upon them. Not exactly true, he reminded himself. They'd all gone through the Colossus training, and his friends had performed better than he would have ever thought. He just wasn't sure how it would translate to real encounters. True, he'd never had any real encounters himself, but his training had been drilled into him from a very young age. Not just over the course of a couple of months.

The group reached the top of the pass. Down the other side was the ranch.

"Yo, hold up, guys," Selby called out to the group.

"Something wrong?" asked Rebecca.

"Nah. Cass? You got a signal on your phone. Folks are probably freaking out about now. Probably oughtta give 'em a heads up."

Cassidi pulled out her phone and looked at it before handing it over to Selby, "Yep. Signal's good up here."

Rebecca's phone buzzed just then. She unlocked it to read the message from Bendi.

"Bendi messaged me while we were out there. Three times." Rebecca was quiet while she read the messages. "Whoa."

Daniel moved in closer, as did Cassidi. Selby was distracted with his own message.

"What?" Cassidi asked impatiently.

"Bendi was trying to get ahold of me. She and Bryn were worried. But now they have Remy and the two escapees!"

"Really?" Daniel asked, looking over Rebecca's shoulder to try to see the messages for himself.

"Really," she replied, angling the phone towards him.

"Hey!" Cassidi said, trying to see as well.

"Okay! Sorry."

"Wait…wait…what was that again?" Selby asked as he sent off his message to his parents.

"Yeah, Bendi's message said that she, Bryn, and Destin — what are they all doing together? — have Remy and the two escapees. Down *there*!" Rebecca pointed down the other side of the mountain to the ranch. "She said they were on their way to the place where Remy parks his truck and to go there if I get this message."

"So, they have *both* escapees? How'd that happen?" asked Cassidi.

"That guy Davi found must be one of them. Has to be. Remy left with him. So, the other one had to be someplace else," Rebecca replied.

"We aren't going to find out for sure standing up here," Daniel said.

"Selby, do we need to wait for your folks to reply?" Rebecca asked.

"Nope. They just did. Let me just tell 'em we're headed down now and I'll message them when we get to the ranch. They wanna meet us there, of course."

"They might be useful, Selby," Rebecca said.

"Yeah. I know. That's what I'm thinkin' too. But I don't wanna tell them until I know it's okay with Remy and Bryn, since they're down there already."

"Good thinking. We all ready, then?" Rebecca asked. In response, they all began making the move over the pass, Selby finishing his message as he walked.

"Hey, Becs?" asked Cassidi.

"Yeah?"

"Did you tell Bendi we were on our way?"

"Oh. No. Need to do that," and she pulled out her phone, slowing down as she, too, sent off a final message before they all continued down the other side of the pass towards the ranch.

****

Juniper was laid out on a makeshift bed inside the storage building. There was no heat, and the air was growing chilly, but at least she was protected from the wind. Her fevered body still reacted to the cold air, causing her to shiver even in her unconscious state. Lucash wanted nothing more than to lay down beside her and warm her up, but Remy and Bryn needed room to be able to check her over and begin to administer small doses of their best guess for the appropriate anti-viral formula. It was a bit of an experiment because they had no way of knowing for certain which one would have the best chances at working. So, Lucash tried his best to stay out of the way, pacing in the background without his eyes ever leaving Juniper.

Destin was sitting on the ground, having no trouble staying out of everyone's way, leaning against the wall and closing her eyes. *Just a few minutes. That's all I need.*

Bendi was doing what she could to help, while watching closely everything Remy and Bryn did. Learning, so that she might actually *be* useful the next time. She was taking Juniper's pulse again when she heard a sound outside. She ignored it, though her heart skipped a beat, in order to finish her task.

"Still high. 110," she reported, just as the door to the storage building opened, revealing Rebecca and the others on the other side. Bendi's face broke into a smile, and then cracked, tears springing to her eyes. She recovered, the smile breaking free again as she ran to her friends and hugged each in turn, including Daniel, who wasn't entirely sure what to make of it.

After their reunion, they all walked to where Remy and Bryn were still working on Juniper.

Remy looked up at them, his face worn, but his smile still warm, "Glad you all made it."

"Where's Davi and Mel?" Selby asked, looking around the room.

"Haven't heard from them yet. One of you want to try messaging them?" Remy asked.

"On it," Cassidi replied.

Rebecca walked over to the pacing and obviously worried Lucash and stuck out her hand in introduction, "Hi. Guess we've not actually been introduced. I'm Rebecca."

Lucash stopped pacing long enough to shake her hand, "Lucash. And Juniper."

"I'm sorry she's so sick. Remy and Bryn are the only two I know of who could help. You're actually lucky Davi saw you."

"Yeah. Thanks. Just hoping this works. I should be there, not her."

"Neither one of you should be!"

"So, who are you guys?" Cassidi asked, cutting straight to the chase.

"Just told you," Lucash replied.

"No. You didn't. You told us your names, but that doesn't really tell us who you are. Why were the Guard bringing you to BRO?"

"BRO?"

"Yeah, that's where the truck was heading. Why were you on it?" Cassidi persisted.

"I—we—could get into a lot of trouble for telling you," Lucash said, worry lines furrowing his brow.

"And you don't think we could get in trouble for helping you and her right now?"

Lucash dropped his head, feeling defeated. When he lifted it again, he looked Cassidi in the eyes, "We're part of a group called the Resistance."

"Yes!" Shelby burst out in enthusiasm. "We *knew* it. Aw, man, this is great. We could learn—"

"*Selby*," Bryn warned.

"Sorry."

Lucash had turned away from the group, feeling more vulnerable than he ever cared to. He wasn't sure what they were up to, and he didn't like knowing they were keeping more from him than he was from them. He was trapped. With Juniper so sick and under their care and with no place else he knew of that he could escape to; he was stuck. He just hoped they really did mean to help Juniper. If they did, all of this would be worth it. Even if it meant trouble with the Resistance.

CHAPTER 35

"Who's BRO?" Lucash asked, looking at Rebecca, since she seemed to be the friendliest voice at the moment.

Rebecca turned to Remy and Bryn, "I think he should know." It was a statement, not a question, though she wasn't sure if they would object or not.

Bryn looked up from Juniper, her eyes meeting Rebecca's, "I agree. My best guess is that Juniper's been injected with the virus, so he definitely has a right to know why. But, Rebecca, there's more that you don't know."

"What don't I know?"

Bendi came to Rebecca's side, placing a reassuring hand on Rebecca's arm, "I found something out, from the scientists' notes. I saw a pattern in them. When I showed Bryn, she agreed with what I thought I saw."

"Okay—" Rebecca said, drawing out the word so that it almost sounded like a question, "so, what was it you found out? And why do you look like you are afraid to tell me?"

"I'm not afraid to tell you. It's just…well…it's big, but we don't know what it means."

Destin, who had appeared to be napping up to now, spoke without lifting her head from its resting position against the wall, "I do."

Everyone stopped any sort of movement, attempting to register the words Destin just spoke. Lucash looked around the room from one person to the next, noting that everyone seemed surprised, though Rebecca, Selby, Cassidi, and Daniel more so than Remy, Bryn, and Bendi. Everyone had turned to face Destin, who still hadn't moved and was giving no indication that she was going to say anything more.

"So, are you just gonna sit there and leave us all hangin'?" Selby asked.

Before Destin could respond, Bryn jumped in, "I'm as curious as you are, Selby, but I don't think now is the time for Destin to speak." She looked at Lucash, speaking to him, now, "Remy and I have given Juniper one of the anti-virals we've come up with. We won't give her anything else until we see what her response is to this. I'm sorry we can't say for sure whether this one, or any of the others we have, will work. The truth is, we don't know because we've not been able to test them on people. Just in the lab."

"I don't understand," Lucash said.

Bryn looked to Remy, still uncertain as to whether or not she should trust Lucash with any information, even though she had just stated that she thought he should know about BRO. She did think he should know but starting down that road meant revealing it all.

"I think we can tell him, Bryn. His girlfriend's life is at stake, after all," Remy said, then turned to Lucash, "Before we tell you, though, we need a little more information about the Resistance. We believe our two organizations want the same thing, but not everyone in our group likes what you guys are doing."

"There isn't a lot to tell. At least not that I know. Juniper and I joined not too long ago. We didn't expect to get called up so soon. If I had known this…" his gaze fell to Juniper. He swallowed a lump in his throat, "We were so ready for our task. We knew we'd likely get caught. Most everyone does. But we were thinkin' it was worth it, you know?" Lucash shook his head, knowing he wasn't making any sense.

"It's okay, Lucash," Rebecca gave him a reassuring smile. "I know how you feel. I lost my brother, Jonathan. It's how I got here." She gestured around the room.

Lucash looked up sharply at Rebecca. For some reason, her revelation calmed him. Made him feel less alone. "I'm really sorry," he said to her, meaning it.

"Thank you. We've only heard of the Resistance from Council News, so we don't know much about them. At least nothing that we can for sure say is the truth."

Lucash grimaced, "Yeah, Council likes to make an example out of us." He paced the floor, gathering his thoughts, trying to make it all make sense in his own head before he spoke the words aloud.

Then he began again, "The Resistance isn't what most people think. It definitely isn't what I thought before we joined. I overheard a couple of guys at work talkin' about the job we were on like they knew who did it."

"Who did what? What job were you on?" Cassidi asked, with a tone that was now more curious than harsh.

"I worked on a road crew. We're Tier 5. I worked on a crew assigned to repair the damage done from Resistance jobs. We're given extra vouchers for doing this work and keeping our mouths shut. So, I do better than a lot of other Tier 5ers. But it doesn't mean I was happy with where I was at. Juniper definitely wasn't. And she's got a little sister who she wants to have a better life than her."

Lucash continued, telling the group about how he'd found out about the Resistance and his and Juniper's decision to join, hoping they could make a difference, even if it cost them their lives. No one interrupted. Even Selby was quiet. He told them about how the Resistance operated, and then went on to describe what he and Juniper had done and their capture and escape.

When he finished speaking, Selby let out a long, low whistle, "That's some story, man."

"It would be if it was happening to someone else. Don't care for it much right now myself. Guess we were pretty stupid to get involved. I thought I was ready for whatever came at us, but I really somehow didn't think it would come to *this*. We hoped that we would at least find out where they were taking The Disappeared. I'd give my life for Juniper, and I don't mind putting my life at risk for the Cause, but now, I'm just not sure that what we did was worth it. How did it get us any closer to bringing down Manglebee? That's what this movement is supposed to be about, but, unless a whole lot more people join in the fight, what good does it do? Even then?"

No one had an answer for him. Lucash's despondence was understandable. They'd all felt that way at times, especially when it seemed nothing was happening. They all trained for the day when *something* would happen, but what?

"It's so much worse than you know. With Council, I mean," Rebecca said.

"She's right," Bryn agreed. "Lucash, you might want to have a seat for what we're going to tell you."

"No. I'm alright standing, thanks."

"Let's start with BRO," Bryn began. "BRO stands for Bovine Research Organization. They began operating here, on Remy and Daniel's family ranching operation. This ranch...we're on part of it now...sits just outside of the Montrose City Unit. Not sure how it works where you are from, but, here, our ranches and farmlands lie on the edges of the city."

Lucash nodded, indicating it was the same in Westlow.

"Right," Bryn continued. "So, the Morgans operate a research ranch. Their family has been working on the optimization of cattle consumption to land unit size and meat output. BRO moved in under the guise of working with the Morgans in improving their research operations and branching out to other cities. That is what they told the family. Of course, they could have said anything. It wouldn't have mattered. BRO was here because Manglebee wanted them here. The only thing is, that isn't why they were really there. I mean, the research wasn't the reason."

"What was, then?" asked Lucash.

"Well, it's still experimental, that's for sure," Remy said in a voice thick with derision.

"They're plannin' another attack, man. A secret one this time. Worse than The Reckoning because no one's gonna know what hit 'em," Selby chimed in.

"Up until now, we're pretty sure it's only been happening in Montrose, at BRO. They've built a facility inside one of the mountains, and they've been working on a synthetic virus. The virus is altered to the genetic makeup of the individuals it is being delivered to," Remy said.

"That's…that's truly crazy."

"Yeah, and they send out the virus in tiny robots. The robots inject the virus during the night when people are sleeping. They have no idea. The robots are sent from a hive sort of thing and then when they're finished, they come back to the hive. They're like bees," Daniel said as he approached Rebecca's side, knowing this conversation was never easy for her. He didn't touch her. Didn't even look at her. Just stood close. Cassidi noticed, but no one else did.

"How do you guys know all this?" Lucash asked.

"Because Remy and Bryn work there," Selby said, "and cuz Becs here got involved after…well, after Jonathan…and then that's how the rest of us got to be here, too. To help Becs."

"What do you mean you work at BRO? Does this mean you're working with Manglebee?" Lucash was starting to panic. It wasn't making sense, what they were saying. How could they be a part of this organization who were apparently trying to kill the people in their town?

"Technically, I guess it does, but not really. I guess we now need to tell you who we are," Bryn said.

Destin remained seated on the floor but was now quietly watching the conversations taking place around her. She knew she was going to have to tell them all what she and Troy had discovered. She wasn't looking forward to it. She really wasn't looking forward to Rebecca finding out first that Troy had disappeared because he found out his dad was working for Manglebee and second the news she had to drop on everyone. She hoped she was right coming to this group instead of telling Melody.

"Everyone here right now is going directly against the orders of Melody, the leader of Colossus in our region and one of the founding members of the whole organization," Bryn said after she told Lucash about Colossus, its mission, and how most of them had ended up out looking for him and Juniper. "And today, we got new information. Information Melody and the rest of Colossus haven't heard yet."

"Why would you do that? Go out of your way to find us?"

"It was the right thing to do," Rebecca responded before anyone else had a chance to. "And, at least for me, I knew I had to. I might not have been able to save my brother, but maybe I could have some part in saving others."

"We were also afraid that they might be getting ready to spread this virus further than here. That they might be escalating their attack," Remy said. "We thought we might be able to learn something from you. If you lived. We didn't know, and still don't, if our concoctions will work. But you can still help us, while we're helping Juniper."

Bryn interjected, "Wait, before we continue, I want to tell everyone what I heard from our informant today. I also have yet to reveal this information to Melody, though she was the one who sent me to speak with him. Originally, I was supposed to talk to two informants, but one backed out. Lucash, I know where they take the Disappeared."

"Where?" Lucash answered in a quiet voice.

"They have prisons in the Borderlands. I know where one of them is, and, as you can imagine, the conditions these people are kept in are inhumane."

"That's no surprise," Cassidi replied sarcastically.

"No. It isn't a surprise to any of us. It confirms what we've suspected. But now we have a location."

"Did the contact say what they were doing with them?" asked Rebecca.

"No, he didn't know. Apparently, though, they have several of them. He didn't know where the others were located, but the one he went to was just outside of Region 1."

"Looks like you got your answer, Lucash," Remy said. "It also seems to me that this is one more indication that Manglebee is getting ready for an attack. He's got the virus and he's got the prisons."

"Remy, I think maybe we should let Bendi tell everyone what she discovered. They might be escalating for an attack, but it might not be what you think," Bryn cut in.

"Okay…Bendi, what've you got for us?" Remy asked.

"As I said before, I was looking through the notes again, thinking I had to be missing something. Something that would tell us more about what BRO was up to. I finally saw something. It was a pattern between their results and what they did next. What I saw told me that they aren't actually trying to *kill* the people they are injecting with the virus."

"*What do you mean by that?*" asked Daniel.

"How does that make any sense?" came Selby's wide-eyed response.

Rebecca found herself at a loss for words.

Bendi's concern for Rebecca's reaction was playing out in front of her, but it was too late to take any of the words back. Taking them back would also not make the truth any less real.

"I don't know why. All I know is that the data show that with each case where there was a survivor, the scientists repeated the virus structure for the next round. The number of survivors increased over time, rather than decreasing. It doesn't make any sense to me either, Selby. I'm sorry." Bendi didn't take her eyes off Rebecca as she spoke, wondering what thoughts were going through her head right now because she wasn't saying a word.

"Makes perfect sense to me," Destin spoke up from the floor, deciding she probably shouldn't hold off any longer.

"How?" Rebecca found her voice.

Destin started talking before Bryn could stop her. She was ready for others to share the burden. "Troy and I were working together today while my dad was at the plant."

"That had to be fun," Cassidi interjected.

Destin ignored the comment. "Made up the key cards, then busted into BRO's Level 3 security."

Sounds of astonishment filled the room. Remy shot a look to Bryn to see if she knew this information. She and Bendi were the only two who seemed unfazed by Destin's declaration. They knew already. Must have been some of what Bryn alluded to when she dropped him off at his truck earlier.

Destin plowed ahead, "We found out some things. Bendi is right. They don't want to kill the people they are injecting. They want to build an army."

"Then why make everyone sick to do it? That isn't how it worked last time. He just forced people into his army or killed them straight out," Remy asked.

"*Because*," Destin said, "he's building an army of robots."

Now everyone looked thoroughly confused.

"Still doesn't tell us what the virus has to do with it," said Cassidi.

"Yeah it does," Selby said, "he's turnin' people into robots, isn't he?"

All eyes turned to Selby, and their looks said they weren't entirely sure if he was being serious. Or just being Selby. But nothing in Selby's own expression indicated he wasn't being completely serious.

"Yes." Destin's simple reply led to an eruption of comments and questions among the group as they struggled to comprehend what exactly this new piece of information meant.

"Are you *sure?*"

"How do you know this?"

"That isn't possible! Is it?"

"The man is crazy. We gotta stop him."

"What are we going to do?"

"QUIET!" Remy's voiced raised above the others and stopped everyone. "Destin, tell us exactly what you know, and how. Start from the beginning, please, and tell us as clearly as possible. I'm afraid we're all having a hard time grasping this."

"Troy and I somehow managed to get through the security system for Level 3. We were looking through a bunch of files about the virus. Mostly, from what we could tell, the files were dates that the virus was being sent out with all the information about the virus and the people it was being delivered to."

"You could see who they're planning on injecting?" asked Rebecca.

"No…well, yeah, but not names. Troy was wishin' there were names so we could tell who they were trying to make sick. At first, we still thought they were trying to make people sick enough to kill them. We changed some of the dosages. At least, we think we did."

"What? You didn't tell me that part," Bryn said in a tone between shock and anger.

"No, I didn't. Already thought you'd be mad, so I left that part out. But Remy asked for all the details, so that's what you're getting."

"I'm surprised," Bryn responded. "And, yes, maybe a little mad. That was a huge risk. An exceedingly dangerous move."

"Isn't it all? I mean, seriously. If Melody doesn't kill every one of us in this room, it'll be a miracle. If Council doesn't find out about us, it'll be an even bigger miracle."

"I know. You're right, of course. But you and Troy potentially just gave us away. If anyone discovers you broke into the system and traces you…"

"Nah, our encryptions are pretty tight. I'd be surprised if someone could break them."

"Listen, I know you and Troy are both exceptionally bright about this, but the risk is still there."

"I know it is, but we wanted to do something. Something that maybe would help us out but would definitely help out a few people whose lives would be saved. At least that's what we hoped. That's why we did it. How's that different from these guys going out there to find Lucash and Juniper?"

"I can see why you think it's the same. But the consequences could be a lot bigger if they discover our own technology. It wouldn't be just you and Troy," Bryn said, a little more softly. "I do understand why you did it. But it *was* a dangerous move."

"I think it's awesome. Who'd have thought ol' Troy woulda had it in him?" Selby said, shaking his head in wonderment.

"I agree," Rebecca stated. "I know it's a risk, but I'm glad you guys did something that might help a few people. And now that you know how, maybe we can do more..."

"Yeah, well, that's not all. Let me finish talking. You might feel differently about everything by the time I get to the end."

Rebecca and the others quieted down and let Destin go on.

"So, after we changed some of the virus doses for people who we think are targeted for the next few nights...we didn't do it all for one night...we went looking for other types of files. Like I said, most of them seemed to be the same kind. Then Troy spotted one that looked different. It was named 'MBD-v04.' Weird thing was, Troy said that name looked familiar, like he thought he'd seen it before. So, we opened it. File name stands for Manglebee Bro Directive. Version 4, I guess. Anyway, it talked about what this whole thing is about. They want to make people sick enough to appear dead but not really *be* dead. That way, everyone thinks the person died, and when they're taken away, they think it's just like any other time a person dies. But it isn't. If they actually survive the virus, they're kept in a coma, and then they move onto the next step. They're implanted with microchips that take over their brains. They turn these people into robots. They can't think for themselves anymore. They're programmed to perform as part of the army Manglebee wants to build to keep us all in line. Guess he thinks people are getting outta control again."

"Not everyone dies?" Rebecca's quiet voice broke into Destin's story.

"Nope."

"Jonathan?"

"I don't know, Rebecca. The document just talked about the plan. We didn't find any information about who survived and is now serving in Manglebee's army. Don't even know where they're being kept, other than 'training facilities in the Borderlands.' That's all the document said. No specific locations."

"I've got to find out. If there's any chance Jonathan is alive, I have to know."

"Rebecca," Bryn, knowing she had to point out the likely reality given the data, spoke up, "I hope Jonathan survived, and if we find that he did, we'll do everything we can to rescue him. But you need to be prepared for the very possible reality that he didn't make it. Most of those injected with the virus did not survive, according to the data in the notebooks."

Tears sprung up in Rebecca's eyes, but she blinked them back, then lifted her chin and straightened her shoulders, replying, "I do understand. But I can't brush off the possibility that he *was* one of the ones who survived. Especially because his symptoms were not as bad as what most people get. He never hallucinated, for one, and for another, he also was able to talk to me and give me information right before he died."

"You're right, Rebecca, that does seem hopeful. I only want you to be prepared. I'd hate for you to have to grieve a second time because you think he is alive now."

"I get it. Thanks, but you don't have to worry. I do understand. I'm just not going to sit by and wonder, though. I have to find out."

"I don't suppose the document said anything about how big the army is already or how big they want it to be?" asked Remy.

"Nope. Very general."

"So, we might be able to save Jonathan, if he's one of them, and a lot of others as well. If we can find them," said Bendi.

"If we can find them," Bryn agreed. "And figure out how to disable the microchips."

"That's Troy and Destin's territory. I'm sure those two can handle it, right, Destin?" Selby said.

"Yeah, well, we could if I knew where Troy was."

"Didn't you just say you two were working on all this together?" asked Cassidi.

"We were," Destin looked to Bryn, who nodded at her to continue. "But we did find something else out. Troy's dad works for Manglebee, and when Troy found out by seein' his name on that document, he took off. Now he won't respond to messages or anything. I've tried and so has Bendi."

Cassidi, Rebecca, and Selby all exchanged looks.

"What?" asked Destin when she saw what passed between the three friends at hearing the news that Troy's dad was involved and Troy had disappeared. They weren't surprised. She thought they would have been devastated.

"We were afraid of that," Rebecca responded. "Cassidi thought she saw someone that looked just like an older version of Troy when she first snuck into BRO, but we weren't sure. We didn't want to tell Troy or anyone else because we didn't know if our suspicions were true. But we definitely didn't want Troy to find out like this."

"Do any of you know where he might have gone?" asked Bryn.

"No. He isn't exactly an outdoorsy type. Mostly just hung out at home or with us when he wasn't at school. Computers are his life. I can't imagine where he would have run. Did anyone try his home?" Rebecca asked.

"We haven't been able to do anything besides message him. We picked up Destin after she messaged me that she had to talk to me, but we had to head out immediately to get Remy, Lucash, and Juniper."

They all seemed to suddenly remember that there were two extra people in the room, one of whom had just heard this entire conversation and had not said a word. Bryn walked back over to Juniper to see if there were any changes. Lucash watched her move, still silent, but eyes now turning questioning.

"She doesn't seem to be getting worse, so that's a good sign. You want to come see her?" Bryn asked.

Lucash needed no other encouragement. He was by Juniper's side instantly, holding her hand in his, raising it to his cheek for a moment before returning it to her side. She wasn't worse, that's true, but she didn't seem to be better, either.

"Will you give her more medicine?" he asked.

"Yes, I'm going to try a bit more of this same one. I only gave her a small dose the first time, in case she had a bad reaction. She didn't, and it seems to be helping, or I'd expect her condition to deteriorate. So, I'll up the dose. I can do that now, if you're ready for me to?"

"Yes." Lucash stepped aside, allowing Bryn to move in, and shifted to the top of the table, so he could still be close enough to touch Juniper.

"What'll you guys do now? Now that you know what Manglebee is up to." Lucash directed his question to Bryn, but only because she was closest.

Bryn didn't respond immediately. Her concentration was on extracting the liquid from the vial into the syringe. The others in the room hadn't heard. They were talking amongst themselves, caught up in the details of the information they'd just been given and what it might mean for them going forward.

"I don't really know, Lucash," she finally said, as she swiveled towards Juniper and lifted her arm, seeking the vein at the elbow that would allow an easy insertion of the needle. Lucash looked away just before Bryn poked the needle through Juniper's skin. Lucash wasn't one to get squeamish. It was just that Juniper seemed so vulnerable right now, and he felt so helpless to do anything about it.

"I want to help. Whatever you guys decide. And I know Juniper will, too. If—" he didn't allow himself to finish.

"We'll do the best we can, Lucash. I'm hopeful now."

"She has to be okay. I know she would really want to help. This girl…once she sets her mind to something, she's unstoppable."

Bryn chuckled at that. "I can't wait to meet her."

"She's amazing."

"Bryn?" Remy asked from the other side of the room, a note of panic in his voice.

"Yes?"

"They got Mel."

CHAPTER 36

Troy did not really know where he was. He had run blindly from Destin's house and had kept on running until his chest burned, his breath so constricted his gasping did little to provide oxygen to lungs or muscles, and he could no longer feel his legs. He could not see through his tears and had crashed into more than one person during his flight from the horror he'd seen on the computer screen. His behavior would have inevitably led to a report or two being sent to DAD of suspicious activity in his own Quadrant. But he was in Quadrant 4, and the citizens there hardly noticed, other than those he barreled over, most of whom grumbled or barked a harsh word before they went their own way, lost in their own heads.

He was squatting in a dirty alleyway, propping himself up with his back against a brick wall. This looked to be a sector where multiple people lived in the same dwelling, stacked one on top of the other. Part of his brain wondered what it was like to live in a place like this. He couldn't imagine it. The living quarters couldn't be big. Not like a house. If whole families lived there, how did they do it? He found himself thinking that he was glad Destin at least had a house.

And then it all came crashing in on him again. Destin's house. The place where he found out that his dad was a villain. He felt tainted, somehow. Poisoned because he shared half his genes with his dad. Another wave of nausea hit him at the thought, and he doubled over, rocking forward onto his hands and knees and losing nothing but stomach acid onto the pavement in front of him. He wiped his mouth with the back of his hand and then again with his sleeve. Troy moved to a seated position, not even bothering to slide down away from the small puddle in front of him.

He could not reconcile the dad he knew with a person who would willingly participate in Manglebee's plot to wage war a second time on the citizens of Anecor. Worse than that, he was turning people into robots. People who first had to endure a painful illness only to lose their ability to control their own mind. Death was the better outcome.

THE BREAKING

For the first time in Troy's life, he felt like he had been doing something that mattered. His skills were being put to work for more than just a school assignment or a personal challenge. He was helping Becs and the rest of Colossus to bring down a government that had been responsible for the death and disorder he was witnessing on the streets of Montrose. Worse yet was the pain he brought to Becs and her family when Jonathan became a target. And his dad was a part of it all. His dad, Trevor Sullivan, was working against his own son.

It made sense of course. At least, in a way it did. His dad's talent for AI meant that he would be the perfect person to design human robots. It didn't just stop there, though. His dad was in *charge*. His name was right there, on the list of people responsible for turning the ideas in that document into a reality. Right alongside Manglebee's name and the 12 Councilors.

Troy heard the sound of voices. An argument somewhere. He noticed for the first time that it had grown dark. He didn't move when the voices grew nearer. Looking down the length of the alley towards the direction of the voices, he saw two silhouetted forms pass by in the space at the entrance to the alley. It was almost time for the New Moon, and street lighting was non-existent in the Quadrant. He could see no details about the two shadowy forms. They passed by without a pause in their argument and without a glance down the alley. Even if they had, they would have been unlikely to have been able to make out the form of the crumpled individual seated on the ground about halfway down the length of the building.

As soon as the momentary distraction passed, Troy's thoughts returned to his family. Something occurred to him; he wondered if his dad's involvement in Council's…activities…was what was causing the new tension between his parents. He hadn't been able to figure it out before. They had never been ones to argue. They'd always seemed so at ease in one another's presence. Their family had always been so close. But something had changed. At the time, Troy just thought it was normal work stuff because of all the new rules in place and with his dad's increased workload.

Troy laughed a hallow laugh. *Increased workload is one way to put it.*

Troy had been confused about the change in his parents' relationship, but he'd also been kind of glad for it. It gave him a freedom he would have never had before. His dad was always gone, and his mom was never there. Never there, even though she was physically present. His parents hardly looked at one another and talked even less. He could relate to Becs. His parents hadn't noticed him for months now, just as hers rarely noticed her, but for entirely different reasons.

Does Mom know?

Surely not. That seemed impossible. Troy thought that if she knew, it would be more than just a tension between his parents.

Maybe not. Maybe both of them aren't who I thought they were. But what about me? What's that mean for me? How am I supposed to go home now? And how am I supposed to keep working with Colossus when it means I'm also going against my own father?

The questions continued to swirl and spin around in his head until he no longer knew what was real in his life. He questioned everything he thought he understood about his family. He stood up, feeling a need to move. Hoping movement would settle his mind. Except he had no idea where to go. Troy wanted nothing more than to go home and collapse in his bed and sleep for days. Let oblivion overtake him. Maybe he'd wake up and realize this was all a dream.

He couldn't go home, though. That was not possible. Even if it were just his mom there, he wouldn't know what to do. Confront her? And if she didn't know, he'd have to be the one to deal with her reaction to the news. He wasn't ready for that. He couldn't even cope with his own new understanding, let alone someone else's. Seeing his dad? That would be so much worse. He wouldn't trust himself right now. No telling what he'd do if he saw his dad tonight. Was it still tonight? Or was it morning?

Troy just started walking. He headed in the direction he thought would lead him to the outskirts of town, knowing no one would find him if he were out in the Borderlands. He wondered what was out there going in this direction. He'd only been to the Colossus headquarters. One thing was for certain.

His dad would not be there, and that was good enough for Troy. He needed some time. Time to wrap his head around this new reality. Time to figure out what to do next.

And time to avoid the worries and fears that he knew were already registering in the hearts and minds of his friends, for there was no way Destin hadn't already revealed what they'd discovered. Facing his friends right now was almost as bad as facing his parents. And facing Becs was probably the worst of all.

So, he walked, passing into the Borderlands an hour before sunrise, and then, he kept going.

CHAPTER 37

"They have Mel?" Bryn wasn't sure she heard Remy's words correctly.

"Yes. Davi just messaged. They took her back to BRO, he's on his way there now…said he just got a signal," Remy responded.

Everything seemed to be rapidly spiraling out of control. For a split second, Bryn wished for the days when progress was almost at a standstill, longed for them, actually. That moment passed away quickly as her mind grabbed ahold of this most recent crisis. When none of the others had been resolved yet.

"What happened? Did he say?"

"He just said they were spotted by one of the guards who chased them for a while. Mel couldn't move fast enough. She told him to keep going and get help. They had no way to defend themselves. He knew it was either just one of them, or both. So, he chose to get away, knowing that he would be able to contact us."

"Tell him where we are and have him come here. I think it's past time for us to figure out exactly what it is we are going to do next."

"Already sent off that message. He said he'd get here as fast as he could."

By this time, everyone had gathered together again, including Lucash. The events of the past 24 hours were taking their toll. No one had slept nor eaten, though the excitement — if it could be called that — fueled their adrenaline and squashed their hunger. As exhausted as they all were, sleep would likely be elusive, even if they had the time for it.

"What *are* we going to do?" Daniel asked the question on everyone's mind.

"I think we first need to ask whether we tell Melody and involve the rest of Colossus," Bryn responded.

"Um, there's another thing too, guys," Selby interjected. He hadn't known when to bring up his parents, but he'd just received another message from them. He couldn't wait any longer.

"What is that, Selby?" asked Bryn.

"My folks. They're wantin' to be a part of all this, and I think they could be useful. They've been waitin' for me to talk to you guys. They're wantin' to meet us here. I held 'em off, but they're gettin' antsy."

"Right. Your parents. I had forgotten about them." Bryn sighed. "I agree that your parents would be a help with their skills. If we bring them on now, we are going to have one more thing to explain to Melody. She will see it as another challenge to her authority."

"Can we bring them here now and not tell Melody yet? I mean, if we tell Melody and the rest of Colossus, they don't have to be around for that. I'm sure they'd understand…wouldn't they, Selby?" Now that the shock of finding out Selby's parents had been told about Colossus had worn off, Rebecca was able to see that the Myers could be a real help. And now that there was a possibility, however small, that Jonathan might still be alive, she wanted all the help they could get. Rebecca didn't know exactly what to think about telling everyone from Colossus, especially Melody, but she had no doubts now about including Selby's parents.

"Yeah, I'm sure they'd be all good with that. They're used to being secretive. Might even like it better if no one else but us knew they were helpin'."

Bryn looked to Remy to see what he thought. It was an unspoken agreement between the two of them. They generally didn't make any moves without reaching consensus, so they were in the habit of checking in with one another before making decisions. Remy nodded in encouragement.

"If you're sure they won't mind, Selby, go ahead and have them meet us here. We will have to catch them up to speed. Hopefully, they won't be too far behind Davi in getting here."

"I'll tell 'em to hurry," Selby said, already punching in the message, providing directions for the quickest route from their house and reminding them to disable their trackers.

Lucash had gone back to Juniper's side to check on her. She seemed to be sleeping peacefully now, no longer twitching and restless with fever.

"Bryn, Remy, I think maybe Juniper is getting a little better," he called over to them.

Both went to see for themselves, along with Bendi and Rebecca.

"She does look better," Bendi said, breathing a small sigh of relief. "This is hopeful."

Bryn and Remy both smiled, and Bryn responded, "Yes, she sure does."

Bendi checked Juniper's pulse, while Remy took her temperature and Bryn checked her pupils.

"Pulse is down. 92…still a little high, but it is going in the right direction," Bendi said with excitement.

"Fever is down, too. 100.8°. It hasn't broken, yet, so she isn't out of the water, but these are good signs," Remy added.

Lucash's face lost its tension, as he bent over Juniper and kissed her forehead. "Did you hear that, Juniper? You're getting there…keep fighting, my girl, keep fighting," he said quietly in her ear.

"Can we give her more medicine?" Lucash asked, face still close to Juniper, but eyes lifted to meet Bryn's gaze.

"Not yet. I don't want her system to become toxic because she has too much medicine. This seems to be working. If she takes a turn for the worse, then we'll give her more. Or maybe a variation of the formula we gave her this time. It might mean that what we gave her wasn't quite the right thing," Bryn said.

A little of the tension returned, as could be seen by a tightening of the muscles along his jaw and slight strain around his eyes. Bryn noticed.

"Lucash, I am now more certain than not that Juniper will recover. She's obviously a very strong woman, so she is doing some of this herself. The medicine is just giving her immune system a fighting chance. It's acting faster than I would have expected. We just have to be a little patient. I know it's hard."

"Thanks, Bryn." Lucash paused, considering something, then asked, "I know you said that what you guys are doin' right now is going against what…Melody, is it?…ordered, but it seems to me that once she heard about everything…well, how could she not want to do something, too?"

Remy took up the response, "You would think that would be the case, but Melody is cautious—"

"Now that's an understatement," Cassidi chimed in.

Remy gave a tight laugh, "True enough. She likes us to think that she trusts us, and maybe it sometimes even seems like she does, but she has a very tight grip on the overall operations. Nothing major happens without her approval."

"Which means nothin' much has been happenin' up til now. Til we broke the rules. *Now* look at all the progress we've been makin'!" Selby said.

"I doubt Melody would consider all this *progress*," Destin said, to which several in the group voiced agreement.

"Yeah, well, she doesn't know what she's talkin' about then," Selby responded, not one to be easily dissuaded from his opinions.

"You might be right, but that doesn't change things in terms of Melody's reaction," Remy said, just as the door to the storage area opened to a disheveled, distraught, and breathless Davi.

"Davi! You got here fast," said Rebecca.

Davi closed the door behind him and leaned back against it before saying, "I didn't have far to go by the time I got a signal.

When I found out where you guys were, I ran all the way." He gasped for air as he spoke, his words coming out in bursts.

"Come on in," Bryn said. "Catch your breath for a minute. We were just starting to discuss the best way forward, but there's a lot you don't know. We'll need to catch you up. We're waiting on Selby's parents, too, so it's probably best just to do all the catching up at once."

If Davi was surprised by what he just heard, he didn't show it. Until he noticed Juniper. "Who's that?" he asked, tilting his head in the direction of the sleeping form on the table.

"This is my girlfriend, Juniper. We are, I guess, the two people you all were out looking for. You found me."

"So, where was she? Looks like she got poked with the virus."

"Yes." Lucash didn't really care for Davi's tone, but he tried to ignore it. "She was really sick, so I had to leave her hidden while I went out to hunt down some food and water. Didn't expect to see anyone else out there except the Guard, who I was hopin' not to see. But it's good you found me because these two gave her some medicine, and it seems to be helping," he said, gesturing towards Remy and Bryn. "So…thanks."

"Yeah. Sure. Why aren't you sick?"

"Don't know. I got injected, too, but nothing happened. I feel just fine."

"Huh. Isn't that something? Wonder if maybe you got immunity."

"Don't know." Lucash turned to Remy and Bryn, "Could that happen?"

Bryn responded, "Sure," she hesitated, "it could happen, but I wouldn't want to jump to that conclusion without running some tests. We do know they were trying out some new generalized virus concoctions. So, it could also be that the dose wasn't strong enough for you, or there was something wrong with the serum."

"Can you test me? Find out which it might be?"

"Once we can get back into the lab, we can."

Bendi spoke up, "Would knowing he's immune help us with anything?"

"Maybe. It might help us with improving the anti-viral if we can determine why he's immune. I'm curious, certainly, but I'm not entirely sure that it's our priority right now. I think we have more pressing concerns to attend to."

"Like getting Mel back," said Davi.

"Yes, absolutely," Bryn agreed.

"What happened?" asked Daniel. "I mean, we know some of it, but…what actually happened?"

"Just like I said in my message. We had bad luck. Guard caught up with us. Mel's fast, but she's a short one, so she had a hard time up on that mountain. It was only one guard, so when she told me to run on, I knew I had to. I didn't think we'd be a match for his weapons, whatever he had on him, since we had nothing at all. I got quite a ways on up and hid. Heard the scuffle when she was caught. I followed back down from a distance to see which way he was going to take her. She was still struggling against him when he tossed her in the back, so she was still alive. They waited in the truck, and I stayed put. No signal there, so I couldn't message you guys. When two of the other three came back, they waited a while longer, but it was dark. They left without the fourth guy, and drove slowly towards BRO."

"She was in the truck! When they passed by us all, Mel was actually in there," Cassidi spoke up, horrified that they didn't know.

"We couldn't have helped her," Destin said.

"*I* know, but *still*."

"The fourth guy is dead," Selby said, "That's why only three came back."

"Really?" Remy asked, somewhat horrified. This would not mean good things for them. "How?"

"He stepped on a soft section on the ridge. It fell away and took him with it. He was after me and Becs," Daniel said. You guys didn't hear the scream?" The others there shook their heads, astonished that they hadn't heard someone yelling as they fell down the side of the mountain.

"We heard it. That's how we met up with Becs and Daniel," Cassidi said.

"Oh, I bet Karl is *not* gonna be happy about this," Destin said.

"No, and neither will Manglebee when he finds out. That puts us in a riskier situation. They have Mel, but they won't let this go. Guarantee they'll be trying to get information out of her. But at least we know she'll likely stay alive for a while," Remy said.

"You know who else isn't gonna like this?" Selby asked.

"Melody," several of the others responded in unison.

A hesitant knock sounded at the door. Selby trotted over to open it, knowing it would be his parents. They were relieved to see him, and his mom pulled him into a brief hug, while his dad grabbed his shoulder with one hand and squeezed. Selby brought them into what was now a crowded storage room full of discarded ranch materials and people. Selby's parents looked a little surprised at the number of people standing in front of them. They seemed flustered at first, but they recovered their composure quickly.

"Mom, Dad, this here is the gang. The best part of Colossus." He made the round of introductions.

"Welcome, Mr. and Mrs. Myer," Remy said.

"Rena and Sid, please," said Sid. "We appreciate you letting us come."

"Yes, well, we're glad you're here. We think you'll be a good addition. However, we haven't cleared this with Melody yet, so, for now, it's just between all of us in this room. Davi arrived a few minutes ago, and we were waiting for you two to be able to fill all three of you in on these most recent events at the same time."

The three recent arrivals were brought up to speed on the most recent discoveries about the virus and Manglebee's plans, Troy's dad and Troy, and, for the Myers, Mel's capture.

"We have to stop this," Rena said, shaking her head in disbelief. "I knew Manglebee was a monster but turning human beings into robots to do his fighting? That's so much worse than I ever imagined."

"Lucash? Lucash?" A raspy, quiet voice called from behind the huddled group. Lucash had been standing near Juniper but facing away from her and had missed her stirring until she called out his name.

"Juniper! Oh my god, Juniper! Are you...I mean, do you know it's me?" Lucash said, suddenly worried that maybe she was hallucinating again.

"Of course, I know it's you...why wouldn't I?" Lucash hugged her and cupped her face in his hands. "Welcome back. You had me scared for a while there."

"Sorry. What happened?" she said, trying to sit up, but then sank right back down, holding her head.

"Don't move too much. You've been really, really sick."

"Hi Juniper, my name is Bryn. Lucash is right. You've been one sick young lady. It's going to take some time before you feel like yourself again, so please take it easy."

Juniper looked at Bryn in utter confusion, then looked back to Lucash for an explanation. "Bryn and Remy saved your life. Maybe mine too."

"Where are we?"

"A long ways from home. Do you remember jumping off the truck?" Juniper nodded. "Okay, good. Because you were already pretty sick then, and you just got worse. Found a hiding spot for you, then followed the truck's tracks."

Juniper nodded, "I remember. Did you find it?"

Lucash smiled, "Yep. Almost got caught by somebody though. Three people were out in those woods, and—"

"That was *you*?" Selby exclaimed.

Lucash looked confused, and then realization hit, "That was you guys out there?"

"It was. Selby, another guy from Colossus who isn't here, and me," Remy said. "Well, guess there's one mystery solved."

"Good thing. Didn't think I'd ever find out," Lucash said.

"Lucash?" Juniper said weakly, trying to keep up with the conversation, but failing.

"Sorry, Juniper. Not important. I found the place, but these guys know where and what it is anyways. I had to go out looking for water and, when I did, this group found me. We're on the same side, Juniper, only they aren't with the Resistance. They're part of something much better because they're doing *more*. More real stuff. And you won't believe it. You won't believe what all is happening—" Lucash noticed Juniper's confusion and realized he had been saying too much and talking too fast. "But you just rest now. You're safe. We're on a ranch in Montrose. In the mountains. There's plenty of time to tell you everything later. Just work on getting better now."

Juniper's eyes were closing again, but she gave a little nod to show she had heard.

"Juniper, before you go to sleep, do you think you can swallow a little water? You need to start hydrating. That'll help that headache you're having." Juniper again nodded. She didn't open her eyes, but when Bryn lifted her head and held a thermos of water to her lips, she took several sips. She was asleep again in seconds.

"Thank you both," Lucash said. "I will never be able to repay you for saving her life. But I'll try. Just know that Juniper and I will do everything we can to help you guys. I know her. As soon as she is able, she will be the first to volunteer for anything you throw at us."

"I'm relieved it worked. Remy and I have been working for months on potential anti-virals. I'm not glad that Juniper was sick, but I am glad that we were able to help her, and at the same time, know that what we've created has been successful. At least with the kind of dose they gave Juniper. That might end up helping in the long run, more than you know."

"Lucash, I'm so glad Juniper is getting better," Bendi said.

"I hate to say this, but should we be planning what's next now?" Rebecca said. "It's getting late, and I think we should decide whether or not to call a Colossus meeting."

"You're right, Rebecca. We need to decide that first," Remy agreed. "Thoughts everyone?"

Over the next hour, the group tossed around their ideas and opinions, giving pros and cons for involving Colossus, and, thereby, Melody, or continuing to operate as an independent group.

They took a vote.

Remy sent out the message.

CHAPTER 38

Trevor's team worked through the night reconfiguring the security system. They redesigned it from the bottom up. None of them, however, were entirely confident that it was any better than the last one. Just different. They'd put everything they had into the system in the first place, so they had no idea how they could make it any better. Their only hope was that different was good enough.

Trevor instructed the team to set up an additional monitoring and alert system. If this person, or anyone else, did manage to break through again, an alert would be sent out immediately to just these team members. Should that occur, they'd be ready with an intervention to cut loose the connection and implement a temporary security patch until they could figure something else out.

"I don't think there's much else we can do," Trevor said as the team finished up on the security system.

"How much longer do we have to keep looking for another level of encryption? We've tried everything, and we're just not finding it."

Trevor was at a loss. How long was he supposed to keep these people here when they'd done everything they knew to do? They had been at this for hours. No sleep. No food. Nothing else to do. Every fiber of his being told him it would be a bad move to let them all go home, but he wanted to go home himself, even if it was just for his bed.

He made a decision, "Go home. Get some food and some rest. At least for a few hours. I doubt Head Councilor will be returning at this late hour."

"Are we coming back here?"

Trevor sighed, took off his glasses, and pinched the top of his nose, squinting his eyes against the headache building behind them. Putting his glasses back on, he replied, "I'm afraid so. Maybe we'll find something if we come back to it with fresh eyes. Report back here…" he checked his watch, "at 7:30. I know that doesn't give us much time, but it's the best I can do."

They all groaned their displeasure, accompanied by muttered complaints, as they finished shutting down their computers. All four team members filtered out without another word, leaving Trevor on his own. He should be leaving now, too. He only had a few hours. He wanted to go home, he really did, but he couldn't seem to make himself move in that direction.

Trevor sat back down in his chair with a thud. He rested his head in his hands. He felt like sobbing, but he couldn't. The emotions got caught up in his chest and stayed there. At last, he peeled himself up, grabbed his belongings, and headed to the garage. When he arrived, he noticed the Guard truck, but no one was around. He was glad for that. He didn't want to talk to anyone right now. He didn't even want to know if they got the prisoners. Actually, that was the last piece of news he wanted right now. He'd rather still hold on to the idea that they got away.

Trevor unplugged an available BRO vehicle and then climbed in, pushed the button to start it, and backed slowly out of the slot. Driving down the darkened dirt road, Trevor wondered if it wasn't time to end the secrecy between him and Mica. Mica deserved to know the truth, but he honestly wasn't sure he could bear her reaction to it. Still, at least she'd know. And he'd either have an ally or another enemy. Either way, at least he'd know, too.

****

On the opposite side of Montrose, in Quadrant 4, a Guard vehicle pulled up in front of a darkened house. It was 2 a.m. If their info was correct, dad should be working the night shift again, which would mean daughter would be home, probably asleep. Their surprise entry would not give any time to conceal a computer, if one was present. The three guards had placed friendly bets on the way over as to whether or not an 18-year-old girl in Quadrant 4 could possibly be hiding a computer. The three guards had had a good laugh at the idea, but one placed a bet in favor of finding the computer, just to make it fun.

By the time they exited the car, their smiles were erased, replaced with the hard looks required on the job. They approached the tiny house with stealth steps, careful not to break the silence that surrounded them. At the door, one of them checked to see if it was locked. It was incredible how many people actually left their doors unlocked these days, though far fewer in Quadrant 4 than in any other Quadrant in Montrose. Upon finding the door locked, one of them kicked it open. With ease. These old wooden doors in this section of town took little to bust free of the lock.

They fully expected lights to turn on and shouting after their loud entrance. Instead, silence engulfed them once more. All three men looked around the dark house, and then at each other.

"Didn't they say the girl should be home?" one whispered.

"Yeah, that's what they said."

THE BREAKING

"Let's look around. Be sure. Who brought their light in?"

A light flashed on in the dark, sending a wide beam through the house, flecks of dust dancing in its glow. The guard holding the light did a quick sweep from where they still stood by the broken in door.

"This shouldn't take long."

They went from the living area, which passed as a bedroom as well, though the men standing there wouldn't know that from looking at it, to the one bedroom. It was also empty of a human presence, including the closet. They checked the only two other rooms in the house: the kitchen and the bathroom. Those, too, they found to be vacant.

"Guess someone got the wrong information."

"Let's just see if we can find this computer, since that's what we came to do."

The three guards began their search, starting in the bedroom, a small and tidy box of a room with one small closet. The closet held three identical uniforms and one other set of clothing. Tucked behind the clothes on the floor next to a single pair of shoes was a box. It was the only thing that was of a size to hold a computer, so one of the men yanked it out and pried off the lid, only taking care because they were ordered not to damage or destroy the computer if they found it. All they found in this box were two more uniforms that looked like they were made for a woman; an old book, faded with age and the words "Grapes of

Wrath" barely discernable; a scarf that would never be worn by a woman in Quadrant 4; and several pressed flowers, dried and littering the bottom of the box with bits of their petals. No computer.

The guards did a sweep of the bathroom and then moved to the kitchen. They opened every cabinet door, tossing contents onto the countertops and floor as they removed them all. To their disappointment, all that was to be found was a few simple meal packs and even fewer serving wares.

"Wish they'd had something good to eat. I coulda used a bite," one guard joked to the other two as they made their way from the kitchen.

"What did you expect from Quadrant 4…a steak?" All three men laughed at this.

The last room to search was the first room they'd entered: the living room. Walking back into the living room, they headed straight for the shelves in the room. One man stepped on a board that felt loose. He stopped, backed up, and tested the board again. His companions watched, a curious look on their faces, before it dawned on them what the first was thinking. One of the men smiled. Maybe he'd win his bet that they'd find the computer after all.

They had a more difficult time prying open the floorboard than they had expected, but, at last, it popped free from its setting. One of the guards inspected it, expecting to find some sort of latch or something that would have held it in place. It was just a simple wooden board. He tossed it aside.

"Shine that light down here," said the guard who was already down on his knees trying to peer in the hole. The guard with the light complied. "Hold up. I see something." The man down on the floor laid all the way down and stuck his hand in the hole, feeling for the object he just barely caught sight of from the beam of the light.

"Aaaahhh!" He suddenly yelled.

"What?" the other two responded.

The guard stood up, shaking his hand off and wiping it on his pants.

"What was it?"

"Don't know, but it had fur. Not the computer." The other two burst out in loud guffaws.

"Right, go ahead and laugh if you want. Next time, one of you gets to stick your hand into the dark hole." And the other two laughed even harder.

When they recovered, they moved to the shelving unit, swiping off every item sitting on top, right onto the floor. They found several containers that held clothing and toiletries, all of which joined the contents strewn across the floor. There was nothing on any of the shelves or in any of the containers that would have held a computer.

The guards had searched everywhere, leaving nothing unturned or unopened. Nothing, that is, except for the well-disguised hiding place in the wall that held the computer they were after.

The guards came up empty-handed, and the one who bet they would find the computer good naturedly laughed off his loss when they'd finished tearing the house apart, creating disorder in the once orderly space.

"I knew there was no way an 18-year-old girl in Quadrant 4 would have a computer!" he said, as they filed back through the unhinged door, careful not to get snagged by the splinters poking out from the place where the door had broken. The three were still chuckling about it as they climbed back in their vehicle and drove away.

****

Manglebee and Henderson had returned to the Capitol. Henderson got an earful the entire way back. The two men were now in the secure meeting room, going over the operational plans. Manglebee was fuming.

"This is moving too slow. We should have been fully operational by now, but, apparently, I have entrusted these tasks to a bunch of incompetent idiots. If things had gone according to plan, this breech of our security system would have been too late."

"Yes. I agree. The question now, however, is what are we going to do about it?"

"Yes. That is the question."

"Head Councilor. I think it's time we convert the prisoners at the camps. We are far enough along in programming, even if they don't yet have the training down for weapons. If we build the army now for hand-to-hand combat, we can work on weapons training concurrently."

"Do you think between you, Gaff, Spencer, Lux, and Cord, you can manage this without ensuing chaos?" Henderson's lack of fear of Manglebee was now paying off, with Manglebee taking him into his confidence and treating him as more of an equal than he did under any other circumstances. Had anyone else been present, Henderson was sure none of this current conversation would have transpired.

"Yes. We will have to work out the logistics, but I think it can be done. We still have the advantage."

"We cannot afford any more errors, such as the ones we saw tonight."

"I agree, sir."

"Arrange a planning session with the other four. I want you to draw up *exactly* how this would work. Every step. I don't care how trivial you think it is, put it in the plans. I want to see that you've thought of everything. Nothing left to chance."

"Yes, sir. We'll get right on it."

"Henderson?"

"Yes, sir?"

"You have 24 hours. Do not disappoint me."

CHAPTER 39

The decision to involve Colossus wasn't an easy one. In the end, it came down to manpower. And brainpower. They would need to figure out how they were going to get Mel out, and they needed to decide where to start looking for this army. Most of them were also of the opinion that they needed to start fighting back. Rebecca wanted to free the prisoners from the location they now knew, with the hopes that it would bring them more help. Selby agreed wholeheartedly. Destin suggested sabotaging the programs for delivering the virus, since she now knew how to get in and what to look for. Bendi suggested that they go beyond that and start administering the anti-virals to those who got sick, if they could find a way to do so anonymously.

The group was counting on Melody being outnumbered. At the last meeting, several in the group had voiced their disappointment in Melody's decision not to look for the two escaped prisoners, Lucash and Juniper. Even stronger than that was the growing sentiment that things were taking too long. Every person in the room believed that there would be other Colossus members who would jump at the chance to take part in any of the actions they planned to propose. They didn't believe that Melody would be able to continue moving at the snail's pace she was used to once everyone found out what they now knew.

No one knew what to do about finding Troy. Rebecca left him several messages, thinking that she might be the one he would respond to, but no such luck so far. She would keep trying.

The responses to Remy's message had come in quickly, so now everyone was on their way to Headquarters. Everyone except Lucash, Juniper and the Myers. Juniper was in no condition to go still, of course, but more important than that was being able to inform Colossus about the four of them prior to introducing them to the group. If things didn't go well, they'd take it from there. Hopefully, it wouldn't come to that, but best to be safe.

It was 2 a.m. when Remy's and Bryn's vehicles pulled into their spots at Headquarters.

"I'm nervous," Rebecca admitted to Cassidi and Daniel, who shared the backseat of Bryn's car with her, while Destin sat in the front. Selby, Bendi, and Davi had piled into Remy's truck.

"Me, too," whispered Cassidi. "I just hope this goes well. Melody scares me."

"I think she scares everyone. That's why she's still in charge," Daniel said, as the three filed out of the car and joined the others.

"Man, it's weird not havin' Troy here," Selby said, as he looked around at their group. With that, the nine of them headed for the door, each of them with thoughts of the possible outcomes running through their brains.

As soon as it looked like almost everyone had arrived, Melody started walking to the front of the room. Remy beat her to it. The group had decided that he'd be their spokesperson. They also thought it was imperative that he start talking before Melody. They did not want her to control the conversation. The other eight moved up beside him, lending strength in their numbers.

Melody stepped back, but she was angry. The rest of the Colossus members looked a little stupefied at the change in procedure. They looked between Melody and the group a few times, but their eyes eventually settled on Remy as he started to speak.

"Thanks for coming. We have a lot of new information to share with you, and then some important decisions for how to go forward. We—" he gestured to the group standing at his side, "wanted to tell all of Region 1 Colossus at the same time so that nobody is left out of the loop or the decision-making process. I know a few of us were unable to make it, but most are here. I will fill those absent in as soon as our meeting is concluded.

Now, I want to be the first to say that the information we received over these past almost 24 hours has been obtained through non-standard Colossus procedures."

At this, everyone looked at Melody to gauge her reaction. Her shock and anger were ill-disguised, "Remy," she said, "I need to speak with you before you continue."

"We can talk afterwards, Melody. This information is too important to wait."

"Remy, that was not a request. I am still in charge here."

"Yes, Melody, you have been the one in control of this pod since the beginning. I understand that. But the information I have is not something I am willing to keep from the group any longer. They all have a right to know. So, I will speak now. To everyone."

The gasps from the Colossus group were audible. Melody opened her mouth to say something more, but Remy turned back to the gathered group and began talking, shutting down her opportunity. The group's attention shifted back to Remy.

"First, we know much more about Manglebee's plan and what the virus is actually about." That sentence ensured that everyone there would continue to listen to Remy. Zeche was the only person aside from Melody who was more angry than curious. He stood by her side, offering his support through his presence.

Remy continued, "But, before I go into that, I want to tell you a few other things because I think they're important too. We need to address them all tonight."

"Where's the other kid from your group? Troy? Why isn't he up there with you?" came a voice from the center of the gathering. Remy wasn't entirely sure who spoke the question. In their earlier meeting, everyone had had a difficult time deciding on whether to tell the rest of their Colossus pod about Troy and his father. They had decided that it was unlikely that anyone would be able to find him until he was ready to be found. Because of this, they had eventually decided not to tell the rest of the Colossus pod just yet. If it became necessary at a later time, they would disclose what they knew about Troy's dad, Troy's discovery of his dad's involvement, and his subsequent disappearance.

"He is one of the one's who was unavailable to come, but he is already aware of most of what I am getting ready to tell you.

So, I'll continue now. The night before last, our scheduled operation inside of BRO was cancelled. Selby, Zeche, and I had discovered upon arrival that two prisoners from another region were being transported to BRO, but they managed to escape. These prisoners were injected with an experimental fast-acting, but non-individualized, form of the virus." At this, some chattering broke out among those gathered.

"I know, this is surprising information, but it's just the beginning, so please let me get through it all before we start discussing anything." Remy waited just a few seconds for everyone to quiet down. "Okay, so those of us who were supposed to go inside met to discuss our options. It was determined that we should hold off doing anything, though several in the group believed we should attempt to find the escaped prisoners in order to try to help them, but also in the hopes that we could get more information. When our meeting concluded, a few of us decided we'd go looking on our own."

"Remy—" Melody's voice came out in almost a growl.

"Let him speak!" someone shouted from the audience. Several other shouts of agreement followed. Melody backed away even further, her rage increasing. She was making every effort to control it. It wouldn't have mattered. No one but Zeche was looking at her. She knew she had no hope of bringing this meeting under control now.

"I reported to BRO to make sure the prisoners had not been found and to inform Bryn of the most recent events and our decision to go looking. Selby left to go talk to his folks," this caused looks of confusion, as he knew it would. "His parents have found out about Colossus because they discovered Selby sneaking in late." This time, the interruption was even louder.

"I know what you're all thinking, but *please*, quiet down! It turns out to be a good thing," he said, speaking over the noise, hoping the words would capture their attention again. The did. "His *parents* are the ones who taught Selby everything he knows. They're also the ones who have the equipment that we've both used and copied. They survived The Reckoning using these skills. There are others out there, too. The others don't know about us yet, and Selby's parents want to keep it that way for now. But. Rena and Sid want to join us, and we would really benefit from their skills."

"Bring them on!"

"I second that!"

"Me, too!" Several calls of the last followed. Remy breathed a sigh of relief, as did Selby, who grinned at how easy that was. His parents would be thrilled.

Remy smiled, as well, and then continued, "Great. That seems unanimous."

"No! It is not unanimous," Melody practically shouted. "This is not how we bring in new members. You and Bryn continue to risk the safety of this organization, and I will *not* stand for it."

"We need people like them!" came the response from the crowd. Several calls of agreement followed.

Remy let the voices from the audience stand as the response to Melody and added, "They will be an excellent addition. In time, perhaps we'll be able to include others with these skills as well."

"Did you find the prisoners?" someone else asked, bringing the conversation back around to where Remy had left off.

"I'll get to that," Remy smiled again, in response. "Selby and I did meet up with the others to help in the search. But, one more thing before I do. Bryn talked to an informant at BRO who provided her with the information that Manglebee is keeping captured members of the Resistance, and other supposed dissidents, at prison camps in the Borderlands. So, it appears these individuals are at least mostly still alive, but only just. As you can imagine, the conditions at these camps are deplorable. The informant had only been to one, but there is no doubt the others are the same. This isn't really a surprise to us, as many of us at least suspected that something like this existed. Now, however, we have the location for one of them." Several cheers went up.

"So, Selby and I joined the others in their search, but Bryn stayed on at BRO so that at least one of us would be there. Before we got too far, Davi here saw a lone individual watching the rest of us. He brought him to us, but before we found out too much, the Guard truck came into view, and we were spotted."

There were reactions from the crowd, but Remy continued speaking. He figured he'd never get through everything if he didn't. "We all split off in pairs. I took the individual with me. It turned out he was one of the prisoners. His name is Lucash. His girlfriend, Juniper, is the other. She was extremely sick, and Lucash had hidden her well. As soon as we were able, we went back for her and took her to a safe place where Bryn and I could treat her. All the others escaped the Guard and two BRO employees who had been sent with them. Except one. One of the BRO employees fell to his death, but one of the Guard captured Mel. She's now at the BRO facility, likely being interrogated. She won't give anything away. We know this. But that is one task we have before us. We need to get her back."

"I'll go!" several people shouted.

"Should we risk that?" came from a few more voices.

"Not sure that's a good idea!" said a couple of others.

"These are decisions we'll have to make. No one will participate in a rescue who doesn't feel they should. There is more to this though. So, let's just wait until the end to discuss it all at once."

Melody searched the crowd for the naysayers, feeling some hope that she would have a few on her side still. She took a mental note of who they were and kept her eyes on their reactions as Remy continued to speak. She wanted nothing more than to storm out of the building, but that would not serve her.

She was better off knowing who she could rally back to the course they'd set in motion more than two years ago.

"Bryn and I treated Juniper with one version of anti-viral that we developed and stashed in a secret off-site location for safe keeping. We are happy to say that she is recovering. Lucash and Juniper *are* part of The Rebellion, but, despite what we've all believed, this organization doesn't operate in the way we presumed." Remy went on to tell the group what they now knew about The Rebellion, as well as Lucash's promise that he and Juniper would help Colossus in any way they could.

Melody noticed that even those who were voicing their concerns about rescuing Mel seemed excited at the prospects of the connection with The Rebellion. This was infuriating.

"With all the headaches The Rebellion created for Colossus, how could anyone want that connection? How can any of you agree to the kinds of tactics these people engage in? The safety of our members is of utmost importance, and you all seem ready to throw it all away for The Rebellion!" Melody was now desperate to regain control. All the years she put into this organization, all her hopes for a well-orchestrated revenge against Manglebee, were slipping through her fingers. This group was all she had now. She could not lose them like she lost her own family.

Remy turned to Melody and his look softened a bit, but his voice remained firm, "I know you take responsibility for the safety of this group, but it is no longer the most important thing to do. It's too late for that. Now is the time for action. We can no longer afford to be so cautious, not with what we now know."

Melody opened her mouth to speak again, but then closed it, not trusting herself to speak. Angry tears threatened to spill. She could not let them think her weak.

Remy faced the waiting group again, "Okay, I am now getting to the most important news we have." The words had barely escaped Remy's lips when the entire crowd grew so quiet you could only hear an occasional rustle of someone's clothing as they shifted position.

"While we were all out looking for Lucash and Juniper, Destin and Troy were working together," several bursts of laughter erupted at this, but the voices were silenced quickly. Destin looked a little embarrassed at the reactions. "They broke through the security wall for BRO's Level 3 system." This caused some commotion, which quieted as soon as Remy told them that this wasn't the big news.

"Once in the system, they discovered what Manglebee is really up to."

"Enough of the suspense! Tell us already!"

"I am getting there. Earlier in the day, Bendi figured out that the scientists at BRO working on the structure of the virus weren't actually trying to *kill* their targets. This didn't make sense at all, at first. Not until Troy and Destin made their discovery.

The point of the virus is to bring people to the brink of death. Everything about them is supposed to signify that they are dead. No discernable heartbeat, no breathing. No apparent bodily functions. In reality, they are in a state similar to a cryogenic sleep. Once the individual is removed following the funeral, they are taken to BRO.

Most of those taken in so far have actually died from the virus, but the number of survivors has increased over time as the scientists have continued to modify the virus. We have not yet figured out who has survived and who hasn't. We only know the basics from the scientists' notes that Bendi interpreted and from the document that Destin and Troy found. For those that survive, though, they are being used to create another army."

Chaos erupted. Remy had a difficult time bringing their attention back to him. Even Melody and Zeche began talking between themselves.

Selby let out loud whistle. That got everyone's attention.

"That isn't the worst of it!" Remy called out in the momentary silence that followed Selby's whistle.

"Not the worst of it? What could be worse?"

"This isn't a normal army. Manglebee is having microchips implanted in the brains of the survivors. They lose all control over their brains, and, therefore, their bodies. He's turning people into robots. This is how he's building his army. And he plans to wage another war on the people of this country because he's afraid he's losing control of the population. He wants to ensure our submission again, and the way he plans to do this is to turn a large portion of us against the rest. Ordinary citizens…people we know…fathers, mothers, brothers, sisters. He believes that we won't fight back when we are confronted with this army."

Now the noise was deafening. Melody looked like she was on the verge of passing out. So much so that Zeche was propping her up, in spite of her protests. It would be several minutes before voices quieted enough to hear any one of them above the general din. Remy and the others expected this. He didn't even make an attempt at this point to calm the group. They knew everyone had to be given an opportunity to process the information.

At last, the noise level died down enough for someone in the audience to be heard when they called out, "If what you say is true, we have to stop him before his plans get too far!"

"I…we…agree. This is why we brought everyone in. We feel like we, as an organization, need to drastically amp up our efforts."

"That is a mistake!" Melody yelled, trying again to make her point. "You will risk the lives of everyone in this room if you do that! Do you not understand that? You could all die if you throw caution to the wind this way!"

"We all *knew* our lives were at risk when we joined," Remy responded. "No one has to participate in anything they don't want to, but we do all have to act. Our lives are certainly all at stake if we don't act. Do you think any of us will be spared when Manglebee's army marches through? Not even Bryn and I will be safe at that point."

A majority in the room voiced their agreement with Remy's words, while no one actually dissented. Melody was definitely outnumbered. Even Zeche looked like he was no longer certain of what he should be thinking.

A voice from the gathered Colossus members called out, "I move to nominate Remy as our new leader!"

"I second that!"

"It's a vote, then!"

Remy was nearly speechless. This was not at all what he'd expected. He looked to the others, who all were smiling, several of them shrugging their shoulders to say they were also surprised at the turn of events. None were unhappy about it, though.

Remy turned back to the others, "I appreciate the vote of confidence. However, I cannot accept—" voices of disappointment rang out, while Melody looked utterly relieved. Remy held up his hand to quiet everyone. "Let me finish. I will not accept unless Bryn is voted in as my co-leader. Our tasks are too great for one person to be in charge of it all. In addition, this group beside me here, they've proven their skills, their willingness to go above and beyond, and their ingenuity in the face of unexpected events. I would also expect that they have leadership roles as well. However, that is not to say that we will have all the control. Each of us is important in determining our course forward. No one among us should have the only voice in what happens going forward. If you all accept, and if Bryn is willing to join me as co-leader," he, and everyone else, looked to Bryn, who nodded her head in agreement, if a bit uncertainly, "then I will accept the nomination."

"Remy and Bryn have my vote!"

"I move to nominate Remy and Bryn as co-leaders," someone else called out, to make the nomination official.

"I second it!"

In a procedure that harkened back to pre-Reckoning days, the group inside Headquarters held a vote, during which they nearly unanimously voted in Remy and Bryn as co-leaders of their Colossus pod.

Melody approached Remy. "You will regret this, Remy."

"Is that a threat, Melody? Because I'm afraid you will have a lot of people here who will not stand by and let anything happen to me." Melody took a step back, realizing the truth of what he said.

"It isn't a threat. I don't need to threaten you. I know you too well. You don't think I do, but I do. You will crack under the pressure, and you will fall when Colossus lives are lost in large numbers."

"We'll see about that," was all Remy would say. He had no need to say anything further. He turned from her and back to the crowd, many of whom had overheard the conversation that just took place. Melody stormed out of the building. Zeche stayed behind.

"Okay, with that sorted, it's time to get to work," he said to the group, motioning for Bryn to come over and join him.

Little did any of them know at that moment how quickly Remy's and Bryn's new roles would be tested, or how they would all have to fight for their country and their fellow citizens, in Region 1 and beyond.

But soon. Too soon. There would be Another Reckoning.

EPILOGUE

CA 5349 awoke in a cold sweat. It was the middle of the night and darkness blanketed the training facility inside. There were no windows in the facility, so CA5349 could not see that the night outside was just as black, with no moon to light the landscape. CA5349 was not supposed to be awake. None of the other CA Individuals were awake.

Images had played through his head while he was sleeping. Images of people familiar to him, but whose names eluded him. His eyes were now transfixed on the ceiling. There was a sound in his brain, something he could not identify, though he felt like he was struggling against a power he could not control. And he was losing the battle. The darkness was claiming him again, but before it did, one clear and cohesive thought entered his mind.

"Jonathan. My name is Jonathan."

And then all was blackness again.

The story of the Undoing will continue with the third book in the trilogy, Another Reckoning. Join Rebecca and the others as they face their enemies and confront unexpected challenges and obstacles in their fight for Anecor!

Hello Readers!

I am so grateful to you for continuing to follow Rebecca's story by reading the second book in The Undoing Trilogy: The Breaking. I hope you're enjoying the adventure and will stick around for the final chapter. If you enjoyed the book, I would really appreciate it if you would *leave a review on Amazon*. As a new and independent author, reviews are the best way to help others discover *The Undoing Trilogy*. Your review does not have to be long! Even a couple of sentences is helpful.

Feel free to contact me at desserae.k.shepston@gmail.com!

Thank you,

Desserae K Shepston

Gratitudes

The completion of this book would not have been possible without the support and votes of confidence I continue to receive from friends and family. I also have my fur babies to thank. They've forced me to take much-needed breaks through their demands for my attention and their propensity for making a bed out of my computer should I step away for the briefest of moments.

I am forever grateful to the readers who have taken the chance on a new author. Your willingness to spend your valuable free time diving into Rebecca's story means a great deal to me. Know that you are appreciated.

I would especially like to thank Gail, Shay, and Kelly for reading drafts of this book. Their feedback and suggestions made it a much better story. I am truly and forever grateful.

About the Author

Desserae K Shepston is writer, traveler, and adventure seeker. She has an affinity for YA novels, especially science fiction-dystopian. In 2018, she left the stationary life and career behind for a life on the road in a 1993 RV, traveling North America with her best friend and four cats, and living her passion for travel and an outdoor life. She wrote her first book, *Travel Cats: tips for beginning an rv journey with your feline family,* after working through the kinks of RV living with cats herself. Also look for her children's book, *The Adventures of Gatsby the Travel Cat in Mesa Verde* and, of course, the first book in *The Undoing Trilogy: The Undoing.* Desserae has lived in Chicago; Garmisch, Germany; Austin; and now, everywhere North America.

Made in the USA
Monee, IL
15 April 2020